Impersonating Aphrodite

KATHERINE WEST

NOTE

This book is a standalone, but the overarching story continues in other books. There are going to be so many more stories in this world! To keep up with books that are coming out and to get some sneak peaks behind the scenes, subscribe to the Lovers of Gods and Heroes Newsletter and let me know which story *you* want to read first!

And… um… while there are characters from mythology in this story, it's very *definitely* adults only. It gets sort of steamy in here, and not just because of *that* bathhouse scene.

Note that the main character in this story is a survivor of sexual assault and parental neglect. This remains in the character's backstory and I've tried to keep details off the page.

ABOUT THIS BOOK

IMPERSONATING APHRODITE
House of the Gods Book 1

Fated mates, forbidden desires and a perilous masquerade intertwine in a galaxy governed by tyrannical gods.

Meggie is a woman with a dull life, a boring job and an extraordinary secret: the power to change her features to look like anyone she chooses. After their mother died, Meggie had to grow up too quickly so that she could look after her younger sister. She doesn't have time for any kind of excitement or romance. She has to earn a living.

When her sister and cousins are abducted by alien warriors, Maggie embarks on a perilous journey into the galaxy to rescue them. They have been sold as slaves to the cruel and vindictive Gorgos, who plans to give them as gifts to the goddess Aphrodite. Accompanied by Brav, Guardian warrior and her fated mate, Meggie decides to impersonate Aphrodite herself to save her family as Brav poses as her faithful slave.

But impersonating the goddess of love is a demanding deception. If Gorgos discovers the truth, he will exact a terrifying revenge. As Meggie and Brav are forced to become more and more intimate, Meggie must confront her own fears, even as secrets from Brav's past threaten to expose them.

Meggie's secret abilities are tested to the limit. Can she save her family in a treacherous intrigue where one wrong step could cost her everything… including her heart?

Prepare to be captivated and thrilled by this steamy science fiction romance series where powerful women and their fated mates traverse a dark and dangerous galaxy—together.

PROLOGUE

<u>Twenty-Nine Years Ago</u>

The archaeologist brushed the last of the dust from the tomb. It was covered in text, but written in a language Genevieve, with her three post-doctoral degrees, had never seen before.

"What is this?" she murmured.

"I've never seen a sarcophagus made of metal," her assistant, who had only been studying for this moment for ten years, commented. He brushed his hand over the smooth, cylindrical surface, then looked down at the rows of identical cylinders. "There's so many of them. If this place hadn't been sealed up during a meteor strike that happened three thousand years ago, I'd swear this had been made yesterday. Is it possible that this is all some set up?"

Genevieve passed her hand over the strange text. "If it's a fake, it's a very elaborate one. The ruins of the city are extensive." She looked up at the solid rock a hundred feet above her. "All of this was sealed in when the meteor struck. And this language—I've never seen anything like it." She noticed that her hand was shaking.

She went to join her assistant in looking at the sarcophagus. The metal still shone like it had been polished beneath its covering of dust.

"I've seen artefacts from this time before," Genevieve whispered, cautiously glancing over her shoulder at the man sponsoring this mission, who had apparently never studied at any university. "They didn't have this shine." She brushed the dust lightly off the surface and gasped.

"Aaron, look!"

"What?"

Genevieve bent low over the sarcophagus, her face an inch from the window she'd uncovered. She cast a wondering glance back at her assistant. "There's a woman in here… and I think she's alive."

CHAPTER ONE

<u>Present Day</u>

"Oh, my *God*, Margaret! How did I not know it was your birthday?"

It isn't, Meggie thought. *It's my mother's birthday.* Her hands shook as she packed up her handbag. She moved slowly, drawing out the process, even though the process involved a conversation she'd otherwise have bailed on.

"How old are you?"

"Forty-six." *Twenty-eight.*

"Oh, my God, you are *kidding* me! How do you look so *young?*"

I lied about my age so I could get this soul-killing job when I was fourteen. "I moisturise."

Elise laughed like it was the funniest joke she'd ever heard. She was probably being polite. Then she sobered suddenly as she watched Meggie slowly gathering her handbag and coat. "You're not leaving already?"

That distress looks real, Meggie thought. But then, given that it was Elise, it probably *was* real. She'd never had an emotion she hadn't shared with the group. "I finish at five." Meggie looked pointedly at the clock that read fifteen past the hour. The last thing she wanted to do was face what was waiting for her when she left here, so naturally this was the closest she'd come to leaving on time in a decade. Goddammit.

"Oh, but can't you wait? I mean, we didn't *know* it was your birthday. Just give me two minutes to whip 'round and get everyone together." Her eyes were panicked, like this was a big deal to her. "We won't have a cake, but we could sing you Happy Birthday." She reached out an impulsive hand to touch Meggie's arm. "Please, Margaret, let us celebrate with you."

Meggie was torn. She wanted badly to agree. Not just because Elise was a nice person, but because she agreed with everyone on principle. It was safer. But face a group of her colleagues wishing her well? She'd rather face a firing squad. She glanced at the clock.

Meggie pulled away. "No—I mean, it's all right. I'm going to a birthday party right now. And I'm taking a week's annual leave."

There. That wasn't a lie. The week's leave had been planned for months. The party she'd only found about this morning. From someone she hadn't seen since she was fourteen. Hearing someone shout Ancient Greek at her in the street was something she hadn't been ready for. She'd had to duck into an alley to rearrange her features.

Elise relaxed. "Really? Oh, that makes me happy, then." She pressed in suddenly for an impulsive hug. "I wish you every good thing this year, Margaret. I tell you what. Wear that pretty green top when you come in next Monday, because we'll be having cake and I'll take lots of photos, OK?"

Meggie was touched by Elise's determination to celebrate her birthday, which was all the more reason to keep the woman at arm's length. But she really *was* in a hurry, and she couldn't think of the right way.

"That… that's sweet. Look, I've really got to go. I'll be late."

"Have a wonderful weekend!"

Oh, God, Meggie thought. *Fun with the family. Help me.*

*   *   *

"Meggie, darling, I'm so glad you came!"

"Happy birthday, Auntie Leona." Meggie's voice was muffled in the baggy beige linen suit that covered her aunt's shoulder as she was engulfed in an embrace that smelled of L'Air du Temps. It was the same fragrance her mother had worn and Meggie's throat was suddenly tight with emotion.

"Oh, Meggie!" Leona buried her face in Meggie's hair. "Oh, my sweet girl, I was so afraid that you wouldn't come."

It had been close.

"Let me look at you, darling. It's been so long." Leona pulled away just enough to examine Meggie's face. "You look so much like your mother, darling. When I saw you on the street, I thought it was Ne—" Leona cleared her throat. "Megara."

Meggie hadn't seen Leona as she hurried down the street on her way to work in the morning, the same way she did every morning. She'd heard someone calling her mother's name and turned to see who was yelling such an unusual word. When she locked eyes with her aunt, Leona burst into a stream of Ancient Greek that Meggie hadn't heard since she was a little girl.

Meggie had to duck into a narrow space between two skyscrapers to change her face. She'd worn her mother's face for so many years that it was her default now. She only changed back to her own appearance when she met with her sister, Teresa. Everyone in her life knew her as a middle-aged woman.

When she'd first learned that she had the power to change her appearance, she'd never thought she'd use that power to make herself look middle-aged. Even with special powers, life was disappointing. Maybe if her mother had survived, things would have been different.

Leona had followed her, pushing through the crowd to find Meggie—now in her own shape—and stared at her, hardly breathing.

"Oh, Meggie," she whispered. "Oh, my darling, is it really you?"

Then she crushed Meggie in an embrace.

Meggie allowed the embrace, but she was filled with bitterness. When their mother died and their father took them away to live in Sydney, Leona hadn't bothered to help her or her sister Teresa. She'd abandoned them. Leona was the reason Meggie was pretending to be her mother in the first place. If their father hadn't turned into a shadow of his former self, if he had looked after them, if Meggie hadn't had to get a job at fourteen to provide for her sister…

Leona acted as if she cared. She cried and held Meggie so tightly, it was as if she'd really missed her. Meggie stood stiffly in her aunt's arms, trying to hide the hurt and wishing with all her heart that this scene had happened fourteen years ago.

She hadn't been able to bear the hurt for long. "I'm running late for work," she said. "I really need to go."

Leona wiped her eyes and gave Meggie one last squeeze. "Oh,

darling, all right. I understand. You're all grown up."

Tears overcame her again for a moment and Meggie had to wait until her aunt could speak again.

"Promise me you won't disappear again. Come to my house tonight. I'm only an hour from the city now. It's my birthday and Cera and Bess are coming. You remember Cera and Bess, don't you? They remember you. Cera still thinks of you and Teresa as her sisters. You were all so close when you were young."

"I… wouldn't want to intrude on a birthday party…"

"I can't think of anything I want more for my birthday than to have my family around me again," Leona insisted. "If your mother had lived, we would have all been together… all this time…" Leona dissolved into tears again.

Meggie hadn't been able to find a way out of it. Leona said she didn't know how to enter a new contact into her phone without calling the number first, so Meggie had to give her real phone number.

And then Meggie had to call Teresa and make her come. And Teresa, damn her eyes, had been excited about it—at least at first.

"Auntie Leona?" Teresa exclaimed as Meggie sat on the steps at the back of her office building in her tea break to make the call. It had taken half her break just to take the elevator to the ground floor, but Meggie wasn't going to call Teresa from her office. This call was private. So now, she was making this very awkward, very private call surrounded by every smoker in her building. "I remember her! She was lovely! Why didn't we keep in contact with her all those years ago? She could have looked after us."

Meggie ground her teeth. She looked around. There were far too many people around and she wished with all her heart that she could make this call in real privacy. Instead, she spoke in Ancient Greek, trying to fashion the nearest thing to privacy she could manage. "Maybe you should ask her why she didn't keep in contact, honey."

There was a pause and Teresa responded in English. "Meggie, you know I don't remember that stuff as well as you do."

Jaw clenched, and still in Ancient Greek, Meggie ground the words into the phone. "She… left… us. Teresa. She… let… us… go."

A longer pause and Meggie hated herself for hurting Teresa. She'd do anything for her little sister. She *had* done just about *anything* for her little sister. And here she was, hurting her.

"Look, we just have to go to this one party, all right? Please try to be on time, Teresa. I don't want to do this on my own. Please?"

Teresa swore to be on time. And she meant it. All the same, Meggie knew her sister. There was no way Teresa was going to be on time. She never was. Meggie dreaded arriving at Leona's house alone, though. And, not so shockingly, Meggie arrived on time and Teresa was nowhere to be seen.

She struggled to make conversation as she pulled away from the hug. "The big 5-0, huh?"

Leona grinned ruefully. "I'm going to have to start dyeing my hair soon. Look, I'm going grey." She pointed to an area near her temples. Meggie looked obediently, but couldn't find the grey in the pixie-cut ash blonde hair.

"I... uh, I can't see any."

"I found a grey hair the other day, cross my heart and hope to die." Then she winked. "Of course, it's not there now because I ripped it out by the roots. But I am going grey." She shook her head. "I honestly never thought I'd get old like this. All this effort, for so many years... it takes its toll. Is Teresa with you?"

Meggie winced. "She insisted on coming on her own. So, naturally, she's late." At nineteen, Teresa often complained that "adulting" wasn't her thing. This drove Meggie nuts, because she'd never had a chance to choose. She'd been forced to become an adult at fourteen. Back then, no-one had cared that it was hard. No one had seen her struggles as she tried to live a life she wasn't ready for yet.

"That's fine. My girls aren't here yet, either. Do you want a cup of tea?"

Meggie trailed behind her aunt as they went into the kitchen. The room was lit by lamps in the corners and was warm and inviting, with a fire roaring in the slow-combustion stove. Meggie looked around. "Have you lived here long?"

"Ten years," Leona answered, putting a kettle on the stove. "Once the girls moved out, I didn't have to keep up a place near their school, so I moved out here."

"Is Dad coming?" Meggie asked uneasily.

Leona paused as she rinsed out a flowered china teapot. "Oh, I don't think so," she said eventually. "After your mother died..."

After Mum died, you didn't care. You didn't call or write or visit when we moved across the state. You didn't see how bad it got. You were the only person in the world who could have helped, and you didn't. You couldn't see that we didn't have shoes for school. You couldn't see that we'd grown out of our uniforms and our skirts were so short that we were sent home from school like we'd done something indecent. You couldn't see that I was the only one making sure Teresa had at least one hot meal a day.

Meggie kept her eyes down. Leona didn't know, and Meggie wasn't going to tell her. It all hurt too much. That was why Meggie had been forced to take the job in the city, use her dead mother's ID and take the kind of job at fourteen that makes you want to kill yourself when you're thirty-five.

Meggie wished so much that things had been different. Their father hadn't wanted them, that much was certain. She'd wished, lying awake night after night as a teenager, wondering how to pay for groceries and school uniforms, that Leona was looking after them instead.

"He looked after us," Meggie lied.

Leona put the kettle onto its cradle and switched it on. "Did he, Meggie?" she asked gently.

Meggie felt like she'd been punched. Her stomach muscles quivered as though responding to a blow. She lashed out.

"Better than your husband looked after his kids," she said nastily. "He was gone before Bess was even born, wasn't he?"

Leona drew back sharply and Meggie cursed herself. Leona was *nice*. She was kind. And right now, she was shaking.

"I am so sorry," Meggie whispered. "I didn't mean it." She reached out for her aunt, but Leona dodged her hands.

"No, it's true," Leona said, reaching up to get two cups out of the cabinet. "Regan and I only had a short time together. But I don't regret it, Meggie. I loved him. And he loved me–"

"Happy birthday, Mum!"

It took Meggie a moment to recognise her cousins. Bess's voice was familiar, but it took a moment to see the girl she'd known and loved in the woman that stood before her. Bess was as fair and blonde as Leona, but her sister Cera had red hair. They both stopped in the doorway.

"Meggie?" Cera asked, her voice disbelieving.

Feeling awkward, Meggie waved. "Hi, Cera."

"Oh, my God," Cera said quietly. "Meggie. Meggie."

There was a knock on the open door. "Can I come in?"

Teresa was behind the other two, dark-haired like Meggie, but much smaller, with a decidedly curvy figure. Cera and Bess turned to see her. Bess engulfed Teresa in a hug with a low cry as Cera walked towards Meggie.

As Leona had said, they'd been as close as sisters when they were young. Cera was a few years older than Meggie, but she'd been the one Meggie had gone to when the other kids teased her. Meggie told Cera, then they didn't tease her again.

Cera came towards Meggie slowly. Up close, she was as tall and strongly built as an Amazon, her green eyes so bright they were almost glowing. She'd never been the type to hug, but she looked like she was working her way up to it.

"Where have you been?" she asked, her voice low. "Mum never stopped looking for you."

Meggie opened her mouth, but nothing came out. Had Leona really looked for them? Her father had told them she abandoned them when they moved to the city. When their mother had been alive, Lewis had been a good father, a loving husband, but he'd changed the day Megara died. At fourteen, Meggie hadn't considered doubting her father's word the way she would by the time she was eighteen, so she'd always taken it for granted that what he'd said was true: Leona had abandoned them.

But what if it wasn't true? What if, in his grief, Lewis had separated them from the rest of their family? What if he'd been the one who kept them apart? Meggie felt like her whole world was shifting.

Slowly, Meggie noticed a noise like a rushing wind, tinted slightly with a metallic noise.

Meggie glanced at Leona and saw the woman's amber eyes go suddenly wide. She dropped the cups in the sink so sharply that one of them cracked. "I have something to show you girls," she said, her voice suddenly brisk. "Come with me." She crossed the kitchen in four quick strides and opened the door to the basement. Meggie blinked. She'd never even seen a house with a basement before. "In here, girls, now."

"I just want a word with Teresa," Meggie began as Cera and Bess obediently went down the stairs. She was still reeling from the thought that their father had kept them from their mother's family.

"*Now*, Meggie," Leona insisted. Teresa came to take Meggie's hand, so Meggie followed her into the basement. It was a large, pleasant room, the many corners filled with comfortable chairs, bookcases and pretty lamps.

It didn't feel so comfortable when Leona locked the door behind them.

Meggie heard the door leading to the backyard open. All four women's eyes flew wide as they heard Leona—quiet, sweet Leona—shout, "*Get the fuck off my property or I swear by all the gods, I will kill you all!*"

Then—male voices. More than one. The sound of barking dogs filled the air.

CHAPTER TWO

Meggie rattled the door handle, pushed at the door, but it was locked solidly.

"Get out of the way," Cera ordered.

Her *eyes*. They were usually green, but right now there was a blaze of gold around the pupils. Meggie stepped back in a hurry, putting herself between Teresa and Cera.

Cera raised her hand towards the door, still several feet away. A blast of power so intense that Meggie could *see* it burst from her palm. The door shattered.

Cera walked through the splinters as they were still falling. Bess scampered after her. Meggie was drawn along with them as Teresa rushed forward.

Leona was out in the backyard. She wasn't dressed in beige linen any more. She wore a long, white dress, like the kind that goddesses wore in paintings. Her pixie-cut blonde hair was now frosted gold at the tips and encircled by a crown of golden leaves.

There were a dozen men surrounding her, all dressed in black and gold uniforms. Guns—or a variant on the same that hadn't been invented yet—in their hands. A dozen more lay dead on the ground. Three of them held Leona, her hands behind her back.

And there was—it could be nothing else—an honest-to-God spaceship parked on the lawn. Its lights illuminated the dark lawn like it was daylight, but its hull was as black as the night that surrounded it.

The man leading them was tall and rangy, dark-haired, his lean cheeks slashed by scars. His eyes—and his weapon—were trained on Leona.

"We meet again, Artemis, after so many years. Come with us peacefully," he instructed, as if disciplining a recalcitrant child. "That way, no-one gets hurt."

Cera didn't give the spaceship a second glance. All her attention was on the men surrounding her mother. She clapped her hands and a noise like thunder rolled around the sky, so loud that it shook the ground beneath their feet.

"I believe she told you to get the fuck off her property," Cera said, her voice oddly sweet. "You should do that. Or I *won't* kill you—but you'll beg me to do it."

She meant it, Meggie realised. The thunder was still rolling. All the men were enormous, every one of them tall and bulging with muscles. Leona, at average height, looked like a little doll between them. Even Cera, at just under six feet, looked small as she strode towards the group, but that didn't slow her down for a moment.

The man with the scarred cheeks took his attention off Leona just long enough to look Cera up and down. His eyes widened and he gave a low growl of approval. "Cera. I would know you anywhere. I will enjoy taking you as my bride."

Twin flashes of lightning arced towards the man. Meggie cried out in fear, the sound lost in the sudden rumble of thunder. She watched in horror as streams of light flew from both Cera's and Leona's fingertips, striking the man in the heart.

Wait. *Not* striking the man in the heart. Bouncing harmlessly off his skin, the light rippling down his body as it found its way to Earth.

"You should be dead," Leona breathed. She glanced at Cera. "Twice. I thought you were mortal, Baelor—human."

"I serve Everius of Rhodes, my lady." Baelor gave a sweeping bow. "I have served him for three thousand years—since I was, as you say, mortal. He has granted me powers even beyond those of the gods."

"I'm not going back to him," Leona stated, but her voice was unsteady.

Thunder cracked overhead like a whip. "You'll do as you're told," the man stated. "Everius wants his wife back. He has found the man you betrayed him with and now both of you are marked for justice."

"He found Regan?" Leona's voice was barely more than a whisper now.

Baelor took a step forward. "He has the adulterer. Everius has good use for his powers. And for yours. Otherwise, an unfaithful wife would deserve death. You are fortunate that he is so forgiving."

Leona's hands clenched at her sides. "I would rather die."

The man laughed. "My dear lady, they all say that. Until they realise they're not dying alone."

The next thing they knew, Baelor had Bess clasped in one arm in front of him. He hadn't walked over to her. No one brought her to him. One moment she was on the verandah stairs, the next moment, she was across the yard, his arm around her chest. She struggled, but he held her tightly.

She went very still when he pointed his gun at her throat.

"Regan got this one on you, didn't he? All of them but the eldest, I imagine, since you only had one legitimate issue from Everius. So, Lioness of the Greatheart clan, will you watch this daughter die first? Then that one. Then that one." He pointed to Meggie and Teresa in turn. His gaze fell on Cera. "That one is the daughter of Everius, promised to me from the time she was a child. That one will be mine. Will you watch as I fuck her and fill her with my child? Or will you come quietly?"

Leona stared helplessly, then took a step forward. "Let her go. I'll come with you."

There was another sound like the wind and the whine of metal. One of the men looked up, his face darkening with horror. He turned back to the man holding Bess. "Hurry up, Baelor, the Guardians are coming!"

Without taking his eyes off Leona, Baelor removed his gun from Bess's neck and shot the man who spoke. The shot wasn't a bullet. It was a ray of ruby light.

"I didn't ask any of you to speak," he said calmly, even as the dead man fell to the ground. "Now, my lady. Walk into the shuttle, or I will kill your bastard daughters here and now."

Leona took a small step.

"Faster!" Baelor shouted, as the sound of the approaching ship got louder. He lowered his weapon and another ray of light shot from the muzzle, green this time. It hit Bess in the thigh. She screamed, collapsing in his hold. A river of blood flowed down her leg.

Leona whimpered and walked faster.

"I swear to God," Cera promised in a low voice, "I will kill you."

Another ship appeared above them.

"Take her into the shuttle!" Baelor screamed. His men grabbed Leona and hustled her even faster to the ship.

The new ship above was approaching swiftly. In seconds, it was above them, and a dozen large men leaped from an open door before it even landed. One of them went right for Baelor, grabbing the arm holding Bess and snapping it like a twig.

Bess fell to the ground.

As he screamed, Baelor shot wildly. The ray of green light headed straight towards Meggie.

Another warrior threw himself in front of her, throwing his arms wide to protect her. His weight landed against her and she felt as well as heard his cry of pain as the ray of light pierced his shoulder. With a snarl, he turned and shot right back at Baelor.

A shimmering, transparent shield appeared around Baelor as he scrambled back to his ship with his men. They stumbled up the ramp as the Guardians shot at them. The black ship rose into the air, even as the ramp closed.

Meggie hurried to Teresa, hands running up her arms. "Did they hurt you, honey?"

"I'm all right," Teresa said impatiently. "Bess—"

The Guardians were already at Bess's side. "Tarn, get her inside, quickly," the tallest Guardian ordered.

"Get away from her!" Cera screamed. She raised her hands again.

The leader of the Guardians raised his arms conciliatorily. "We're not here to fight you, little girl."

Little girl, Meggie thought, just as Teresa whispered, "Oh, he is *so* dead." No one called Cera names like that if they wanted to live.

He took a step forward. Cera shrieked and flung lightning at his feet. Meggie's arm went around Teresa to hold her tight. Once again, the man was unharmed. As Cera clapped her hands and thunder rolled around them again, the man disappeared and reappeared.

Before Meggie had a chance to shout, "Behind you!" he'd already appeared behind Cera and grabbed her hands. He wrapped her arms around her waist and held her securely. She struggled, but although she was very tall and strong for a woman, she could barely even move in his grasp. He towered over her, his thick arms enfolding her body, both her wrists held in one massive hand.

"Let me go!"

"Not until you're safe," he growled. "We're not here to hurt anyone. My name is Jessan. These are my men. We are the Guardians of the House of Valor. We're just here to talk to Artemis."

"And who the fuck is that?" Cera snarled.

"Me," Leona replied. She came to stand in front of Cera and put her hands on her daughter's shoulders. "Calm down, honey. It's OK. I know who they are. They're friends of your father's. Your sister needs help. You have to let them help her."

Cera wasn't able to twist in the giant's grasp, but she looked behind her, as if seeking the truth in his face.

Something passed between them. Meggie didn't know what it was, but something had happened in that momentary silence. Cera's eyes were wide, but when she spoke, it was in a shaken whisper. "Please, let me go."

He released her. "Don't try anything," he warned. "I won't allow you to hurt my men."

Cera was rubbing her wrists. He frowned and reached out for her again. She dodged out of his reach. "Did I hurt you?" He followed her and caught her hand gently. "Let me see."

Meggie's mouth fell open as Cera *let him*.

He turned her hand over in his palm and ran his finger lightly over her wrist. A golden glow stroked over her skin. Cera's wide eyes were on him the whole time. "I apologise," he said, his voice so low that Meggie had to strain to hear him. "I didn't mean to hurt you."

She stared at him and there was another moment when Meggie was sure that something wordless was passing between them. Even Leona stared, shocked, at the sight of her forceful daughter struck silent.

Eventually, Cera whispered again, "Please, let me go. It—it's healed now. I just—I think I need to sit down."

He let her hand go, but she swayed. "Let me support you," he urged gently, holding out his arm. Cera went into his embrace like she'd known him all her life.

The one who broke Baelor's arm scooped Bess into his arms as if her curvy figure weighed nothing at all and headed for the house. Leona was right with them, Cera and the giant following behind.

The man who had protected Meggie with his body was down on one knee. She approached him cautiously. "Can I help you?" she offered.

He lifted his dark head and when their eyes met, it was like a current went through her.

"Do I know you?" she asked.

He didn't have time to answer before two Guardians hastened to his side. "We'll lift him for you, lady," one said, a tall, blonde man with gentle green eyes.

"He's a heavy son of a bitch," the other complained, equally tall, but even broader, a mane of dark hair spilling over his shoulders, his jaw shadowed by a wild beard. His eyes were the same green as the blonde man's.

"Watch your mouth in front of her," the man between them groaned.

The dark man apologised, lifted the wounded man's arm around his shoulder, and he and the blonde man supported him into the house.

Meggie followed them inside.

CHAPTER THREE

The man carrying Bess laid her on the sofa. She was already unconscious, her face pale, her hand falling limply off the edge of the sofa. "I have to get to the wound," the man said. His name was Tarn, Meggie remembered, from the huge one who'd given the order to take Bess into the house.

Leona jerked as the man put his hands into the hole made by the blaster and ripped Bess's trousers open. Her pale thigh was covered in blood. He swore softly at the sight. Cera stepped beside her mother and put her arm around her shaking shoulders.

"I'll get some tea towels," Meggie offered. She ran into the kitchen and came back with a handful of linen. "We can use these to stop the bleeding."

She was right beside Tarn as he laid his hands right over the pulsing wound. Blood seeped through his fingers. Meggie's hands were right behind his, ready with the tea towels when she saw the golden glow.

She dropped the tea towels in shock and fell to her knees beside him. "What are you doing?" she asked. The golden glow from his hands intensified until it looked like Bess's thigh was bathed in bright light.

"Healing her," he replied.

The blood stopped flowing. As Meggie watched, the wound closed, new skin sealing over the mended flesh. Bess's eyes opened and sought out the man who knelt above her. She raised her hand to his face. "I know you," she murmured.

With cries of joy, Cera, Teresa and Leona fell upon Bess, who laughed a little weakly and assured them she was fine. Bess held her mother at arm's length and stared at her mother's changed appearance. "Mum... when did you change your clothes?"

Leona stroked her daughter's cheek. "This is my goddess-form, darling. You'll find your own one day, when you come fully into your powers."

Still shocked by what she'd seen, still with her hands full of tea towels, Meggie turned back to the man who'd been injured. He was sitting on a kitchen stool, a Guardian either side of him, leaning against the kitchen bench. "Let me help you," she offered.

He sat up obediently. He groaned as he shrugged the black uniform jacket from his shoulders. She caught it and threw it over the bench. There was a jagged hole in both the jacket and his shirt— and in him. There was a lot of blood around the edges of the fabric.

"Uh, can you unbutton your shirt?" she asked.

"It goes over the head," the blonde man offered helpfully.

There was no way she was going to ask him to raise his hands above his head for her to remove his shirt with a wound like that, so Meggie reached into the kitchen drawer and took out a pair of scissors.

"Fill a bowl with warm water," she ordered the blonde man, and he took the mixing bowl that had been draining on the sink. It took him a moment to figure out how to work the tap.

"I just have to cut here," she told the wounded man, ducking in front of him and pulling his shirt tail out of his waistband. She was quick with the scissors, slicing up the front of the shirt, then pushing it off his shoulders. She couldn't help but notice that his shoulders bulged with muscle, the skin smooth and silky, his chest patterned with a smattering of dark hair that was somehow unbearably masculine.

She laid her hand gently over the wound as she waited. The blonde man returned with the bowl of warm water, clearly pleased with himself. At her quizzical glance he said, "I figured out your alien water system, my lady."

"You're such a show off, Kairn," the wounded man grumbled, and the man with the wild hair and beard let out a laugh.

"Let me see this wound," Meggie said firmly, refusing to be distracted.

She took a tea towel and moistened it with water. There didn't seem to be any fresh blood flowing, so she cleaned the blood away from the muscled expanse of his back to allow her to see the wound clearly.

The damp tea towel in her other hand, Meggie reached out with her fingers to touch the wounded skin. "Is this healing already?" she asked. The wound looked like it was already a week old, fresh pink skin puckering at the edge.

"What?" the man asked. He turned his head and caught her gaze. Again, that moment when his dark eyes met hers made her feel weak at the knees. Her hand was still on the bare skin of his back. "Already?"

The blonde man drew in a sharp breath. "Brav, she must be your—"

The giant who led them clapped a hand on the blonde's shoulder. "You're doing an excellent job at healing him, my lady," he said.

"But I'm not doing anything," Meggie protested. While she said she wasn't doing anything, though, she noticed that when she took her hand away from him, the wound stopped healing. When she touched him, a faint golden glow seeped from her fingertips to the wound, drawing it closed.

"You are more powerful than you realise," Jessan stated.

Meggie snatched her fingers away from him. "I'm sure Cera could do a better job—"

The wounded man caught her hand. "Don't want anyone else touching me," he rumbled. "Just you."

He wasn't just saying that, Meggie realised. He really meant it. The look in his eyes was so intent that Meggie was frightened by it. She shoved his shirt back at him and stumbled over to the table. Brav, she thought, trying out the name in her mind. Brav.

Teresa was already sitting there, the one with the blonde hair standing behind her as if he, like Cera's giant, were standing guard. The dark, wild-haired Guardian was on one knee beside her chair, leaning down so his face was even with hers as he said something that made her laugh.

"Teresa, stop it!" Meggie snapped.

Teresa looked up. The sudden dismay and consternation on her face made Meggie feel terrible. "Stop what?" Teresa asked innocently.

"Stop encouraging them," Meggie hissed. Even Cera snapped out of her daze at Meggie's sharp tone. Brav, lounging against a wall, just watched her impassively.

"Cup of tea!" Leona announced loudly, as if to forestall any further arguments.

The man behind her was carrying the tray and set it down at the table. Cera's giant pulled out a chair for Leona at the head of the table. Cera shot him an approving glance. Meggie saw the glance and saw the way the giant responded to it, standing a little straighter at her approval. What had passed between the two of them in those silent moments?

"Girls, there are things I probably should have told you a long time ago," Leona began. She busied herself with the cups and the teapot and didn't meet their eyes. "To be honest, I didn't know how to begin. I didn't know if you'd believe me. I didn't want to spend the rest of my life locked up because you thought I was crazy.

"This affects all of you—Cera, Bess, Meggie, Teresa. Our family is descended from an ancient line of people called the Alterrans. We were the first people on Earth. We were special. We had powers. You've all seen Cera's powers today. She's the strongest I've ever seen. Even as a child she was remarkable."

Cera's lip quivered, like her mother's kind words hurt. The giant laid a hand on her shoulder. "The strongest any of us have ever seen," he rumbled as Cera fought to control herself. Meggie wondered how he knew she was upset when he was standing behind her and couldn't see her face.

Leona went on. "Our people were the first on Earth. Those of us descended from the great Houses had special powers." Her lip twisted regretfully. "In our arrogance, we even styled ourselves as gods. I was known as Artemis. My father—your grandfather, all of you—was Zeus. We were powerful. Immortal, unless killed in battle.

"The Earth was menaced by demons, created by the man Everius to conquer it. We had to pay a heavy price to defeat him. All the gods—myself, and my sister Megara included—were placed into stasis and our powers concentrated on creating a barrier around the Earth so Everius couldn't return. We slept for thousands of years. Some were sent to the Moon, but many of us slept in Atlantis, the ancient, sacred city of our people."

"Many of us?" Meggie asked. "You and who else?"

"Most of the gods. You know their names, Meggie. I know that your mother taught you our history. Zeus. Apollo. Athena. Hades.

Poseidon. And many, many more. Among them was my sister Megara—your mother, Meggie—and Cera. Cera was only four years old then. They told me I should leave her behind and let her be cared for by my friends."

"And your husband?" Teresa asked. "Was he in stasis, too?"

"My husband—my first husband—was Everius, the Steward of the Earth, who wanted it for himself." She drew in a shuddering breath. "He was your father, Cera, and Baelor spoke the truth out there. Your father promised you to Baelor when you were just a child." Leona swallowed hard. "I fulfilled my duty, and you were born, Cera. I loved you so *much*, from the moment you were born.

"Then I met Reganus. We fell in love. Regan is your father, Bess." She gave a little laugh. "So, I suppose, there were four of us in cryo-sleep that you knew, because you were born after I woke."

"What woke you?" Teresa asked. "Were you supposed to sleep so long?"

"The energy source that powered our cryo-sleep chamber was stolen when tomb-raiders found the place where we slept. Megara woke first. I woke some time later as I felt the shield start to fail. For the last twenty-nine years, I have been spending all my power on maintaining the shield."

"You should have said something!" Cera's voice was sharp. "I could have helped you."

Leona shook her head. "You are powerful, darling, but you don't have shielding powers. Your powers are for attack, not defence. You got that from your father."

Cera went very still at the implication that her father had been violent. "Is he still alive?" she asked.

"I don't know." She tilted her head back to look up at Cera's giant. "Is he?"

Jessan nodded. "Everius lives. He has… augmented his lifespan in other ways. His House is more powerful than ever."

Leona's lips tightened, but she didn't say any more about her husband. She looked down at the table before her. "Oh! I forgot to pour the tea." She reached out for a cup but knocked it over accidentally.

Bess took the cup from her mother's hands. "We don't need tea, Mum."

Leona's shaking hands clenched into fists to control herself. "I suppose it's for the Guardians to speak now. Why are you here? Why now?"

The man behind Bess spoke. He had a rich, deep voice and spoke carefully. Jessan's voice—and Brav's, a little voice whispered in Meggie's mind—had been rougher. This man had been taught to speak properly, taught to speak in public, Meggie was willing to bet on it.

"My name is Tarn of Gerea. I serve with Jessan, our Captain, and Brav, Kairn, Mac and the others standing guard outside and in the ship. We, among many others, are the Guardians of the House of Valor. We serve the Intergalactic Alliance, a federation of star systems dedicated to peace and order.

"Several months ago, we received word that the House of Everius had conducted raids on Allied space. His powers grew exponentially until he became a serious threat to the Alliance. There was no explanation for this development of his powers. It could only be that he had either a new ally or a new resource. There was no-one known in the universe that had powers like those that Everius was using now—at least, not known any more.

"We learned Everius had found Reganus, floating in space, in cryo-sleep. He is now using Regan's powers to claim more territory and harass the Alliance. He has brainwashed Regan. We were tasked by our Council to find Regan's mate. She is the only one who might be able to get through to him. Goddess—Artemis—we beg you to come to him."

Leona was shaking all over. She shook her head, but she said, "Regan is alive?" A nerve ticked in her jaw and her eyes grew suddenly bright. "By Olympus... by my own father's name! We thought he was lost. Regan—beloved–" She buried her face in her hands for a moment, shoulders shaking with sobs. Bess put her arm over her mother's shoulders.

"I remember him," Cera said quietly. "Papa. I loved him. He loved me."

"Oh, Cera!" Leona exclaimed, reaching out to take her daughter's hand. "He loved you so much. And you, Bess, if he'd had a chance to get to know you, he would have loved you the same way." She sniffed. "I have to go to him, girls," Leona said. "I have to. I traded Regan for the Earth once, I can't do it again."

"And you're just trusting that they're telling the truth?" Bess asked dubiously.

"They're telling the truth." Cera and Leona spoke at once.

"How do you be so sure?" Bess asked.

Leona smiled at Cera and took her hand. "You get that power from me," she said softly. Then, replying to Bess, she said, "We can speak mind to mind, Bess. Telepathy. We can tell if someone is lying."

Jessan leaned forward, placing his hands on the back of Cera's chair and Cera didn't even move away. "I'm sorry to have to rush you, but I must stress the urgency of this mission. There are several systems about to fall to Everius. Lives are at stake. We must move as swiftly as possible—within the hour, if it can be done."

Leona nodded firmly. "I can be ready in a few minutes." She rose to her feet, then paused, her gaze going from daughter to daughter, from niece to niece. "Oh, girls, I'm so sorry to leave you."

Bess stood up and went around the table to embrace her mother. "This is important," she stated. "We understand, Mum."

"Oh, Bess." Leona dropped her face to bury it in her daughter's shoulder. "Bess, I should have told you all this years ago." She pulled away, her eyes wet with tears. "I need to go. Oh, Bess, Bess—when I come back, your father might be with me."

"I'll help you pack," Cera said firmly. "Come on, Mum."

"I'll come, too," Bess said.

Meggie and Teresa were left alone with the Guardians, and Meggie had never wished to help someone pack more than she did at that moment. Kairn, the Guardian who had been standing behind Teresa, laid his hand on the back of the chair Cera had vacated. "Do you mind if I sit next to you, my lady?"

Teresa blushed. "Oh, no, not at all."

Meggie hadn't even had time to scowl before Brav was standing beside her, far too much muscular, bronze chest exposed for Meggie's peace of mind.

"May I?" he asked. He sat down before she had a chance to sort out her conflicting emotions.

She wanted to say "No" because how dare he invade her space? When she'd spent fourteen years trying so hard to keep everything together? But then, she wanted so much to say "Yes", wanted so much to just stop holding everything together, just for a minute.

"We have to leave soon," Brav said, "but there is something I'd like you to have first."

"Oh, I–" She didn't even get a chance to say that she couldn't possibly accept anything before he was pulling his watch off his wrist.

"This is called a *custodia*. It's a communicator. It's simple to operate. Voice activated. Just raise it to your face and tell it to call me—or Jessan, or Kairn, or any of the others." He pressed the watch into her hand and she was grateful he didn't buckle it onto her wrist. "Call anytime. I mean it. If you need anything—anything at all—or even if you just want to talk, I'll be ready."

"Must work pretty long-distance," Meggie joked, but it fell flat.

"It's keyed to my personal code. It will reach me across the galaxy if necessary. I mean it, Meggie. Call anytime."

Meggie struggled to find something to say and blessed Teresa when she spoke up. "Speaking of communicating, how is it you're speaking English?" she asked.

The blonde man beside her shook his head and looked up at Cera's giant. "Will you explain, Jessan?"

The giant nodded. "I have some powers of my own, though nothing like the powers the Alterrans had. I simply opened your minds to understand and made sure that you could be understood. Out in the galaxy, communication barriers are a thing of the dim, distant past. Every baby has their mouth and ears opened shortly after they are born."

Leona and her daughters were back barely more than a minute later, Cera pulling a suitcase that didn't look like it was heavy.

"I'm ready," Leona said firmly.

The Guardians rose. Meggie stood, too, unsure what she was supposed to do. But then Brav was looking at her so intently she forgot to be nervous. The others went out, leaving them alone.

"You know I'm coming back to see you again, don't you?" he asked softly.

Meggie's hands were shaking so hard she didn't know what to do with them. She wanted to whisper, "Yes." Wanted to lean towards him and sigh. But—God!

What was she *thinking?* She stuck her hands in her pockets to hide the way they trembled. She had to be strong. She had to look out for herself. She'd spent years—*decades*—learning to protect herself. Now was *not* the time to lean into a stranger and sigh.

She shrugged and spoke coolly. "I literally have no power to stop you. Do what you like."

He frowned. "You have more power than you know. I would do anything for you, Meggie. All you have to do is ask."

He looked so intent. So sincere.

"Fine," she snapped—or tried to. The breathy tone that had entered her voice made it hard to snap. "Go, then. Go and leave me alone right now. That's all I ask of you."

He flinched, like she'd hit him, and took a step back. His eyes searched her face, trying to see if she really meant it. Meggie felt like she'd hurt herself just as badly as she'd hurt him, but she'd had half a lifetime of pretending she was OK. She didn't want to engage in further conversation. She turned and followed the others from the house. She heard Brav's slow steps following her.

Leona threw her arms around each of them in turn and whispered quiet, desperate goodbyes into their ears. When she got to Meggie, she whispered, "Meggie, darling, I'm only leaving for a little while. I wish with all my heart that we had more time to talk. You know I love you, don't you?" She pulled away just enough so she could see Meggie's face—and so Meggie could see the sincerity in hers. "I loved my sister so much. I love you and Teresa every bit as much as Cera and Bess. I know that Megara would have been so, so proud of the beautiful, brave woman you've become." She pulled Meggie back into the embrace. "Don't be afraid, Meggie. Be happy, my special, grown-up girl."

Meggie had to swallow hard, but nothing could stop the tears that flowed down her cheeks. She saw Teresa was crying too, and put her arms around her sister, letting her press her head into Meggie's shoulder.

A moment later, Leona had disappeared up the ramp into the spaceship with the Guardians and the door pulled closed smoothly behind them.

The ship barely made any noise as it rose—just the same sound Meggie had heard earlier—a sound like wind with the faint tang of metal. Another moment and it had risen so high into the air that Meggie couldn't see it anymore and it was just another star in the sky.

She looked around at the others. Teresa had moved away and was hunting in her pockets for a tissue among the million other small things she carried with her everywhere. Bess was hanging on to Cera, who was still staring up at the dark sky.

A thought struck Meggie. "Are you talking with *him?*" she asked Cera. "Telepathically?"

Cera's eyes jerked downwards. She looked uncomfortable. "It's hard not to listen when someone is talking to you," she said evasively.

"How long have you known you had these powers?"

Cera looked up. She wasn't so easily cowed. "All my life," she said. "Not speaking mind to mind, since no-one ever spoke to me, but I've always been able to tell what someone else *really* means, no matter what they say out loud. I've always been able to move things without touching them. Always had... a way with electronics. I can make my car start without a key."

"Good God," Meggie breathed. "Is there anything else?"

"Maybe," Cera admitted. "To be honest, I tried not to find out how far it went. I didn't want to know."

"And you never *said* anything to anyone?"

"Tell people I'm a freak?" Cera snapped. "Absolutely not." Her lips were thin. "Let them find out the hard way."

"Cera, don't say you're a freak!" Bess exclaimed, putting a hand on her sister's arm.

"Why not?" Cera countered, her eyes still hard. "As it turns out, we're *all* freaks. Mum included."

"Mum most of all, I think," Bess said, letting go of Cera and wrapping her arms around her waist. "All that talk about her protecting the planet. Do you think you'll be able to maintain the shield, Cera?"

Cera nodded, but she looked uncertain. "I said I could, didn't I?"

"Let's go inside," Teresa suggested. "It's kind of cold out here, don't you think?" She wrapped her coat tighter around her and flashed them all her beautiful smile so that her dimples appeared in her plump cheeks.

CHAPTER FOUR

Meggie couldn't sleep that night. She was in an unfamiliar bed—that didn't help. Cera had insisted they stay overnight. She admitted, finally, when Meggie informed her she'd had quite enough birthday cake and was leaving now, that she wasn't as sure of her ability to maintain the barrier as she'd made out.

Cera's eyes were hard as she admitted her weakness and then turned it into an ultimatum. "So, you're staying here, where I can protect you. Mum always kept a room ready for you."

Meggie hadn't believed it, but it was true. Leona had kept a spare room for Meggie and Teresa for their whole lives, even during the last fourteen years, when the two girls had been living across the state with their father.

Meggie had never even slept in the room until tonight. Her cousins had been like sisters when her mother was alive. Now she was terribly afraid they were little more than strangers. Bess was warm and welcoming, practically sharing her life story over birthday cake and tea, but Cera's hard expression didn't invite intimacy. Bess had told them about her job in the diplomatic corps and her brute of an ex-husband. By the end of the evening, Meggie still wasn't sure what Cera did for a living.

She lay awake and resisted the urge to toss and turn. Teresa was fast asleep, curled up on her side. Meggie didn't want to wake her. So, she lay on her back, every muscle burning with the urge to toss and turn, and tried to sleep.

She kept thinking of Brav. The way he'd sought her out, like she was special. The way that his dark eyes had held hers. The way he'd insisted on her taking the communicator. Making sure that this wouldn't be their only meeting.

In the darkness, with no-one around but Teresa, asleep in the next bed, Meggie allowed herself to think about him. He'd been reaching out to her constantly. Everything he'd done had called to her. She took the communicator off the bedside table and wrapped it around her wrist where it clasped itself seamlessly, fitting her narrow wrist as easily as it fit his.

No man had ever given her a gift before. No man's eyes had ever followed her around a room as if she was special and beautiful. She'd never had a boyfriend. She'd never had time for relationships at all, and once she was earning enough to not have to hold two jobs down at once, she'd been too concerned with raising Teresa.

She looked over at the still, sleeping form. Teresa was only nineteen. Hardly more than a baby. But she was stubborn and strong and smart and Meggie loved her more than anything else in the world. Teresa had been five years old when their mother died, Meggie fourteen.

She hadn't understood at first, after her mother died, how bad it was going to get. Their father had moved them out of their country childhood home almost immediately. To this day, Meggie wasn't sure why he'd done it, but she remembered hating it. Remembered hating her new school, hating their dingy new home, and hating him.

Then gradually, she'd realised that he wasn't going to start cooking for them. He wasn't going to worry about the things they needed for school. When Meggie came home from school, trembling with excitement, and told him she'd been approved to do a course that would allow her to take the first steps in becoming a teacher—something she'd dreamed of all her life—he'd thrown the permission slip in the bin.

"We don't have time for this shit," he snarled.

"But, Daddy, it doesn't cost–"

"And who'd look after your sister?"

That was when Meggie realised that it really was up to her. She put her dreams about the course aside and started looking for a job she could do on the weekends. At fourteen, she couldn't find a company that would take her without her father's permission. She knew he wouldn't give it, but she also knew she needed the money—needed money that he didn't control, so that she could look after

Teresa.

It wasn't until she'd thought of her mother's things—the few things Meggie had squirreled away before her father threw them out—that she realised what she could do. She had her mother's handbag. Inside it was her mother's purse. And her driver's licence.

She'd stood in front of a mirror and done her makeup carefully, then looked at the tiny picture. She looked like her mother to begin with. It was a simple matter to use her powers to shift her features to make herself look older. If she dressed in her mother's clothes, could she be taken for an adult?

The answer was no. A fourteen-year-old cannot impersonate a woman in her thirties. But then she'd been interviewed by Colin Walt.

He'd eaten her up with his eyes from the moment she walked into his office. By now, she'd been turned down by manager after manager. Something about the hunger in his eyes told her he wasn't going to turn her down—but also that she should run.

She didn't run. She needed this job. Both she and Teresa had been sent home from their two different schools this week, because they'd grown so much over the summer that their uniforms were now very short. They weren't allowed to come back to school until they were decently dressed.

Decently dressed. The phrase had stung badly. Decently dressed. And here she was, wearing her mother's best suit and her mother's face, not sure what to do with her legs when she sat down. She crossed them nervously. Colin Walt watched the movement and licked his lips.

She got the job.

Three months later, Colin was fired following a series of allegations of sexual assault. Meggie didn't speak up. She'd been too afraid someone might find out the truth about her. She hadn't told anyone, ever, about the things he'd forced her to do. She'd still needed her job, and at least she and Teresa had school uniforms now. Uniforms and books and shoes and a hot meal every day. So, every weekend, she put on her mother's clothes and her mother's face and pretended to be happy about it, for Teresa's sake.

At least she hadn't had to worry about the time relationships would take from her already full schedule. After Colin, she hadn't wanted anyone's hands on her ever again.

She'd been so successful in keeping men at arms' length that no-one had ever come close to breaching her defences. Not until Brav, who looked right at her and left her trembling with only a few words.

That's it, she thought, and swung her legs out of bed. *I'm getting a cup of cocoa.* A cup of cocoa and a stern talking-to. That's what she needed. Stop thinking of things she couldn't have. Like sleep. Like love.

She put some milk in the microwave to heat up and sat down at the table to study the communicator. *Custodia*, he'd said. *Voice activated. Just raise it to your face and say my name and I will come to you.*

She jumped up when the microwave dinged and cursed herself. She hadn't wanted it to ding, in case it woke the others, so she'd set it at ten minutes, sure that she'd remember to stop it before it went off.

She took the milk out of the microwave carefully, holding it at arms' length. It was probably super-heated now. If she jostled the cup, it might explode. She turned around.

There was a man behind her.

Meggie screamed and threw the cup full of hot milk directly into his face. His scream echoed hers. The hands that had been reaching for her came up to scrabble at his face, already turning a scalding red. She backed away, but he was too quick for her. One hand shot out to grab her arm, twisting it so that she dropped the empty cup.

His other hand came around in a powerful punch to her face.

Meggie collapsed. She'd been hit before—by her father, by Colin—but never punched. She felt like her cheekbone had exploded. He was snarling with rage, holding her up by her arm as he hit her again. And again. She sagged, aware of nothing but the pain that was blacking out her entire world.

As she hit the floor, her fingers closed on the communicator and brought it to her face. "Brav," she whispered, mumbling because her face didn't feel the same shape anymore. "Help."

A big boot came down on the communicator—and on her fingers that held it. She screamed through a mouth that couldn't open properly. He drew back his foot again and kicked. The darkness finally took her.

She woke—she had no idea how much later. It was still dark. Her vision was blurry and pain was still exploding through her whole body. He was gone. She tried to say, "Teresa," but the pain of speaking overwhelmed her and she passed out again.

She woke again. It was daylight. She could see her own blood on the tiles, among the crusting remains of the spilled milk. She saw what had happened to her fingers and her gorge rose. She gagged. A few moments later, she lost consciousness again. She wished she would never wake up.

*   *   *

But she did wake, and the next time she woke, she was in a different room. It was difficult to tell if it was day or night—the room was lit with artificial light and she couldn't see a window. She wasn't on the floor. She was on a bed.

She moved her jaw experimentally. It didn't feel broken anymore. She looked down at her right hand. The fingers were straight and smooth, the skin unmarked.

"Hi," a soft, deep voice murmured from beside her. Meggie turned her head, relieved that she could still do so.

Brav was standing beside her bed. His dark hair was mussed and his jaw was covered in a layer of stubble, but his dark eyes were as warm and gentle as ever. He reached out a hand to touch her cheek.

"How are you feeling?"

Meggie flexed her fingers and was relieved to find that she could. She raised a hand to her cheek and her fingers brushed his as she probed her cheekbone. "I think I'm all right," she whispered. "I could have sworn… did I have a dream?"

"No dream." Brav bent over her and stroked her hair behind her ear. "You've been through a lot, sweetheart."

"I—did someone hit me?"

Brav nodded. "Everius sent more men to your house last night. One of them beat you. Badly." His fingers trembled against her ear. "I think the only reason he left you was because he thought you were dead." His voice broke on the last word. "So did I, when I found you."

He dropped to the seat beside her bed and took her hand in both of his, warming it in his large palms.

"When you activated the communicator, I heard you say my name. I heard you scream. I came to you as quickly as I could." His voice dropped to a low, hoarse whisper. "Gods, Meggie, I hope you never have to feel how I felt when I found you."

Meggie didn't know what to say. She hadn't known him more than a few minutes, but he seemed like he really cared. So, she changed the subject. "How is Teresa?" she asked. "Cera and Bess? Are they all right? He didn't hurt them, did he?"

Brav's hand tightened around hers for a moment and Meggie felt like the bottom had dropped out of her world.

"There was more than one of them, Meggie. Everius's men move in squads of twenty-four. I think…" he looked down at their joined hands. "I think they took the others captive. I can't find any signs that they were hurt. It looks like they were taken from their beds and didn't have a chance to put up much of a fight, while you were awake, and able to fight back. I think that's why he… brutalised you."

"Captive?" Meggie cried. "But, why? Why would anyone…" her voice trailed off as she realised the answer to her own question. "Because of Leona. Because of Cera's powers."

Brav nodded. "Everius wants to stop Artemis from bringing Regan back to himself. He needs Regan's power and he knows Artemis could stop him. As soon as we left Earth's atmosphere, we were attacked." His gaze flicked up to meet hers once more. "I'm at fault for you being attacked, Meggie. I thought we had cleared them all out. I didn't know that there was another ship within light years of Earth."

Meggie wasn't the least interested in assigning blame. She pulled her hand from his and sat up. "I don't care who is to blame," she stated, and meant it. "All I care about is saving my family. Where are they now?"

"I'm tracking their ship, but in this shuttle, we cannot match their speed." His jaw was tight.

Meggie swung her legs over the side of the bed and had to pause for a moment as dizziness hit her. "What about Leona's power?" she asked. "Can she find them? She's supposed to have super powers, doesn't she?"

"Artemis is far from here," Brav explained. "Other Guardians are carrying her to Desiderus Nonus with all speed. You and I are alone on this shuttle. I deserted my post to return to you."

"Alone?" Meggie's feet had just hit the floor. All of a sudden, she felt like the floor wasn't where it was a moment ago. "As in, just you and me?" An involuntary chill wracked her and she swayed.

His hand caught her elbow. "Careful!" he exclaimed. "Yes, Meggie, we're alone." He saw her settled steadily on her feet. His voice dropped low again. "Don't be afraid of me, Meggie. You're safe with me, I swear."

In one swift move, he dropped to one knee. "I swear I will do everything in my power to protect you. I will guard you. I will serve you. I will honour you. Ask me anything, and I will do it. I will give my life for you. My life is yours, my lady. Forever. So, do I swear it."

He bowed his head. He was so tall that even kneeling, his head was barely below hers. Something inside her she couldn't name made her reach out a hand and place it on his dark hair. "I accept your oath, warrior," she said, and felt something inside her click into place. It felt right—so right—and she swayed towards him.

Even she didn't know what she was going to do. She froze in the very act of bending towards him.

He spared her any further embarrassment by rising to his feet and bowing. "Excuse me, my lady. You need to rest. I must see to the ship."

"Wait!" What was she thinking, prolonging this? All she knew was that she didn't want him to leave her. He turned, an expectant expression on his hard face. He was ready for her to speak, and she didn't know what to say. She looked down. She was still wearing her bloodstained nightgown. "Um, I need to get changed. And—I don't know where I am."

She hadn't intended for her voice to sound so small, but she saw it touch him. His expression softened. "I have replicated some clothes for you, based on what you were wearing down on Earth this afternoon." He gestured to a small pile on a shelf opposite the bed. "Are you well enough to dress yourself, or do you want my help?"

Meggie's blush rose so fast she was concerned for a moment that she was going to rupture something. "Oh, no, I can dress myself."

"I will be in the hall if you need me." He bowed again and closed the door behind him.

Meggie moved to the shelf and took the clothes down. They were... serviceable. Of course they were serviceable, and nothing more, if he'd based them on what she was wearing to the party. All her clothes were... serviceable. And nothing more.

As she slipped the nightgown over her head, she was very aware of him, standing outside her door. She stood there for a moment, bare, staring at the door. On impulse, she raised her arms and took her hair out of its braid, so that the chestnut tresses spilled over her shoulders. Her hand dropped to stroke over her flat belly, down over her hips and thighs.

She was too slender. She hadn't been so slender as a child, but she'd spent years making sure that Teresa had enough to eat and sometimes there wasn't enough to go around. Now, it seemed like her body had forgotten to develop curves.

He'd seemed interested in her. What would he think, if he saw her like this? Would he like her body? She'd never willingly shown her naked body to anyone, but for a moment, she wished he would open the door, stride across the room, and explore every one of her secrets.

Her hands were trembling as she dressed in the newly-generated clothes. He'd given her a black, knee-length skirt and a white blouse. There was even a pair of plain, black court shoes. He hadn't included any underwear, and Meggie realised this was because he hadn't seen her underwear. He probably thought her breasts were naturally that prominent. Meggie looked down. Her bust didn't look that impressive without support. Her lips pursed in disappointment.

Too thin, she thought. *No bum, no boobs. Why would a man like him be interested in me? I must be going mad.*

She went to the door and waved her hand over the panel beside it as he had. It slid open smoothly.

He glanced down her body. *He's looking at the clothes*, she told herself sternly. *As if anyone would be interested in you, especially like this.*

His gaze snagged on her neckline, and she realised that the outlines of her breasts and nipples were plainly obvious through the soft, white fabric.

He jerked his head up so that he was looking at her eyes and swallowed hard before saying, "Uh, I'll show you the kitchen."

Meggie followed him, her own eyes a little wider than usual. Had she imagined the way he'd looked at her? To be honest, she was finding it a bit difficult not to devour him with her eyes, too.

He was tall, probably at least six foot four, with dark hair and dark eyes. He wore the same black uniform as all the Guardians, with a high collared tunic and very… she devoured him with her eyes… very well fitted trousers. She detailed the width of his shoulders, the way the muscles in his arms strained at the fabric of his jacket, the muscular buttocks and thighs flexing as he walked.

The shuttle was small, no larger than the tiny home Leona had lived in when Meggie's mother was alive and the two families were still in contact. There was one bedroom, where she had been recuperating, a cockpit at the end of the hall, a bathroom and living area between them. There were blankets and a pillow thrown messily over a sofa.

Brav snatched them up in a hurry and bundled them into a chute in the wall, then turned to indicate the table. He was clearly trying to distract her from the fact that he'd been sleeping on the sofa while she was in the only bed. Meggie was touched by this evidence of his thoughtfulness. "What sort of food do you like?" he asked, going to the table and pulling out a chair for her.

CHAPTER FIVE

Meggie sat down as he pushed in the chair behind her and suddenly realised that she had no way of answering that question. What did aliens eat? How could she describe Earth food to someone who had never eaten it? Did they even eat? What would three thousand years of divergent evolution do to the human gastro-intestinal system?

"Umm…"

His hand, large, warm and gentle, fell onto her shoulder. "That was a stupid question, wasn't it? Why don't I get us a selection and you can try a bit of everything?"

Meggie nodded in relief. He went to a blank space in the wall and pulled out a small bench beneath it. He tapped an empty part of the wall and a screen appeared. "Two servings of Forlaria, two servings of Joradan bread and two servings of Calreian roast, please." He glanced back at Meggie. "And two servings of Averones for dessert."

A hatch in the wall opened. A tray rolled out of it, onto the bench. Brav carried it back to the table.

Meggie sat up a bit straighter. The scents wafting from the food on the tray smelled *delicious*. Then she sat back. What was polite, when eating with an alien? Was she allowed to have her elbows on the table? Should she chew with her mouth open or closed? Should she eat everything put in front of her, or should she leave a little on the plate to show that the serving size was plentiful? All of a sudden, the hungry feeling in her stomach changed to flutters of anxiety.

"These are foods from my homeworld," he explained, setting the tray on the table. "I was taken from there when I was five years old, but I can still remember my mother's cooking."

"Taken?" she asked, distracted from her anxiety for a moment. "You were taken away from your family?"

He froze for a second, halfway to his seat, before gathering his composure. "Yes. I was taken. I never saw my family again."

"Oh, Brav, I'm so sorry." She reached across the table to lay her hand over his. He stared at it, like no-one had ever taken his hand before. He curled his fingers around hers before she could pull away in embarrassment.

"I… appreciate your compassion," he murmured, and finally looked up at her. He was looking for something in her face, she realised, so even though she blushed, she didn't look away. He seemed to find what he was looking for because his hand tightened around hers, squeezing gently. "You have a tender heart, don't you, Meggie?"

The blush was in full force now and she had no idea what to say, but she still couldn't look away. He raised her hand to his lips for a brief kiss, just the barest brush of his lips over her knuckles. "Your heart is beautiful, Meggie." He lowered her hand.

"Have you seen cutlery like this before?" he asked, indicating what was very obviously a knife and two-pronged fork.

The moment passed. Meggie drew in a deep breath. All he'd done was hold her hand and kiss her knuckles. So why was she so weak in the knees?

Your heart is beautiful, a little voice repeated inside her head. That was why she was weak in the knees. Because he'd said the most swooningly romantic thing anyone had ever said to her. *And more than that. Because he sees you. He's paying so much attention that he sees your heart.*

"Uh, yes," she replied, picking up the knife and fork, noting surreptitiously that he was holding the cutlery the way she would expect.

"Now, be aware that all of these are sensation foods. I've included something rich, something comforting, something cool and something hot."

Sensation foods? That was an odd way to put it. Still, she followed his lead and cut herself a slice of the meat.

It tasted delicious: rich and warm. Warm clear down to her toes, in fact. She glanced up at him to find him watching her.

"Do you like it?"

"It's wonderful," she told him. "In fact, I don't think I've ever eaten anything better." She ate another slice and her cheeks began to flush.

"Try it with the bread," he urged. "Rich foods go so well with comfort foods." He broke off a piece of bread, dipped it in the gravy on his plate, and ate it, closing his eyes for a moment in pleasure.

Meggie followed suit, but she didn't close her eyes. Her eyes flew wide open.

"What was that?" she asked, twisting around in her seat to look around. "Did someone just touch me?" There was no-one else in the room and Brav was still across the table from her.

"Joradan bread is a comfort food," Brav explained, as if that was any explanation at all.

"Comfort food, fine," Meggie snapped. "But I felt like… like someone gave me a hug." *And not just anyone,* she thought to herself. *That was Mum, I'd swear to it. For a minute there, I could swear I smelled her perfume, felt her arms around me. I'd swear it.*

Brav frowned slightly. "Don't your people find hugs comforting? Perhaps the food reacts differently with your physiology. I'll get you something less complex." He reached for her plate.

"No, wait." Meggie held on to her plate. The sensation of being embraced at the table by a woman who'd been dead for fourteen years was unnerving, but he was right. It *was* comforting. "Explain it to me. What are sensation foods?"

"Foods that cause sensations," he replied simply. "The roast will make you feel warm and full and relaxed—that's how we describe a *rich* food. The bread is comforting. It will make you feel comforted. For many people, comfort takes the form of an embrace from a loved one, often from a parent or a beloved."

"What did you feel when you ate the bread?" she asked, curiously.

"I felt your hand on my back, the way you touched me down on Earth when you were tending my wound."

"Oh." Meggie was touched—and confused. "I think—I think mine was my mother. The way she used to hold me when I was a little girl."

Brav nodded. "I used to sense my mother when I ate comfort foods, too." He looked down at his plate. "I was so small when I was taken away… I have very few memories of my parents now. For a long time, the only time I could remember them was when I ate

Joradan bread. And then, for the past five years, when I ate Joradan bread I felt nothing at all."

Meggie wanted to get up from the table and go to him, wrap her arms around his massive shoulders, bury her fingers in his thick, dark hair and cradle his head against her. Nothing sexual, she told herself, but she wanted to give him comfort. Wanted to give him a warm, safe space where he could relax and be at peace. He was a huge warrior, easily twice her size, but she knew instinctively that he needed what she could give. She wanted to be his safe harbour.

It must be the bread, she decided, looking away. She'd never had thoughts like this before. It had always been so easy to keep everyone at arms' length. And now she was a heartbeat away from wrapping her arms around him and drawing his head to her breast.

She tore off another section of bread and ate it. This time, she enjoyed the sensation of her mother's arms around her, the scent of her mother's perfume, the warmth of her mother's love. "I feel like I'm getting a hug from my Mum," she said. "She died when I was fourteen."

"What was she like?"

And then Meggie found herself pouring her heart out. She hadn't spoken about her mother with anyone for years, not even with Teresa. She'd worried that talking about their mother would make Teresa sad, that it would remind her of everything they'd lost. Now, being able to tell Brav about her mother's bright, swift smile, her determination and protectiveness, her wisdom and patience, was just as comforting as feeling that embrace one last time.

"What's the drink?" Meggie asked, reaching for the glass of transparent, green juice.

"Something cold," Brav answered. "It doesn't have an emotional sensation beyond being refreshing, and a physical sensation of coolness. It's called Forlaria. To be honest, it's something children drink more than adults, but I have fond memories of Forlaria on hot days after I'd been playing out under the suns."

Meggie took a tentative sip, then drew in a deep breath. Brav's eyes dropped to her cleavage as it heaved up and down, then back to her eyes immediately. "Oh, that *was* refreshing!" She took another sip. The cool sensation was like a short, sharp thrill of cold, racing along her nerve endings. It was like jumping into a cold pool after a sauna.

"What's this last food?" Meggie asked, finally pushing her plate away. In the end, she hadn't worried about whether she should clean her plate or leave a portion. The food was so delicious that she didn't even think about manners again until she was chasing the last of the gravy around the plate with the last of the bread.

The last food before her was shaped like little balls. They were the size of small grapes, covered in a golden-brown coating, with a little pot of creamy sauce with little brown flecks in it like vanilla. "Are these sweet or savoury?"

"Savoury," Brav answered. "We like to end the meal with an intense sensation. Not necessarily something sweet, but something strong. The little balls are called Averones. They're made out of a special kind of cheese with a coating of spices before they are fried. You dip them in the sauce like this. But be careful—the sauce is *very* spicy."

For all that he'd warned her the sauce was *very* spicy, he dipped the little ball into it until it was covered and popped it into his mouth.

"I might try one without the sauce, first," Meggie mused, cautiously.

Meggie speared one on her fork and brought it to her mouth. The sudden burst of flavour and texture on her tongue was so intense she had to close her eyes. "Oh, my God," she moaned. "So good!"

The balls had a crisp coating on the outside, while the inside was creamy and soft. The spices in the coating mixed perfectly with the creamy, rich interior. She speared another one, dipped it a little way into the sauce, and ate it. Her eyes went wide.

"Oh, my God," she moaned, eyes watering as it seemed like the whole inside of her head heated up. "Oh, my God!"

Brav was out of his seat in a moment, his expression concerned. "Meggie, is it too strong for you?"

"Yes!" she cried. "Good *God*, give me something to drink!" She grabbed for the glass of Forlaria in front of her and swigged. It did nothing—*nothing*—for the burning in her mouth that was so intense it was going to fry her brain in a minute. "Brav, help me!"

He knelt by her chair, his arm along the back of it. Her mouth was open, trying to get air inside to cool the burning flesh. Brav put his hand on her cheek to turn her face to his, then leaned down and kissed her.

Or was it a kiss? It was hard to say. Her mouth had been wide open and his tongue entered her immediately, stroking over her own. Meggie would have protested, but the gentle invasion seemed to ease the burning. He slid his tongue over the roof of her mouth, around her teeth, inside her cheeks, then back to curl around her tongue again.

By now the burning had passed, and all that remained was the pleasure of his tongue in her mouth. Meggie moaned into his mouth and he slanted his lips over hers for what could no longer pretend to be anything other than a kiss. The arm he'd laid across the back of her chair moved to encircle her shoulders. The other hand slid from her cheek into her hair.

Her hands came up to grip his arms, the way she'd wanted to do when she'd been tending his wound. She sucked delicately on his tongue, curled the tip of her own around his and felt the growl deep in his chest as he pressed her closer.

Then he pulled away. He was breathing faster, she noticed. So was she. She'd never been kissed like that in her whole life. Never.

"Forgive me," he rumbled, his voice hoarse. "The spices in the sauce—they can only be neutralised by saliva. My people have eaten this kind of food for centuries, so our saliva has adapted to cool the burning sensation."

I want his tongue in my mouth again, Meggie realised. Her eyes flicked up to his, then away, then back again. It was shocking! She'd never wanted a man like this. She'd never been bold. Never, ever, ever. She swallowed hard.

"It was delicious," she said, her voice husky with desire. "And I'm hungry, Brav." She pierced another Averone and dipped it into the sauce.

His hand caught her wrist before she could bring the morsel to her mouth. "Careful. If you eat another, you'll need me to soothe the burning again. You can eat them without the sauce. Or I can get you other food, if you're still hungry."

She held his gaze. "This is what I want, Brav."

Meggie didn't even try to break free of his grasp. She just leaned forward and plucked the Averone off the fork with her teeth. This time, knowing what to expect, it wasn't such a shock. She enjoyed the way the coating shattered in her mouth, enjoyed the creamy flood of cheese, enjoyed the swelling heat.

Then she swallowed and turned to Brav, running her hand up the tight muscles in his arm to his neck. She pulled him closer. "So hot," she murmured as the familiar burning began, then slanted her lips over his and speared her tongue into his waiting mouth.

There weren't nearly enough Averones on her plate. By the time her plate was clear, Brav had hold of the fork and was feeding her, dripping the sauce over her lips and licking delicately at them to ease the burning, before thrusting his tongue into her mouth for a passionate kiss. Meggie's hands were in his hair as she ate at his mouth as much as the food.

He drew back. Took his arm away from her shoulders where he'd been crushing her against his chest. Disentangled his fingers from her hair.

"Brav?" she asked, feeling a little hurt at his withdrawal.

He ran his hands through his hair. It was a mess, after the way she'd been running her own fingers through it. Surreptitiously, she cast a glance down his body. There was a huge bulge in the crotch of his trousers, so he'd been as affected by their passionate kisses as she was. So why had he pulled away?

"I… I must see to the ship," he said. He'd said that before, and Meggie recognised it for the excuse it was. He didn't wait for her to reply, just strode from the room, the door sliding open and closed automatically.

Brav

He'd had his tongue in her mouth. And not just to ease the burning. She'd used the spicy Averone sauce as an excuse. She'd *wanted* his tongue in her mouth.

Brav had never been so aroused in his life, and all he'd done was kiss her. Kiss her, crush her soft form to him… penetrate her mouth. All he could think about was everything else he wanted to share with her.

She'd never know how close he'd come to plucking her out of her chair and carrying her back to the bedroom. Or just to the sofa, so close behind him. Or, godsdammit, just sliding her out of the chair and taking her on the floor. She wasn't wearing anything under that little black skirt. Her small, perfect breasts were bare beneath the white silk.

He knew their passion had shocked her. From the first moment her trembling hands had touched his skin, back when she was tending his wound on Earth, he'd known that she was inexperienced. He'd read it in every single one of her responses. And he was ready to go slow. Ready to give her the time she needed.

To be honest, to take the time he needed, too. Even his brother Guardians didn't know what he'd gone through when he was captured by Aphrodite six years ago. He'd never spoken a word to them about what he'd had to do before he was free.

When he first saw Meggie, he'd recognised her at once. Like all Guardians, he'd gone before the Mirror of the Fates when he graduated. They'd shown him the face of his mate as she would be when she was old enough to meet him and he'd gone away as thousands of Guardians had gone away before him, knowing that his mate was on a protected planet and it was unlikely that he would ever see her again.

He'd lived for her, though. Her sweet face was all that had gotten him through his time as a slave. The compassion he'd seen in her eyes even then had been enough to make him determined to be the best that he could be. He'd spent his life training and fighting, defending the weak—but it was all for Meggie.

He didn't have one doubt in his mind that she was the one he'd been designed for. Every cell in his body had recognised her. Any fears or hesitation he might have had melted away in the glory of his immediate love for her. He would do anything for her. Die for her. Live for her. Wait for her.

But, godsdamn. After a kiss like that, walking away from her was the hardest thing he'd ever done.

CHAPTER SIX

<u>Meggie</u>

Meggie didn't know what to do. Brav had left her in the living area, the plates still on the table. She couldn't clear the table. She didn't know where the plates were supposed to go. There was a sofa, but there were no books and she couldn't see anything resembling a TV. What did aliens do to fill their time?

Probably check on the ship a whole bunch, she thought bitterly.

She sat on the sofa, but was very swiftly bored. She lay down, but the thought of lying on the bed he'd been sleeping in was a bit confronting. She wandered around the room. Eventually, she wandered back to the bedroom.

Lacking anything else to do, she curled up on the bed and went to sleep.

Unknown to her, the lights in the room dimmed in approximation of artificial night, and eight hours later, slowly brightened to simulate the dawn. The light woke Meggie. She had no idea how long she'd slept. It could have been minutes, hours—days, for all she knew. She hadn't been wearing a watch when she'd gone downstairs for cocoa, just the communicator that was still on her wrist.

All she knew was that she was hungry.

She'd gone to sleep in her clothes. She didn't have any others. She slipped off the bed and pushed her feet back into the low heels that looked just like the awful, boring shoes she wore to work every day.

Standing up brought realisation of a new problem. She had to go to the bathroom. *Right now.* And she couldn't remember him showing her a bathroom.

There was another door leading out of the bedroom and to Meggie's intense relief, it opened onto a bathroom.

It wasn't *quite* like a bathroom on Earth, but there was something to sit on that had a hole in it, and that was good enough. The toilet didn't even seem to need to be flushed. There was no water in the bottom. When she stood up, a thin film of fluid coated the walls of the toilet, then drained away. It looked perfectly clean.

There was a shower—or a sort of shower. Behind a clear partition, a section of the room had a ceiling studded with little holes, and there was a showerhead attached to a hose, very similar to the one Meggie had at home. She felt very brave as she attempted the controls.

There was a panel beside the showerhead, so Meggie just pressed buttons until a warm stream of water was flowing from overhead.

No wonder Kairn was so proud he'd managed to figure out how the tap worked.

She stripped off and stepped in. It was delightful—like being caught in a rainstorm on a hot day. Her shoulders relaxed as the water poured over her, streaming her hair down over her body.

After a while, she decided that she wanted the water just a tiny fraction warmer. Greatly daring, she reached out to the panel to increase the water temperature and pushed a button.

The water shut off completely. Meggie pouted in disappointment, realising suddenly that she didn't have a towel.

A moment later, her concerns about linen were eclipsed by a much bigger problem. Steam started pouring out of vents in the wall. Meggie yelped in fright and backed away, but the vents were all around her, even beneath her feet. *Steam,* Meggie thought. *Or... gas. Oh, God, I'm going to die!*

She turned to leave the cubicle, but the door had closed behind her. Her shaking hands slipped on the locking mechanism. The steam was hot. *I'm going to die!* she thought again. In her panic, she couldn't get the door open and resorted to just shoving at it.

"Help!" she screamed. "Brav, please! Help!"

Even above the noise she was making shoving at the locked door frame, she heard the pounding beat of his boots as he ran down the hall. He jerked the bathroom door open and met her frantic eyes.

"What is it?" he demanded. "What's wrong?"

"What's *wrong*?" she shrieked. "Get me the *fuck* out of here before I burn to death!"

Eyes wide, he opened the cubicle door. She rushed out of the shower, straight into his embrace. His arms came around her slowly as she cannoned into him. "Meggie—sweetheart–"

"*Please*, just get me out of here!"

He reached out a long arm to a wall panel that opened to display rolled up towels. He swathed her in the soft fabric and swept her up into his arms. "I've got you, sweetheart, you're OK."

Meggie wished she could stay cradled in his arms forever, but he laid her on the bed just a moment later. She kept her arms tight around his neck, but instead of lying on the bed beside her, he knelt on the floor beside it.

"Sweetheart." His voice was warm and deep in her ear, as soothing as the hand he was stroking up and down her back. Her hair was still streaming wet and probably soaking the bed beneath her, but she couldn't do anything but tremble in his arms and press her face into his chest. He didn't push her, just held her gently, soothing that hand up and down her back and murmuring the softest words she'd ever heard.

Eventually, she stopped shaking. He drew away a little and that gentle hand moved to push the wet strands of hair away from her face. She was sure her eyes were red, and a towel isn't exactly the most flattering garment, but nothing in his face showed distaste. He looked... *so tender*, Meggie thought. *He looks like he really cares.*

"What happened, sweetheart?"

Meggie's fingers tightened around his shoulders for a moment. She swallowed hard. "I feel so stupid," she admitted.

He leaned forward to press a kiss to her forehead, devastating her with the sweetness of it. "Tell me, baby. I just want to make it better."

Meggie had to clench her teeth for a moment. She'd never had anyone outside her family care for her like this, never. Brav had only known her for a little while, but his emotions were clear on his face.

"I thought I'd have a shower," she admitted, lowering her gaze to study the black braid sewn into loops around his high collar. "I mean, there isn't anything else for me to do around here." Her eyes flashed up to his in a moment of sudden defiance. "After all, *I* can't run out of the room every three minutes to 'check on the ship.'" Her gaze dropped again. "I figured out the shower. That was fine. I just thought I'd warm the water up a little. Then the water just *stopped*. And this awful steam started coming out of the *walls*. I thought it was going to scald me. And then I thought…"

She had to press her lips tight together as she remembered her fright. She'd been seriously worried she was going to die.

Brav's hand was still stroking her, gentle little circles on her bare shoulder now. "Go on, sweetheart."

"And then I thought, what if it isn't steam? What if it's gas? What if it… what if it could hurt me? I don't know anything about this world. I was so afraid I was going to die because I couldn't work a damn shower." She pressed her face against his chest again, embarrassed.

His hand came up to cradle her head against him and her embarrassment faded. "I was scared," she admitted. "Seems silly now, but our showers don't work like that."

"Nothing to be embarrassed about," he rumbled. "The fault is mine. I should have demonstrated how everything works. I forgot that everything in our world is going to be new to you." He drew her away from him so she could see him smile. "In fact, we should start now. First of all, you're going to need some more clothes."

"Oh, I–" She cut herself off, and sat there, embarrassed again.

"What is it, sweetheart?"

"Nothing."

He tilted his head in an obvious question.

"Fine." She sighed. "I was going to say I don't want to be a bother, but I need clothes. So, I'm naked *and* a doormat."

His eyes flicked down to where she was holding the towel around her body. "I don't know what a doormat is," he admitted and his voice lowered, "but Meggie," he reached out and traced the line of the towel across the swell of her breasts, "you never need to apologise for being naked around me."

Naked, a doormat, *and* aroused. What a combination. Meggie scrambled off the bed. "OK. Um. Where do I get clothes?"

Brav rose to his feet in a smooth movement. *Bet **he** doesn't skip leg day*, Meggie thought, watching the muscles bunch in his powerful thighs. Meggie routinely skipped leg day at the gym. Along with every other day. There wasn't any spare money for gyms.

"Let me show you the replicator," he offered and Meggie's eyes went wide as she realised she'd just been staring at his thighs. *Does he think I was staring at his crotch?* Meggie wondered. She'd been staring in that general location, after all. Her cheeks flamed as she followed him to the wall.

Another blank section of wall. "How do you even find *anything?*" she asked. "Everything is so well tucked away."

"This is a small shuttle." He shrugged. "If everything wasn't tucked away, it would be a mess. Larger ships will have things configured differently. It's written on the panel, though." He indicated a series of marks in a vertical line at the right of the panel. They were finely engraved, and Meggie hadn't even noticed them until now.

"I thought that was just decoration," she admitted.

"What?" He frowned and turned to her. "Decoration? Meggie—I'm sorry, I never even thought to ask. Can you read?"

Her face flamed, but she stood her ground. "Of course I can read," she retorted. "I just can't read *this* language."

"Of course not." It seemed to hit him for the first time how out of her depth she was. "Meggie, please, I want you to feel you can come to me. Last night when you'd never eaten sensation foods— the trouble in the shower this morning…" He swallowed hard. "I'm deeply shamed that I didn't see to your comfort before introducing you to these new experiences."

Meggie put her hand on his arm. "Please don't feel bad," she murmured. "Show me how I can make myself some clothes."

He showed her how to operate the replicator. Everything the machine produced was created out of energy collected when they passed close by a sun and discarded items went through a recycling process where they fed back into the replicator. He assured her she could make as many clothes as she liked, of any type, in any style.

"What do women in your world wear?" she asked. Brav obligingly ran the replicator and handed her a bundle of soft, white fabric. Meggie shook it out.

"So, women wear dresses in your world, too, do they?"

"Sometimes. They can wear other clothing if they wish, but this kind of dress—a chiton—is the most common type of garment. It's worn everywhere, from the home and family gatherings, to the most formal events. Since it's just as easy to replicate complicated clothing as it is to replicate simple clothing, there is no social status attached to fancy clothes."

"Can I try it?"

"Of course." Brav bowed. "I'll wait in the hallway while you get dressed."

Meggie dropped the towel and slipped the dress over her head. She had to bundle her hair up into the discarded towel to stop it from wetting the fabric. The dress was sleeveless and the fabric was very soft and very white, falling in graceful folds from her shoulders to her ankles. "You can come back in, now," she called.

Brav returned. He looked her up and down. "You look lovely, Meggie," he murmured. "But I forgot the belt. Here, let me." He ran the replicator again, and returned to stand in front of her, holding a length of golden rope in his hands. "There are several ways women wear their belts. Some just tie them simply around the waist, and let the ends hang in front. Will you let me show you?"

For answer she raised her arms out from her sides and grinned. "Go on, Brav. Dress me."

He chuckled, and wrapped the long belt twice around her waist, tying it in front so the ends hung nearly to the floor. "See how you like that."

Meggie… was not a fan. A soft dress, tied at the waist, did not flatter her slender figure. It made her look like she didn't have one. She stared at herself in the long mirror and plucked at the fabric, trying to make it look better. Brav came up behind her. His hands came around her waist to settle over hers and still her restless movements.

"Let me show you the other ways," he offered.

Trying to pretend she wasn't upset, Meggie nodded. She wished that she'd thought to change her appearance the first time he'd seen her, but he knew what she really looked like now. She'd had the chance to look hot while she got to know a handsome man and she'd wasted the opportunity.

Brav saw her struggles, though, and after he untied the belt, he smoothed his knuckles over her cheek. "You are beautiful, Meggie, do you know that? So beautiful, no matter what you wear."

She met his eyes gratefully, but had no idea what to say in reply.

This time, he tied the belt higher, wrapping it several times around her ribcage and crossing over itself. "This looks nice," Meggie told him when he was finished. Pulling the soft fabric in beneath her small breasts made her appear more curvaceous.

"There is at least one other way of tying the belt I'd like to show you," Brav said, still behind her.

Meggie met his eyes in the mirror. She felt a lot happier now, realising that it was just that the previous style didn't suit her, not that she herself was inadequate. "Sure," she said.

He untied the belt again. "This method crosses the cord between your beautiful breasts," he informed her.

Meggie stopped breathing for a second. "Show me," she whispered.

He looped the belt around her ribcage, then up between her breasts. Her breath came faster as his hands brushed the sensitive undersides and she was trembling when he finally tied the belt behind her. "What do you think?" he asked.

Meggie stared at herself. Her breasts pushed against the fabric, outlined by the golden cord that continued down, wrapping around her ribcage. The fabric fell in flattering folds around her hips and thighs to her ankles. He'd pulled up part of the fabric at her waist to make its own little pocket, and it also added to the drapery across her body. "I like it," she breathed.

Brav's eyes were fixed on her body in the mirror. "I like it too," he murmured. She watched his Adam's apple bob as he swallowed hard. "You look amazing, Meggie. You look like a goddess."

Meggie couldn't help the instinctive preen, the way her shoulders went back with pride, thrusting her breasts forward a tiny bit more. Brav growled in approval. His hands came up to curve around her arms, stroking down the length of her arms until he took her hands. "I think we should get some breakfast now."

Well, it was better than checking on the ship again.

"One more thing," he said, before they left the cabin. "I'd like you to wear this again."

It was the communicator he'd given her, back on Earth.

"But I thought it was smashed when I was attacked!" she exclaimed.

"I fixed it. I want to know that you are safe. I'll feel better if you're wearing it."

She held out her wrist and allowed him to fasten the communicator to it this time.

He kept hold of her hand as they made their way to the dining area. His hand engulfed hers and she felt small and feminine as she walked beside him. He only let her hand go when they were standing in front of the food-prep area.

Like last night, he pulled out the bench under the wall, then ran his hand down the line of what she now knew were letters engraved into the surface of the wall. "This says 'Food Preparation,'" he told her. "I'll sit down with you later and show you all the letters, so you know what you're reading. Unfortunately, it won't be a matter of just learning the alphabet, because it's written in the Common language. When Jessan gave you the ability to communicate, that only applies to spoken language, not written words. But that can be a task for later. Right now, I'll show you how to make any food you want."

Like the replicator in her room, this one was powered by energy gathered when they passed close by a sun. Meggie's initial attempts at making orange juice ended up with a glass of neon orange flavoured water, a thick orange soup that smelled sour rather than tangy and lastly a solid lump that was closer to brown than orange.

"I'm not even touching that," Meggie took a step back from the replicator. "I don't even want to smell it."

Chuckling, Brav took some tongs and disposed of the lump in the garbage chute, as he had with the previous attempts.

"How can I describe a food this thing has never seen before?" she asked. "It's going to take me years to just get breakfast. Brav, I don't think I can wait that long for breakfast."

A broad smile split his face at her pitiful joke. "Don't worry, sweetheart, there is another way we can program the machine." His hand came up to stroke her cheek again, then pressed lightly to her temple. "It's just a bit more… intimate."

"OK." And if she breathed it like she wasn't capable of speaking out loud anymore, who cared? His touch on her face was devastating.

He made a soft, rumbling sound deep in his chest. "Unfortunately, the intimacy isn't with me. It's with the replicator."

Meggie blinked, the spell broken. "What?"

"The replicator." He reached out and brought a small patch, barely more than an inch across, to her face. "I need to place this on your temple. May I? It won't hurt. It will just allow you to control the replicator with your mind."

"Mind control?" Meggie asked, dazedly, then laughed unexpectedly. She'd heard of mind control before, but never mind control of machines!

"It's the most efficient way. Do you want to try it?"

"OK." A more practical OK this time, without the breathy, husky tone that said "OK" was code for 'Take me now.'

He placed the patch on her temple. It was cool, but not uncomfortable, and adhered lightly to her skin. "Now, think of the food you want the replicator to produce. The size, shape, colour, texture, taste. Then press this button for the replicator to produce it."

Orange juice, Meggie thought. *Orange juice, orange juice, orange juice. Sweet, tangy and bright.* She'd never thought so hard about orange juice before. Tentatively, she reached out for the button and pushed it.

A glass appeared on the tray, which was a better start than the brown lump. As the glass materialised, a liquid appeared in it.

"How does it look?" Brav asked.

Meggie brought the glass to her nose and sniffed. "It looks right. Here goes nothing." She raised the glass to her lips. The sweet, tangy, bright taste of orange juice exploded in her mouth. "Mmm, Brav, tastes so good." She opened her eyes to surprise an expression of naked hunger on his face, quickly controlled. "Do you, um, do you want some?"

She held out the glass to him and he took a swig. "Delicious," he declared. "You're good at this, Meggie. You got it on the first try. I suppose it makes sense, given your heritage."

"My heritage?"

Brav handed the glass back to her. "Artemis said that you were her sister's daughter, isn't that right?"

"That's right."

"Well, this technology is designed to work with your kind. It has a special affinity with your thought-patterns and your abilities." Something flared in his eyes. "I never thought I'd say this, but I'm a bit sorry we're not on one of Aphrodite's ships."

"Aphrodite? Wasn't she a goddess?"

Brav nodded. "She is a goddess. The ruler of a suite of systems in this sector. She is the goddess of love. Of pleasure. And that's what her ships run on: pleasure. She doesn't bother harvesting power from a nearby sun. She leans back in the control chair and the Master of her Wardrobe sticks his head up her skirt. Since she is truly god-born, unlike all the other so-called gods, her pleasure feeds the ship's engines."

Meggie's eyes went wide. "You mean that… literally…"

"Literally. You look a little like her, you know. Same dark hair, same dark eyes." A corner of Brav's mouth pulled up in the tiniest smile. He'd gotten so grim while he was talking about how

Aphrodite powered her ships. "But your eyes are soft. Hers are hard. Like granite. She cares only about what she wants. But you…" His hand rose to trace the golden cord that crossed between her breasts, over the soft fabric of her chiton. "I think I'd enjoy helping you power the ship."

Meggie's breath was coming faster. His fingertip was still between her breasts. "I've always been a helpful person. If that's what the ship needs…"

Brav leaned forward.

And an alarm went off.

Both of them closed their eyes on a heartfelt sigh, then chuckled together in a way that seemed as intimate as any kiss. "Come on," he said, taking her hand. "That's important. I set up an alert for the shuttle to tell us when it found the ship that took your sisters."

He took her into the cockpit. In front of them was a large display screen. Meggie stared at it, trying to figure out what she was looking at. It was difficult, because it was so dark. There definitely wasn't another ship there that she could see.

She was about to make a smart remark about how she couldn't see anything. Then he groaned, soft and low. "Oh, Meggie. Meggie, I'm so sorry–" and the bottom fell out of her world.

CHAPTER SEVEN

Everything went quiet inside her.

"No," she said, before she even knew what she was saying 'No' to. There was nothing on the screen. Just black. Just the black depths of space, and some little things that reflected the lights from their shuttle.

"No," she said again, as a larger piece of debris slowly slid past her view. Debris. That's what it was. Debris. From something larger. Something made of the metal pieces that were now shredded and spinning gently in the exterior shuttle lights.

His hand landed on her shoulder. "Meggie, I'm so sorry."

"There isn't anything to be sorry about," she insisted, but she didn't turn to look at him where he stood behind her. All her attention was on the spinning debris before her. "No, Brav, you've made a mistake. You got the trails crossed or something. Or this is just a piece of a ship. Maybe they did it to throw you off the trail. There—there aren't enough pieces for a whole ship."

Brav cleared his throat. "It was vaporised," he said gruffly. "Meggie, it would have been instant."

"No, you've made a mistake. I'd know if something ha-happened to Teresa. I'd just know. She's a part of me. Bess and Cera, too. I couldn't lose all three of them in one moment and not *know*." She shook his hand off her shoulder. "No, Brav. We'll find them."

"Meggie —"

"*Stop* saying my name like that!" she cried, whirling away from him. "Just *stop* it, Brav! Sit your ass down in that chair and get us the *hell* away from here! We need to find them!"

He didn't sit. He didn't move. He didn't even flinch as she threw herself at him, battering him with nerveless hands. He let her beat at him until she collapsed against him, then his hands were there to hold her up.

"No," she moaned. "Brav, no."

He put his arms around her shoulders. Her hands curled into his jacket and she held on for dear life. On a broken, shuddering indrawn breath, the tears came. She didn't know how long she wept there, but she knew there would never be enough tears to ease her grief.

When her knees buckled, he lifted her easily into his arms. "I've got you, Meggie," he murmured. He carried her back to the bedroom and laid her on the bed. She clung to him, but he gently extricated himself from her clinging hands to go into the bathroom.

He came back with a damp washcloth in his hands, a thing recognisable in any universe. He cleaned her face and that was when she realised that she'd stopped crying. It hurt too much to even cry.

Brav sat beside her on the bed and wiped her face. She stared at him, unable to even understand what was happening. It was like something inside her had broken. Once her face was clean and he'd tossed the washcloth onto the bedside locker, she leaned forward to rest her face against him again.

"Don't leave me," she whispered, not sure if she was talking to him or Teresa.

"I'm here," he replied, stroking her hair. He swung her legs up on the bed and came down beside her on the narrow surface. He gathered her into his arms so that her head was resting on his chest and again his hands were soothing in her hair. "I'm here, sweetheart."

"Sorry I cried all over you," she whispered, embarrassed, but knowing that she was going to cry again and probably soon.

The gentle stroking of her hair never paused. "I've shed my share of tears, Meggie. When I was taken from my family. When I lost one of my brother Guardians to battle or disease. And six years ago, when I thought I'd never see freedom again. It's OK to cry, Meggie."

She cried. Eventually, exhausted, she slept. She dreamed of Teresa, hands bound in the dark with Bess and Cera as everything around her went very bright then very dark, and when she woke, she cried again. Brav's hand soothed her the whole time. Finally, she fell into a deep, dreamless sleep.

*   *   *

She woke to another alarm. It was loud and intrusive. Her arms and legs were tangled with Brav's and for one of the worst moments of her life, she didn't recognise him.

"No!" she screamed, kicking and flailing. "Get off me! Get off me!"

He was off the bed in an instant, bending down so his face was level with hers. She slapped him—as hard as she could. He caught her hand against his cheek and held it there, holding her terrified gaze with his own.

"It's me, Meggie. Brav. Look at me, sweetheart. It's just me. You're safe."

"Safe?" she repeated, feeling fear run like cold water along her bones. "Brav?"

"Yeah, sweetheart. It's OK. Let me go see what this alarm is about and I'll come back to you."

He let her hand go and rose to his full height. She struggled off the bed, her limbs heavy and uncooperative. "What's that alarm?"

"It's a proximity alarm, sweetheart. I have to go. We've got company."

"I'm coming with you," she stated.

She expected him to fight her, but he just nodded, took her hand, and brought her along with him into the cockpit. He guided her swiftly into one of the seats in front of the console and took the other. She had to swallow hard as she looked at the viewscreen. The last time she'd looked at it, she'd seen the remains of the ship that had taken Teresa from her. She struggled not to heave when she saw a piece of debris still floating in front of them.

"I can't see them," she whispered.

"They're beyond visual range. Space travel is very fast, sweetheart. You won't be able to see them until they're right on top of us."

He shut off the shrieking proximity alert, then something else started to beep. "What's that?"

"They're hailing us," Brav informed her. He flipped a switch. "This is Shuttle Alpha Valoran. State your designation."

A lazy voice came from the comm panel. "This is Gerea Prime,

Shuttle Alpha. Would you care to explain what the fuck happened here?"

Brav glanced at Meggie and coughed uncomfortably. "Uh, Gerea Prime, be advised I have a lady with me." To Meggie, he said, "It's my brothers."

The lazy voice turned sharp. "Which lady?" it demanded. "Cera, baby, are you there?"

Meggie recognised the voice as Jessan. She leaned forward, over the comm panel. "No, it's..." she had to clear her throat. "It's Meggie. The others..." Even with a clear throat, she couldn't say it.

"Their ship was destroyed." Brav said it for her, reaching out to cover her hand with his. "Meggie and I have been following their trail for the last 37 hours. We arrived here three hours ago." His voice lowered. "There was nothing left but debris."

"And?"

Brav shook his head, although Meggie was pretty sure the conversation was audio only. His voice hardened. "Nothing but debris," he reiterated.

"The fuck there was," Jessan growled.

"Watch your language," a voice said on Jessan's end. Meggie thought she recognised Tarn.

"There's something," Jessan insisted. "A life pod. A shuttle. Fuck, a *bubble*, I don't know. But they are *not* dead."

Meggie's face twisted and the tears ran down her cheeks again. She put her face in her hands and her shoulders shook as she tried to restrain the sobs.

"Turn your fucking viewscreen on, Brav, and look me in the godsdamn eyes when you lie to me!" Jessan roared.

Brav flipped a switch. His voice was hard. "Watch your tone," he snapped. "She's been through enough."

Meggie removed her hands enough to look up at the screen. Jessan was right in front of the camera. He was furious, his face puce with anger, white lines of strain bracketing his lips. His lips pressed tightly together when he saw her and he took a step back from the camera. "Don't cry," he rasped.

"My sister is dead!" she shouted back. "Don't you tell me not to cry!"

Pain ripped at her belly and she slid out of her chair to kneel beside Brav and bury her face in his knee. "Jessan, control yourself," Brav gritted. "You're not helping."

There was a moment of silence as Jessan took a deep breath. "Sister, listen, please. They're not dead. I'm telling you. I'm not making this up. Do you remember when we were at your aunt's house and Cera and I spoke together without words?"

Meggie nodded, but didn't look up. Brav's hand cradled her head.

"Sister, *I can still hear her.* Cera isn't dead. And she isn't alone. There are two others with her she loves."

Meggie looked up, her tears evaporating. "What?"

"I said, I can still hear her. Cera is alive. And I believe your sister and hers are alive, too."

He went on, but Meggie could hardly hear him past the rushing in her ears. She struggled to her feet, and Brav caught her when she fainted.

When she awoke, she was on the other ship. She was lying on a different bed, and five Guardians were seated on chairs nearby. To a man, they had their heads bowed, their hands clasped and their elbows resting on their knees. One of them was speaking softly. He was the blonde one who had sat beside Teresa in Leona's house. What was his name? Kairn.

Brav launched himself out of his seat when he saw she was awake. His big hand was warm and gentle on her brow. "Sweetheart, are you feeling any better?" His other hand took possession of hers.

She sighed, and it still shuddered a bit. "Better now," she assured him, curling her fingers around his big palm. "Brav, where are they? Are they far away?"

"We don't know where they are," Jessan admitted, rising to his feet to stand on the other side of her bed. "All we know is that they're still alive."

"But… why don't you just ask them? If you're in contact with Cera. Even if she only describes her surroundings, won't that help?"

Jessan shook his head. "It isn't like that. I can't—I can't get through to her right now. She's reaching out for me, but she can't hear me."

"Are we too far away?" Meggie asked.

Jessan's lips pressed together tightly for a moment and those white lines of strain appeared around his mouth again. "No." He swallowed hard. "She can't hear me because she can't stop screaming."

Meggie was glad she was lying down, glad she had Brav's firm hands anchoring her to the bed, anchoring her to life itself, because

Jessan's words terrified her so much she feared she would faint again.

She opened her mouth to speak and found that not a word came out of it.

"Why is she screaming?" Brav asked. "Is she… physically hurt?"

Jessan shook his head. "No, I don't believe she is physically hurt. But she's frightened. Very frightened."

"It isn't like Cera to be frightened," Meggie got out eventually.

Jessan's face was grim. "I know."

Kairn rose to stand beside Brav. "We found another trail, my lady. We believe that the Malia ship was overcome by slavers."

"Malia?" Meggie asked.

"It's the name used by Everius's smallest squads. It's similar to the word for honeybee, and to the word for evil."

"How do you know it was Everius who took them?"

"There was one moment when someone came into their cell," Jessan answered, his voice tight. "A moment of light and terror. He gave them water." Meggie was pretty sure there was more that he wasn't telling, because for a moment he looked like he was going to kill someone. "I recognised the uniform."

"What do we do next?" she asked.

"We're tracking the ship," Tarn assured her, coming to stand at the foot of her bed, so that only the dark wild man who'd brooded behind Teresa was still in his chair. "They're taking a direct route, so it seems like they don't know they're being followed."

"Where are they going?" She knew she wasn't going to like the answer.

"Clarion Quint," Tarn answered.

"A slave market," Jessan elaborated.

"We can't outpace them," Tarn went on, "but we should arrive only a few hours after they do."

"How long does it take to sell a slave?" Meggie asked, hardly able to believe what she was saying.

"Hours," Brav answered quickly, and she wondered how he knew. "First, the slaves have to be sorted, evaluated, tagged, prepared. There will be a lot of them. It's chaotic. It will take time."

"Do we have money?" She felt stupid. She didn't even know how money worked out here.

The faces around her were tight. "Everything we have," Jessan growled. "All of us."

Meggie looked from one stern face to another. "Why would you do that for us?" she asked eventually. "You don't even know us."

"Cera is my *mate*," Jessan growled. "I will give my life for her."

"And Bess is mine," Tarn added.

Kairn patted her hand. "Your sister Teresa is my mate."

Finally, the dark man who'd hung back all this time rose to his feet. "And mine," he announced, his voice a deep growl.

Meggie blinked. She looked from him to Kairn. "But you said Teresa was *your* mate."

Kairn nodded. "Mac and I are bond-brothers. We both love your sister. We will *both* cherish her." He looked around the room. "Gentlemen, I believe that's our cue. We will leave you two alone now."

He bowed and left the room. All the others except Brav followed. Mac was the last to leave. He hesitated at the doorway. "I don't have fancy words," he growled, "but I will love her all my life."

The door slid shut behind him. Meggie and Brav were alone. Brav smiled gently down at her and stroked the hair from her face. "I'm yours, Meggie," he murmured. "I've always been yours."

Meggie stared at him, drowning in his silver eyes. "How do you know?" she asked. "What does it mean when they say that my sister is their mate? They sounded so serious. But they've just met. Haven't they?"

Brav reached out and brought a chair close to the bed and sat beside her. He didn't let go of her hand the whole time. "It has to do with what we are, Meggie. And what you are."

"I don't understand."

"I'll explain it to you, sweetheart. You're an Alterran. One of the race of the gods, who first populated the Earth. You saw the affinity you had with the replicator. Your kind were the template that our civilisation is built on. Thousands of years ago, the Guardians of the House of Valor were just humans, just ordinary guards. Then the best among us were selected for—improvement."

A shiver ran down her spine. "What does 'improvement' mean, Brav?"

He shrugged. "We were treated. Genetically altered. We became bigger, stronger, faster. Some of us, like Jessan, developed powers like the Alterrans have. We are trained from childhood. If we survive the training, the best of us are still selected for improvement. When we are changed, we are changed to be a match for one particular woman, one Alterran, who is fated to be our mate. We are literally designed for her."

"Are you–?" Her voice trailed off.

"Yes, Meggie." He bent his head and kissed her hand. "I was designed for you."

"How do you know it was me, though?" She struggled to sit up and his hands were there to help her. As he'd always been there to help her, she realised. She didn't even need to ask. He just saw her need and moved to meet it.

"We are shown on the date of our graduation." He smiled fondly at the memory. "I graduated far too long ago, but I remember it like it was yesterday. It will always be one of my most cherished memories, because it was the first time I saw *you*."

They were taken into a darkened room in Solace Station, he explained, where the young were trained. There, the triple-faced goddess who wove the fates of the Guardians with the Alterrans showed them the face of their mate in a mirror. There was wonder in his eyes as he recounted the story.

"Even though it was seven years ago, I saw you as you are today. I thought of your face every day for the rest of my life since then. When I saw you on Earth, I could hardly believe you were real."

Meggie blushed. "I hope you weren't disappointed. I'm quite a bit older now–"

His caressing finger on her lips stopped her rambling. "You're so beautiful I can't believe how privileged I am to call you my mate. My Megara." He whispered the name like it was sacred.

She started. "No one but Leona knows my real name," she breathed. "Everyone thinks Meggie is short for Margaret, but it's not. I was named after my mother. How did you know?"

"I've carried that name in my heart ever since I became a Guardian. You're the only one for me, Meggie. Forever."

"But…" Her hands twisted in the folds of her dress. "Does that mean I have to marry you? I mean, I like you, but what if I didn't? What if it turns out that Bess can't stand the sight of Tarn? What if Teresa is horrified by the thought that not one but *two* men want to claim her? She's so innocent, Brav, so young!"

"I was designed for you, Meggie," he answered. "I am yours. You are my mate. I am bound to you forever. That places no obligation on you, or on your sisters. It's up to me to win you. Up to Tarn to win Bess, up to Kairn and Mac to win Teresa." A smile twitched at his lips. "And to be honest, I'm looking forward to watching Jessan grovel at Cera's feet, because he will, you know. He'd do anything for her, the same way I'd do anything for you."

Meggie stared at him. It was all so strange. Designed for her? How could that be true?

But he was everything she'd ever dreamed of. She needed his gentleness. She needed his attentive care, his steady strength. She'd been through a lot in her life. Losing her mother had shaken her and she'd never been steady since. Trying to look after Teresa when their father didn't bother to see to their needs. Getting a job at fourteen, pretending to be older. Tolerating Colin's hands and mouth on her because she needed that job.

She shuddered in disgust.

Physically, Brav was everything she'd ever dreamed of, too. He was tall and muscular, with thick dark hair and flashing dark eyes. What woman *wouldn't* be attracted to him? But behind her attraction to Brav was her memory of everything Colin had done to her. Everything he'd required of her, so that he would keep her secret.

"Meggie?" he asked. Her eyes flew up to him for the briefest of moments, enough to see the frown furrow his brow. "Meggie, I meant it. You don't have to do anything you don't want to do."

"Well, that's just it." She spoke too quickly and the words tumbled over each other. "What if…? Brav… I think I've given you the wrong idea. I don't… I can't." She kept her eyes down and shuddered again. "That kiss last night was a mistake. I don't know what I was thinking."

He wasn't even touching her. She was sure if he touched her, her skin would crawl, because it wouldn't be *his* hands on her, it would be Colin's hands, all over again.

"It wasn't exactly a kiss, though, was it?"

Her eyes darted up to his for another brief, brief moment. His expression was bland.

"It was the Averones. The sauce was too spicy for you. I understand that."

She'd begged for his tongue in her mouth. For a moment she almost wished that he would ignore her protests and kiss her again. Wished that he would press her back into the bed and show her that making love wasn't something to be afraid of.

But if he did, she'd scream and scream and she wasn't sure she'd ever stop being afraid.

"It's all right, my lady," he said, and his voice was suddenly distant and professional. "I know that this is a lot to take in. You will need some rest. This cabin is yours. You will not be disturbed here. If you need anything, use the communicator."

He bowed and left her alone. She locked the door behind him.

CHAPTER EIGHT

<u>Brav</u>

Outside Meggie's room, Brav's knees failed him. The sound of the lock closing behind him nearly undid him. He slid down the wall. That expression of fear in her eyes had cut through him like a knife. After all they'd been through, how could she look at him like that? It felt like a betrayal and he fought the feelings rising within him. Why didn't she trust him?

He'd give his life for her. That went almost without saying. He was hers. Every bone, every muscle, every cell in his body was hers. Completely hers.

And she didn't want him.

He tilted his head back against the steel wall, trying to find a steady spot in the world again while everything whirled around him. He ached to go back in there and show her he wasn't going to hurt her. But there was not a damn thing he could do that wouldn't do the very opposite. The only way to show her he loved her right now was to leave her alone.

He didn't even hear Tarn approach.

"Rough day?" Tarn asked.

Brav buried his face in his hands. "Gods, Tarn, you have no idea."

Tarn sat down beside him. "You shouldn't have gone off by yourself. The others have taken Artemis to Desiderus Nonus. We would have gone with you. You know that."

"You had the mission to think about. I don't even know why

you're here."

Tarn let the moment stretch out for an extra heartbeat. "Brav, we're family. We're here for *you.*"

Brav drew in a deep breath. "I get it. Your mates are in danger, too. I should have said something instead of just running. I know that you want to protect your mate just as much as I want to protect mine."

"We're here for you, too, Brav. We're your brothers. We'd go through fire for you, the same as you would for us."

"Ha." It wasn't a funny sound. Brav scrubbed at his face with his hands, then faced the other man with a bitter look. "Before," he said succinctly.

"Always," Tarn insisted. "Look, I don't know what happened to you before you came back to us last year. You've done a damned good job of keeping it secret. Even Jessan can't pry it out of your mind, and he's tried. But there is not one damned thing in this universe that can change the fact that you're our brother. Not one damned thing."

Brav remained stubbornly silent. He wasn't sure if he was glad or sorry that they didn't know.

Tarn rose to his feet. "Get up. It's time to eat. Jessan's waiting in the dining room to kick your ass."

He wasn't wrong. Jessan's eyes narrowed when he saw Brav enter the dining room. He leaned back in his chair and crossed his arms over his massive chest. "You've got three seconds to make your excuses."

Brav faced him directly. "My mate," he retorted.

Jessan nodded. "Fair enough. But by all the gods, Brav, the next time you disappear without telling anyone, I'm going to lose my fucking shit. You're part of a team here, and that means letting us help you. I'm nearly out of my mind worried about Cera. Don't make me worry about losing you, too." His voice dropped briefly. "I can't lose you again, brother."

Kairn and Mac came into the room and Jessan scowled at them. "Someone hurry up and get that godsdamn replicator running," Jessan snarled. "I feel like I haven't eaten for days. Where do you think you're going, mister?" He leaped to his feet, both hands on the table and leaned forward threateningly as Brav left the room.

Brav's voice was hoarse as he replied, "I'm going to see if my mate wants something to eat."

Meggie

Meggie heard the chime coming from the door and was proud of herself when she waved her hand over the panel to unlock it. She might not be able to read, but at least she was able to open the damn door now. *It's all about progress,* she thought to herself.

Progress. When she couldn't even bear the thought of having the man she loved put his hands on her.

The man she loved? She thought about it, almost as though she was tasting the thought like a new food. The man she loved. It felt right. Brav was the man she loved.

And there he was, on the other side of the door.

Her heart skipped a beat, even though he'd barely left her five minutes before.

"We're having supper," he said without preamble. "Would you like to join us?"

Meggie nodded. "OK," she replied, wishing that her voice didn't sound quite so small. Brav bowed and gestured for her to accompany him. He didn't take her hand this time and she found she missed it.

He led her to a large open room with a massive table in the centre of it. The Guardians were already busy ferrying dishes from the replicator to the table. Tarn saw her first, his hands full of a huge serving dish of roast meat. He stopped in his tracks, smiled and bowed.

The others saw him, then turned to her and did the same, even Jessan, who had nothing near Tarn's grace.

"Um, thank you," she said. "I—I don't know what to do."

"Just smile at us, my lady," Tarn replied graciously. "We're all in love with your sisters. We want to make a good impression. If you smile at us, it makes us feel like we've got a chance."

That made Meggie laugh and relax a little, though Brav stiffened behind her.

Tarn put the roast down then came to offer Meggie his arm. "May I see you to the table, my lady?"

Blushing, she agreed. Brav stayed in the doorway and she wished he would come with her. She felt a little lost without him.

Tarn steered Meggie to the head of the table. "Oh, no, I couldn't," she protested. "I'm shy, Tarn, really shy."

Kairn deposited a bowl of fruit in front of her. "You're going to have to get used to being the centre of attention, my lady. You're the only woman on a ship with five men. There's not one of us here who wouldn't rather talk to you than anyone."

That just made her blush all the more, but she let Tarn edge the seat in behind her as she sat.

With all of them working, it didn't take long to set the table and load it with food. Meggie stared at the feast laid out before them. Obviously, men who were twice her size were going to eat more than she did, but she'd never translated that into the sheer volume of food on the table.

Tarn sat on one side of her, and Brav sat at the other. She'd been half afraid that he was going to avoid her all evening. Jessan sat at the other end of the table and Kairn and Mac sat at his left and right hand. She somehow suspected that Tarn and Brav usually took those places, but tonight the head of the table had shifted a little.

"We usually say a prayer before we eat together as a family, my lady," Jessan announced. "Would you like to give thanks for the food?"

If Meggie blushed any harder, she was going to develop a medical condition. Still, she nodded. She hadn't said it out loud for years, but she still remembered the words her mother had spoken over her meals. She repeated it, in the same little rhythmic tone her mother had used that was somewhere between speech and song.

"The birds of the air ask their food from the sky. The beasts of the field find sustenance from the earth. The fish in the sea slake their thirst in the mighty waters. We give thanks for the food before us. We give thanks for the sky and the earth and the sea. We ask blessings for all those around this table."

"We give thanks." "We give thanks." They all said it, murmured low in their deep voices, their heads bowed. Only Brav looked directly at her as he said, "We give thanks."

They were eager to serve her. She loaded her plate with more food than she could possibly eat, protesting all the while, but they insisted that she try at least a little of everything.

Meggie agreed, then a thought occurred to her. "Um, none of this is very, uh, spicy, is it? I had some Averones last night and it turns out I'm not as good with spicy foods as I thought."

Every eye around the table turned to Brav.

Averones, Tarn mouthed around a toothy grin.

"Averones, huh?" Jessan asked. "Sensation foods. *Fancy.*" There was a wealth of scorn in that one word. "What else did he give you?"

Glancing at Brav, Meggie answered, "Um, it was a roast. I forget what kind. And bread. And a drink. I'm sorry, I forget the names."

"Calreian roast," Brav supplied shortly. "Joradan bread. Forlaria. And Averones to finish."

They all looked disappointed. "That's *all?*" Kairn asked after a long pause. "You fed your mate sensation foods and that's all you gave her?"

Brav picked up a small fruit that looked like a grape and pegged it playfully across the table at Karin. "We'd just met. She'd been injured. And mind your own godsdamned business."

"You'll have to ask him about other sensation foods later, sister," Jessan smirked. He caught the grape Brav threw at him easily.

"Just not at my table," Tarn said, moving the grape-like fruits out of Brav's reach. "Forgive them, my lady. Not one of them knows how to behave."

"Is this your ship?" she asked, trying her first slice of bread. It was soft on the inside and crusty on the outside, slathered with butter just the way she liked it.

"Yep, it's his ship," Jessan answered for her. "You wouldn't think it to hear him talk like an aristocrat, but Tarn here drives the shittiest ship in Gerea."

"Jessan!" Kairn exclaimed while Mac growled at the rough language. Their protectiveness made Meggie feel warm and happy.

"It belonged to my great-grandfather," Tarn explained.

"Exactly," Jessan. "It's *old.*"

"It's *vintage.*"

"It's a crap-bucket."

"Language!" Tarn admonished as Meggie held back a giggle. "Anyway, it keeps the godhunters off my ass—tail."

Jessan bowed from the waist without rising from his chair. "You're welcome to stay with us in this *vintage* crap-bucket, sister, if you wish."

Meggie couldn't help her grin. "Certainly," she said. "Why do you call me 'sister'?"

Jessan looked down at his plate. "Cera's my mate," he said. "She called you her sister. So, you're my sister, too." He scowled around the table. "Unfortunately, these are all my brothers, so you just got yourself a vintage crap-bucket of family here, whether you want it or not."

Meggie was touched. Cera had described her as her sister? She hadn't known. She'd been practically alone for so long, with no-one else to rely on. Now she had Cera and Bess for sisters as well as Teresa, and five huge Guardians for brothers. Her gaze slewed to Brav, as it always did. Scratch that. Three sisters. Four huge Guardians for brothers. One huge Guardian that belonged to her body and soul.

*　　　*　　　*

They reached Clarion Quint the next day. Meggie had never really considered the concept of orbital traffic before, but as they got caught in the endless procession of ships, moving with imperceptible slowness, she realised that some things are the same everywhere.

From orbit, Clarion Quint looked a lot like Earth. It was blue and green and round, it was just the patterns that were different. Another planet.

"Come into the dining room and we'll let you know what's going to happen," Tarn invited. Aside from Brav, he was the one she felt most comfortable with, and Brav was barely speaking to her right now.

The other Guardians filed in and sat around the table. Brav pulled out a chair for her, then sat beside her, but didn't speak.

"The slave markets on Clarion Quint are extensive," Tarn began, calling up a map on the surface of the table. "Every major city on the southern continent is a trading hub."

Meggie stared at the map and despair began to grow inside her. "It's so vast," she whispered. "How will we ever find them?"

Brav's hand found hers in silent reassurance.

"It's a market planet," Kairn explained. "Forgive me for saying it so bluntly, my lady, but it's important that customers can find the… the merchandise."

Her sisters. Merchandise. She wanted to throw up. She looked at the map. How many other people's sisters were also merchandise down there?

Kairn pointed to a spot on the map. "This is where the women are sold."

"But that's a whole city," Meggie protested. "It would take us years to find them and we've only got hours!" Her hand tightened in Brav's grip.

"A set of three would bring a high price," Brav said. "That

narrows it down some. Cera's abilities narrow it down a good deal more. There is only one auction house in Orvis that would handle the clientele who would bid for her."

Meggie felt like she was shaking all over. "Why is that?" she asked.

"Cera's abilities make her dangerous," Jessan said. His face was taut. "Right now, she is wearing a collar that inhibits her abilities, but it can't hold her forever. Her powers mean that she would be in great demand, but it also means that most buyers wouldn't have the means to control her." He enlarged the map and pointed to a specific part of the city. "Here. She would be sold here."

"What if they're separated?"

Jessan shook his head. "They won't be separated. They're related." His lips compressed briefly and when he spoke, his voice was rough. "They're worth more as a set."

Meggie was surprised by the low growl that echoed around the table, and she realised that each of the Guardians had contributed to the angry, possessive sound, even the civilised Tarn. Brav caught her gaze. "We'll find them, Meggie."

Seeming to come himself, Jessan sat up straighter. "We'll go down to the surface at the top of the hour, sister. We'll bring your sisters home to you."

It took a moment for his words to sink in. "Wait... I'm not staying up here while you're down there."

"Yes, you are, sister. That's the plan."

"To hell with the plan!" Meggie cried. She rose to her feet. "I'm going with you." She turned from Jessan to Brav. "I'm not asking. I'm going down to the planet with you."

"Absolutely not!" Brav shot to his feet. "If you think I'm taking you down there, you're much mistaken, my lady!"

"I'm not going to sit around here and wring my hands while I wait to see what happens!" she shouted back.

She could practically hear Brav mentally counting to ten. When he spoke, his voice was tight. He was clearly trying to be reasonable.

"You don't know what it's like down there. Last night you were so shy you didn't even want to sit at the head of the table!"

"I don't see what that has to do with anything!"

"No, you don't. Because you don't know what it's like down there. This is the women's market, Meggie. The only women down there are slaves. If you were to come with us, you'd have to pretend to be my slave, and I know damn well that you're not ready for that."

"I'd do anything to save my sisters." She faced him, feeling like a kitten facing down a German Shepherd.

His hand came up to caress her cheek in an unexpectedly tender gesture that tore at her heart. "Sweetheart, I just want you to be safe. I don't want to be the one to scare you."

She let her voice lower to match his. "I'm going to be scared anyway, Brav. I'd rather be scared with you than scared and alone."

He sighed and closed his eyes for a moment.

Chairs scraped across the floor as all the other Guardians stood. "Told you it'd be better if she came with us," Jessan remarked. "You've got–" he looked at his wrist device, "just over half an hour to prepare her. We'll meet you in the embarkation room."

They left Brav and Meggie alone. Brav hardly even seemed to notice that they'd gone. He was still touching her cheek. "You can change your mind at any time, Meggie. I want you to know that."

"I'm ready, Brav. Tell me what I need to know."

Reluctantly, she thought, he withdrew his hand from her cheek. "Fine," he said. His voice was stern. He stepped back. "Strip."

Her mouth fell open. He raised his hand as if to strike her. Meggie took a stumbling step back. "Brav, you wouldn't," she whimpered.

"No, I wouldn't," he growled. He stalked forward and took her by the shoulders. "But if you're going to pretend to be my slave, you need to be obedient. Instantly obedient. Any slave who hesitated to obey her master like you just did *would* be punished." He let her go. "Now, slave. Strip."

CHAPTER NINE

Heart pounding, Meggie raised her hand to the golden cord wrapped around her chest.

"You belong to me now," Brav growled. "Your body, your life, to do with however I please. If you think you can pull this off down there on Clarion Quint, you need to be able to do this for me."

Meggie pulled at the golden cord. The dress fell loose from her shoulders. She dropped the cord. What was he going to do? And was he really going to do it *here*, in the dining room, where they'd eaten dinner and breakfast with his brothers?

He leaned forward and spoke into her ear. "I want you naked, slave. Now."

He walked past her. Meggie's trembling hands smoothed the soft, white fabric from her shoulders. The fabric of the chiton puddled on the floor around her. She'd replicated underwear for herself, so she pulled those off, too. She stood there, naked, in the middle of the dining room, where anyone could walk in on them. She wrapped her hands around herself.

"I—I did it… Master," she whispered.

"Good girl." He sounded like he was a distance away from her, but Meggie couldn't bring herself to turn around and find out. He said something indistinct she couldn't make out. She swallowed hard as she heard his footsteps returning to her.

She flinched when she felt something settle onto her shoulders. It took her a moment to realise it was another dress. Her trembling hands came up to catch at the edges of the fabric and she realised it was practically see-through.

"Brav, do I have to… to wear this?" It was so thin it could barely be described as a garment.

"This is what slaves wear." He came around to face her, closing the front of the gown to shield her. She realised that even though he'd commanded her to strip, he hadn't even looked at her naked body.

"But… but it's open all the way down the front."

He raised his hand. "You also wear these."

These turned out to be a golden metal bra, and a sort of belt with an ornate flap that hung down over her front to her knees, but it was barely more than six inches wide.

"You need to be comfortable with me doing anything I want to you. Raise your arms a little so I can get this around you. Be a good girl for your Master, slave."

She needed to be comfortable with him doing anything he wanted to her? And, apparently, what he wanted right now was to dress her. He clasped the golden bra around her chest. The belt hung low on her hips, the flap doing very little to preserve her modesty. Behind her, there was nothing but a single layer of transparent fabric between her bare ass and the world.

This is what you wanted, isn't it? she asked herself. *You can be brave. You told him so.*

Brav stepped back to admire his handiwork. Meggie stood there, heart pounding, and let him look. She realised that this was the first time he'd looked at her since he ordered her to strip. He'd kept his back turned or his eyes down until she was covered. By the time his eyes came back to her face, she couldn't help but notice the bulge that had grown in his trousers.

"You will do what you are told," he informed her, his voice rough. "No matter what, you will obey without question, without hesitation. You will only speak when spoken to and you won't speak to anyone but me. Is that understood?"

"Yes, Master."

Her breathing was coming faster. She'd never admit it, but the scenario was kind of hot. His next words went right through her.

"Good girl. Now, undress me." Her wide eyes flew to his. His face was still fierce. "If you can't do this, you won't last five minutes pretending to be a slave." He ducked his head. "You can say no, Meggie. You can say no and go to your room and wait for us. You don't have to do this."

She raised her chin. "I'm going," she snapped, and her hands went to the belt of his coat.

He just stood there while she attended to the task he'd set for her. His uniform jacket parted beneath her fingers, revealing a white shirt made of the same fabric as her chiton. The shirt fastened at the neck with a small tie, then billowed around his body like a pirate's shirt. She pulled the tails out from his trousers.

"Raise your arms, Master," she whispered. She pushed the shirt up his body, but he was so tall that she couldn't get the shirt off his arms.

He wasn't helping, she realised. Watching, to see what she'd do.

Reaching out with her foot, she hooked an ankle through the nearest chair leg and pulled it close. She stepped up onto it and drew the shirt off his arms. When his face was free of the fabric, she realised he was grinning.

"Next time," he said, "you can just ask me to bend over a little." His arm went around her waist and his eyes dropped. Her heart stuttered when she realised that being up on the chair meant that her breasts were on the same level as his face. "Although, I like this method. I like it a lot."

His arm tightened around her waist.

"If I was really your Master, I'd suck you, Meggie." His other hand came up to circle the edge of the metal bra. His nimble fingers found a small button. She gasped as the bra opened up, leaving her nipple shielded by a layer of thin fabric with just a metal ring to surround her breast. His finger circled the metal band. "If I was your Master, I'd have the right to do anything I wanted to you. Would you let me, Meggie?"

Hardly knowing what she was doing, Meggie's hands slipped into his hair.

"Yes, Brav," she whispered.

He leaned forward so that his lips were a fraction away from her nipple. He breathed out and her nipple puckered at the intense sensation of his breath on her sensitive peak.

Then he closed the metal cup over her breast again. Meggie gave a small whimper as the cool metal pressed against her nipple when she'd wanted his hot mouth.

"Come down, slave girl," he ordered, but he held out a hand to help her get down from the chair.

Her hands dropped to his belt. The taut muscles of his belly shivered as she brushed his skin. His hands closed over hers. "You don't have to do that, sweetheart," he murmured.

"I can be your good girl, Master."

A deep rumble sounded in his chest. "You are my good girl, Meggie. But you don't have to take off my pants. Unfortunately, all I need is a new shirt."

He reached out to snag a pile of fabric off the table that she hadn't even noticed.

The shirt was just a long vest, open in front so it showed the muscled contours of his chest and the smattering of chest hair that had so fascinated her when she'd tended his wound. As he turned his back to her so she could slip the vest over his arms, she saw the pinkish line of the wound she'd tended back on Earth. Her fingers traced it and she watched his response in the play of muscles in his back.

They joined the others in the embarkation room, a small alcove by the entrance to the ship, with bench seats either side where the other Guardians were waiting. They stood when she entered, but she noticed that they all kept their heads bowed. Not one of them looked at her, except for Jessan, who kept his eyes firmly on her face.

"Are you sure, sister?" he pressed.

"I'm sure."

"Fine. Let's go, then."

Jessan led the way, followed by Brav, holding Meggie's belt. Tarn was on her other side, Meggie realised. Kairn and Mac were behind them. They'd placed her in the middle. No one was even catching a glimpse of her.

The moment they stepped off the ramp, Meggie was glad they had her surrounded. She'd never been in such a busy place before. There were thousands of people around them, all hustling in the same direction. She allowed herself to be carried along by the Guardians as they all headed to the markets.

Each market was held in a square, surrounded by tall buildings. There was a raised section for the slaves to be displayed at the head of the square and the buyers shouted their bids. She only glimpsed the stage briefly as a woman was led towards it.

"Do I hear thirty gold orinchs?" the auctioneer called, and a desultory bidding followed.

"Eyes down, slave," Brav rumbled.

Meggie obeyed, knowing that even in this he was protecting her. She'd never be able to unsee the things she saw here. She stayed close to him and kept her eyes down, letting him lead her along, his hand fisted in her belt.

She heard the auctioneer as they walked away. "Sold, for sixty-five gold orinchs to the gentleman in green!"

They stopped a few times to ask questions. The cacophony of voices around them was so loud that Meggie couldn't even make out what Jessan was saying. Eventually, they stopped for longer than before, and Jessan turned back to the group.

"They're here," he rumbled. "Three women, one collared. They're Lot 3052." Meggie saw a nerve tick in his jaw. "Premier band. Fucking Cera always has to be so fucking conspicuous."

"What does that mean?" Meggie asked.

"Interested buyers only," Jessan replied, his eyes on Brav. "It means that anyone who is going to bid for them is going to have to be vetted first. Only one of us can bid. Brav—that means you and Meggie will have to go to the bathhouse. Meet the other bidders."

"A bathhouse?" Brav's voice was appalled. "Fuck, Jessan. I can't take Meggie into a bathhouse."

"Would you rather she went in with me?" Jessan shot back. "They wouldn't believe a real buyer wouldn't be accompanied by a slave. It's the only way to get them out, Brav."

"I'll go," Meggie offered. "Brav—I trust you."

He looked down at her, anxiety roiling in his eyes. "The bathhouse means you'll have to be my attendant, Meggie. You'll have to undress me and wash me. And… there will be other men in there, too, attended by their own slaves. We won't be able to fake it in there. If we're caught, you'll be sold, and I'll be taken to the authorities for judicial punishment."

"What exactly does 'judicial punishment' entail?"

"Flogging, at the very least. Maybe execution."

Meggie stood very straight in the circle of the Guardians. "I can do anything I have to do to save my sisters, Brav."

She heard Jessan's choked sob of relief and told herself to be brave. He could still hear Cera, she was sure of it. Was she still screaming? Meggie steeled herself and told herself that she was ready for anything.

The bathhouse was a large building in a side street just off the main plaza. It backed onto the warehouse where her sisters would be held. The other Guardians left them at the door and took up positions around the bathhouse so they could be called if necessary.

A doorkeeper took Brav's money and led them inside.

*   *   *

They went down a lot of stairs. As they went down, the sounds of the street behind them receded and the air grew warm and slightly damp. A man greeted them at the foot of the stairs.

"Honoured Master, may I have your name, please?"

"Brav of Mohara."

"Mohara!" the man bowed again. "A fair planet, and a system blessed with many beauties." He smirked at Meggie. "Not the least of which is in your company, honoured Master."

Brav stepped in front of her. "She's *mine,*" he snarled. "Keep your fucking eyes off her!"

The man took a step back. "Yes, sir. I hope you understand, though, that today the tepidarium is only for bidders interested in a very *special* lot."

"Three females, one collared," Brav stated. "Lot 3052. Call me interested." He shoved a coin into the other man's hand.

"Oh, very nice," the man crooned. "Right this way, sir. I will show you to your cubiculum."

Meggie followed close behind Brav. Other men were walking around the bathhouse, clad in only loincloths. They looked at her curiously. She kept her eyes on Brav's broad back in front of her.

The man showed them to a small room. "Loincloth, towels, essences, oils," he explained, waving his hands at linen and bottles on the shelves. He indicated a pair of platform wooden shoes. "Tyrrhenian pattens. Your clothes go here. Be advised that all bidders are required to be out of the tepidarium by nightfall. You will be called in time to be ready for bidding."

Bowing, he left the little room, closing the rattan door behind him.

Brav bent casually over Meggie and whispered in her ear, "We're being watched." He raised his voice. "Undress me, slave."

If he hadn't already pushed her beyond her comfort zone in the dining room, Meggie was sure she wouldn't have been able to do it. Instead, she just bowed her head and said, "Yes, Master."

She slipped around behind him and slipped the vest from his

shoulders, folded it carefully and put it on the shelf the man had indicated. Her fingers were steady on his belt. She slid it from its loops and rolled it up like she did this every day.

She indicated the bench seat. "Would you sit down while I remove your boots, Master?"

He sat, then held out one foot after another so she could remove his boots. Then he rose to his feet again, so she could finish undressing him.

She had a moment of nerves when she realised that she didn't know how to unfasten his pants. They didn't have a zipper. Brav hadn't said anything earlier about how his pants closed. He probably thought that she already knew.

He noticed her hesitation.

"Come here," he ordered, pulling her closer, both hands closing over her buttocks and pulling her flush against him. He rolled his hips into her and she felt herself turn to liquid in his arms. "Like this," he said, and brought her hand between them. To an observer, it would have looked like he was making her stroke him. Instead, he was guiding her fingers to the fastenings, showing her how to slip them free. "Now get my pants off, slave."

"Yes, Master." She pushed the trousers down his lean hips, her hands brushing his buttocks, his thighs. He rested his hand on her shoulder as she pulled them off his feet.

It shouldn't have been a surprise when she looked up, still kneeling at his feet, and saw that he was erect. And at eye level. She reached up to touch him.

His hand caught her wrist before she made contact. "Hurry up and give me that loincloth, then fold my clothes so I can get into the baths."

"Yes, Master."

She handed him the loincloth. He wrapped it around himself like he'd done this a thousand times while she folded his trousers as she'd folded his other clothes and placed them on the shelf. He slipped his feet into the wooden pattens.

"You'll have to take off your breast-piece," he told her. "Slaves don't wear them in the baths."

Meggie unfastened the metal bra. Brav's eyes went to the outline of her nipples through the nearly sheer fabric, then back up to her eyes. He cleared his throat.

"Bring some soap with you, and the towels. No, not that one, that's massage oil." He pointed to another row of bottles. "Follow me," he ordered. "And keep your eyes down. I don't want you looking at the other men in the bath, do you hear me?"

"Yes, Master."

CHAPTER TEN

She followed him, keeping her eyes on his back again, but this time it was bare. It wasn't a hardship to keep her eyes on his naked back. Her eyes traced down his body. She'd seen him naked. She'd been a moment away from wrapping her hand around his cock. Who was she kidding? She'd been a moment away from opening her mouth for him.

They went into a large room, cladded in marble. Her sheer dress clung to her almost immediately in the warm, humid air. There were more cubicles around the walls, each of them at least ten feet square, but open to the centre of the room where there was a large, octagonal slab of marble. There were other people in the cubicles. Meggie's eyes darted around. Only one was empty.

The other cubicles were all taken by a man and a slave girl. Or *girls*, she realised, when she saw that one man was sitting up against a marble wall with one girl straddling him, while another fed him her nipples and yet another reached between his legs to fondle his balls.

She jerked her eyes down, but she knew they were as wide as saucers.

Brav went straight into the empty cubicle. "Get some water in the bucket and bring the dish," he ordered.

Meggie went to the tap he'd indicated and filled up the wooden bucket. She grabbed the wide, shallow bronze dish, stuck it under her arm and tried to lift the bucket with both hands.

She felt like her arms were coming out of their sockets. Brav's muffled chuckle didn't help. He uncoiled himself from the wooden bench and came to help her. He carried the full bucket with one hand across the width of the cubicle.

"I think I need a stronger slave," he murmured, giving her a smile that was just for her.

"If you're looking to sell her..." a voice came from across the room. They both turned.

At least it wasn't the one with the three slave girls. This man had just one. He was short and squat with a very round belly, a round face and even rounded ears that stuck out from his head like handles. He smiled encouragingly at them as his slave washed him.

"I'm always in the market for a new pleasure slave. She wouldn't have to lift anything heavy. So, if you're looking to sell her...?"

"She's not for sale," Brav said gruffly. "I'm training her. I'm Brav of Mohara."

The round man inclined his head. "Gorgos, Senator Primus of Jiliar. So, you're here to bid on the three virgins?"

Only Meggie saw Brav's hand clench into a fist at Gorgos's casual words. He gave Gorgos a tight smile. "Like you said. A man's always in the market for a new woman—or three."

"Sisters, can you believe it?" Gorgos threw back his head and laughed and the slave took the opportunity to wash between his chins. "Gods, what a gift. And just at the right time, I tell you." He leaned forward conspiratorially, as if he wasn't on the other side of the room. "I'm getting them as a gift. For Aphrodite. Three virgins—that will make all my problems go away like that!" He snapped his fingers.

"Aphrodite?" Brav asked casually, then looked down at Meggie. "Come on, slave. Make a lather and wash me." He unwound the loincloth from his lean hips without ceremony and gave his attention back to Gorgos as he sat down naked on the wooden bench. "Is Aphrodite coming here?"

Standing behind Brav, Meggie couldn't help but stare. He was naked. He was *naked.* Her hands shook as she tipped some liquid soap onto the cloth. It formed a creamy lather that felt silky smooth and slippery between her hands. She went weak at the knees thinking how glorious that smooth, slippery lather was going to feel when she touched his skin.

"Well, not here," Gorgos admitted. "She's coming to Jiliar. For a, uh, *visitation.*"

Brav raised an eyebrow. "A visitation?" he asked. Meggie, having taken as long as she could making a lather, stood behind him and smoothed the soapy cloth over his broad shoulders. Brav ignored her. "No wonder you need three virgins." Meggie let the cloth trail over the bulging muscles in his arms and he lifted his arm so she could wash it easier. "But, I'll give you fair warning, you should find another gift. I need these three. I've been sent by the goddess Hecate. One of these girls has powers. Hecate wants to train her. You don't want to cross Hecate."

"I don't want to cross Aphrodite, either!" Gorgos complained, shaking a finger at Brav. His slave washed under his arm.

"Aphrodite doesn't want girls," Brav informed him. "Aphrodite likes men. The bigger the better. You should get her a set of guards." Meggie's hands came around his shoulders to wash his chest.

Gorgos laughed again. "Ride her ship by day and ride her pussy by night, eh?"

Brav's returning smile was thin. "That's what she likes. What would she even do with three girls?"

Meggie, copying the other slave girl across the way, used the bronze dish to sluice water over Brav's soapy body. God, he was gorgeous. She'd had her hands practically all over him. And now, watching the other slave girl kneel before Gorgos and start washing his legs, Meggie was ready to change that from 'practically' to 'actually.'

She came around in front of Brav and knelt before him. Brav looked down at her like he'd nearly forgotten she was there. "Master," she whispered. "Let me."

She put her hands on his knees to push them further apart. He'd gone soft while talking to Gorgos, but when she opened his legs, she saw him start to get hard again. He bit off a curse as she moved forward and, abandoning the cloth, ran her soapy hands up and down his thighs. The powerful muscles in his legs flexed under her touch as her hands slipped higher and higher with each stroke.

He wasn't looking at Gorgos anymore. All his attention was on Meggie as she knelt between his legs, running her soapy hands over his skin. Some of the water had splashed on her dress, rendering it completely transparent. The outlines of her nipples were clear through the fabric.

Across the room, Gorgos groaned. Meggie looked over. His slave had bent her head between his legs and was bobbing her head up and down. Meggie looked back to Brav. But not to his eyes. Brav's hands landed on top of hers to still their movements.

"I'm determined to buy those girls," Brav warned Gorgos again, but his voice had gone rough. "Hecate won't take 'no' for an answer."

"Good gods, man," Gorgos complained. "Who cares right now? Let your slave suck you off and we'll talk about it later. Gods, yes." He grabbed the back of his slave's head, forcing her further onto his cock.

Meggie looked up at Brav. "Master," she whispered. She watched his eyes go heavy with desire. She slipped her hands out from under his and took hold of the dish, still beside her. Carefully, she rinsed the soap from his legs. "One place left to wash you," she reminded him. She reached out for the cloth, then made sure she'd worked up a good lather on her hands.

Brav leaned forward. "Meggie, you can pretend," he whispered, his voice so low that no-one could hear him but her. "You don't have to."

She turned her head and felt the scratch of his cheek against hers. "I want to," she whispered, astonishing herself as much as him. Greatly daring, she caught the lobe of his ear between her teeth and scraped lightly.

His whole body convulsed with a shudder of desire. As she watched, a bead of clear fluid appeared at the tip of his cock.

"Yes," he gritted, then leaned back and opened his legs to grant her better access.

She swiped the bead of fluid from his tip first, smearing it across his head lightly. Brav threw back his head and gripped the edge of the bench, the muscles of his belly shivering with delight.

She should be terrified, she thought. She should be out of her mind with fright. Colin had made her do this. More than once. She should be thinking about how awful it had been with him, but she wasn't. She was completely focused on Brav. Somehow, this scenario was making it easier for her to act on her desires. She'd never done this willingly for any man. She wanted to do this for Brav.

Her hand was gentle as she explored him. He was hotter than she'd expected, pulsing with life, the skin silky smooth. The soap made her hand slip along his length. She curled her fingers around him as she pulled back up towards his tip. Her fingers didn't even meet.

She made a sound of pleasure as she gripped him tighter and started to work him with her hand. He heard the sound and echoed it.

She looked up at him as she established a rhythm, her hand moving slickly up and down. With her other hand, she massaged the precum leaking from his tip, using her palm and rotating it around his head.

She never thought she'd enjoy this act, but feeling the silky smoothness of his skin, his heat, even his scent had her fascinated. When she looked up at him, she saw that his gaze was fixed on her: on her face, on her breasts, on her hands, working industriously between his thighs.

He was losing himself in her. She could see it. The rest of the world had faded away for him, as it had for her.

She let him go. He groaned as if in agony, and she smiled with feminine smugness as she reached for the basin. She was very gentle and slow as she poured the water over his soapy shaft, pouring with one hand while she rinsed the soap from his straining flesh with the other.

"Gods, sweetheart," he groaned. "Your soft little hands on me feel so good!"

"I know what else will feel good." Meggie washed the last of the soap from his skin, then bent forward. His hands landed in her hair and she felt them shaking.

She opened her mouth and closed her lips over the very tip of him in a tender, sucking kiss. Above her, she heard his muffled curse.

Then a gong rang.

Meggie looked up. The gong rang again. Gorgos's slave was rinsing her mouth out and getting to her feet. Gorgos looked over at them and laughed again.

"That'll teach you to talk so much in the baths!" he crowed, wrapping the loincloth around his hips.

Meggie looked up at Brav. He drew in a deep breath and guided her to her feet. "Come on," he said, his voice deep and rough. "Apparently it's time for the auction."

He wrapped the loincloth around himself. "Gods, Meggie." His voice was still ragged. "If your sisters are virgins—there's no way we'll have enough money to buy them."

"But they can't be," Meggie protested. "I mean, I don't know about Cera, but Bess was married. Teresa is... well, I'm pretty sure she's innocent, but Bess was married for years."

Brav sighed. "We can only hope they're not. In the world of the flesh markets, virginity is expensive."

They returned to the cubiculum. By now, Meggie was uncomfortable in her wet gown, and very aware of the way her breasts and thighs were on display. She'd felt sexy and powerful when she was kneeling between Brav's legs. Now she just felt dirty.

Once inside the cubicle, Brav reached for her.

I'm his slave, she thought. *I can't back away.* For the first time since they'd started this, she felt like she was actually trapped. Her eyes widened and her heart pounded in her chest as she stared at him.

Brav just took hold of her shoulders and drew her into a gentle embrace. It was so unexpected that Meggie began to cry. She leaned into the embrace, her face against his chest and wept.

"It's OK, sweetheart," he murmured, his hands so gentle on her shoulders that it just made her cry harder. "It's OK. I know that was intense, but it's going to be all right. We'll get out of here, and everything will go back to the way it was."

She let him soothe her, until her tears had eased and she was pressed softly against him.

He let her go. "Let's dry off and then I'll get dressed, OK, sweetheart?" His hand was under her chin, raising her face to his.

"My dress is all wet," she complained.

His grin took her by surprise. "I bet you haven't had this before," he said, and reached out to push a button on the panel beside the door.

Meggie shrieked as warm air came out of vents in the floor and ceiling and rushed around them. She felt like Marilyn Monroe above the subway vent and clutched at her dress as the wind blew her skirts in all directions. In moments, both she and her dress were dry.

Brav had turned slightly away from her and unwound the loincloth. He reached for his clothes and started to dress.

"Let me," Meggie urged.

Brav shook his head. "They won't be watching right now, sweetheart. They'll be too busy preparing for the auction."

Meggie took the shirt from his hands. "Let me, Brav."

Brav's expression was inscrutable, but he raised his arms, allowing her to help him dress. Once he was dressed, he helped her put the metal bra back on. "Although," he murmured, for her ears alone, "I rather preferred you without it."

They came out of the cubicle just as Gorgos and his slave exited the cubicle beside theirs.

"For a man who took his sweet time in the baths, you were quick enough once you got the door closed," he commented jovially.

"What do you mean?" Brav asked.

Gorgos nudged him, as if they were friends. "I heard you, when you two were alone in there. Well, heard *her*, anyway. Never heard a man get a woman off quicker than that. If you ever want to share your secret, let me know!"

Brav fisted his hand in Meggie's belt again. "Trade secret," he snapped. "Let's get to the auction."

Meggie had expected that the auction would be held outside like the others, but it wasn't. Apparently being in a Premier band meant that you didn't have to mix with the rabble. It was in a room, like a large boardroom, with chairs ranged around in a half circle. The masters sat. Their slaves stood behind them.

Meggie moved to stand behind Brav's chair, but he refused to let her go. "No," he gritted. "I don't want you out of my sight. Sit at my feet."

Gorgos was watching them. Apparently, he liked the subservient way Meggie knelt at Brav's feet, because he pushed his slave to sit at his feet, too.

Then the auction began.

CHAPTER ELEVEN

The lights dimmed and a sliver of light appeared at the other end of the room, outlining a door in blue light. A sleek, expensive voice came over a PA system.

"Gentlemen, for your pleasure, it is our very great privilege to present a Premier band offering. This lot is unique and will suit the most *discerning* bidder. Each one is a precious gem, but together, they create a fabulous diadem that will become the pinnacle of any true collector's hoard."

Before them flashed holographic images of the three women, but not as Meggie had seen them before. They were dressed scantily, their hair and makeup overdone, their bodies contorted into a parody of sexy postures. It was all she could do not to shudder. Neither Teresa nor Bess nor Cera would ever have willingly posed like this. Her nails dug into her palms. What had they done to them, or what had they threatened to do to them to make them pose like that?

"Three virgins, gentlemen. Sisters." The voice lowered. "Imagine what you could do with three virgin sisters."

"Actually–" a little man stuck his head out from behind the door. "There was, um, a glitch. It turns out they're not actually virgins. Wait!"

Two of the buyers were already up and out of their seats.

"Wait! They're a bargain, I swear! Come back!"

The disappointed buyers did not come back. After a moment, one more rose to his feet and left. "No," he said. "They must all be virgins. It was a requirement of sale. My Master will accept nothing else."

Only three men remained seated: Brav, Gorgos and another man with a lean, hawk-like face. The little man darted behind the curtain and the voice came over the PA system again.

"The first is nineteen." The display showed Teresa and something inside Meggie sobbed silently. "Brunette. Ready to learn just how to please you. They're very flexible at this age. And look at those lush curves. This one is a double handful, gents!" The hologram rotated and something about the angles of the body made Meggie realise that it was fake. Holographic Photoshop. Whether it was Teresa's face pasted onto another model, or an extrapolation of what they thought Teresa looked like, this definitely wasn't her real body.

"The second part of our offering today is twenty-nine." Elizabeth (it was impossible to think of the hologram as Bess) appeared before them. "But don't let her age fool you. This one knows how to please a man." The fake Elizabeth blew a kiss and pouted as Meggie was pretty sure Bess had never pouted in her life.

"And the highlight of this Lot is before you now." Cera appeared, her red hair loose over her shoulders as her eyes promised both sex and death. They could paste her face over a fake body, but they couldn't change the expression in her eyes. "Part three. Thirty-two years of age, and barely broken in. And she's not just any pleasure slave, gentlemen. She's *special.*"

The Cera-hologram before them suddenly spun and thrust out her hand. Sparks shot from it in a tiny display of fireworks. She turned and did it again, this time looking seductively over her shoulder at the bidders as she shot fireworks towards the ceiling.

"She is more powerful than any female we have *ever* offered for sale at this hallowed institution. Telepathy. Teleportation. Lightning and thunder. And maybe many more! To control this powerful creature, she comes fitted with a Romian shock collar to inhibit her powers until the moment it suits you to unleash her on your enemies.

"All of this can be yours, gentlemen." The three holograms appeared together again. Meggie closed her eyes as the holograms kissed each other and Gorgos made a sound of desire. "Three beautiful women, sisters, ready to obey your every command. We will start the bidding at three thousand gold orinchs. Do I hear four thousand?"

Three thousand? They only had five thousand to offer. Meggie wanted to weep as Gorgos quickly raised the bid to four thousand.

The hawk-like man raised the bid to five thousand. She shook from head to foot. Two bids, and they were already out of the race. It couldn't be true. They had to save them. They couldn't let her sisters fall into Gorgos's hands.

Brav stood up. Meggie looked up at him despairingly. He wasn't leaving already, just because they'd been outbid, was he?

He made a slicing gesture with his hand that silenced the other bidders. They were already up to seven thousand between them. "I don't have time for this," he stated. "I want this Lot. I will pay five thousand in cash today and give you the deed to a starship. Gerean Couril Class, valued at thirty *thousand* orinchs. That is my offer, take it or leave it."

The other two bidders glanced at each other. The auctioneer came out from behind the curtain, walking right through the holograms of the women to bow to Brav. "Honoured Master," he fawned. "What a generous offer! We would be most honoured to accept."

The hawk-like man unfolded himself from the chair. "I bid you good day, gentlemen," he said, and left the room.

"No," Gorgos complained. "Noooo. I want this one!" He stomped his feet where he sat, then jumped up. His voice whined nasally. "This is an auction and the auction isn't over yet! He's willing to pay thirty-five thousand. I'll pay thirty-six thousand. No, wait. *Forty* thousand!"

Brav glanced down at Meggie. She knew what that look meant. He had nothing left to offer.

But she did.

She crawled over to Gorgos. "Let him buy them today," she said throatily, "and I'll be yours."

He inspected her closely where she was kneeling at his feet. "You look like Aphrodite," he said slowly. "I could use a woman who looked like Aphrodite."

"You could use me any way you like," Meggie purred.

"And I would," Gorgos mused, a cautious, dreamy smile lighting his face.

Meggie was startled when Brav reached for her, grabbed her by the belt and physically dragged her away from Gorgos. "No deal."

The auctioneer smiled condescendingly. "Well, it looks like we have a winner here. Lot 3052, sold for forty thousand gold orinchs to Gorgos of Jiliar!"

Brav helped Meggie to her feet silently.

"You should have given me your slave," Gorgos commented. "I would have let you win the auction if I could have a woman who looks like Aphrodite suck my cock." He got that dreamy smile on his face again as he looked her up and down. "I'd make her suck me, then I'd beat her until she was dead and then I'd fuck her."

Brav bent and threw Meggie over his shoulder. She closed her eyes tightly, not wanting to see Gorgos as Brav strode from the room.

He put her back on her feet when they were outside. It was fully dark now. He took her by the shoulders and shook her. "What were you thinking, offering yourself to him like that?" he demanded. "Did you hear what he said he would *do* to you?"

"I had to do something!" she cried. "Now my sisters are owned by that… that man!" She pressed her hands to his chest. "Brav, what are we going to do? He'll kill them—Brav, worse, he'll–"

Jessan loomed out of the shadows, followed by the other Guardians. His face was paper white. "You lost the bid."

"I offered everything," Brav said shortly. "I even offered your ship Tarn. Thirty-five thousand."

"I would have given it, gladly," Tarn said.

Jessan looked at Meggie. "What is he planning to do to them? It sounded like you knew something."

Meggie couldn't say a word. She couldn't repeat the horror of what Gorgos had said. Brav's hand fell heavily on her shoulder to steady her.

"That won't happen to your sisters," he said flatly. "They're a gift for Aphrodite. He won't dare so much as bruise them. He will look after them because it's in his best interests to do so. He's afraid of Aphrodite and so he damn well should be if he's getting a visitation. He needs to offer her a valuable gift. He won't touch them."

Meggie started to shake again. She'd never heard anything so awful as what Gorgos had said to her. She turned to Brav and buried her face in his chest. His arms came around her shoulders.

"What happened?" Jessan asked.

"Meggie offered herself to Gorgos as collateral. Because she looks like Aphrodite, he wanted to take his frustrations with the goddess out on her. He made a particularly vile threat."

"You offered yourself?" Jessan's voice was incredulous. "Sister, we would never have asked that of you." Even wrapped in Brav's arms as she was, she felt Jessan's hand on her shoulder. "Never."

"So, we'll ambush them," Kairn said. "We'll go round the back of the warehouse and grab them as they're being transported. Brav, you get Meggie back to the ship."

Meggie felt rather than saw Brav shake his head. "It wouldn't work. These women were just sold for forty thousand orinchs. They'll have more security than you've ever seen in your life. No, better to wait until they reach Jiliar. Gorgos won't be as accustomed to providing security for flesh transfers as the markets."

"Maybe we can buy them from Aphrodite," Tarn suggested. "I'll go back to my grandfather. Beg him. He may be able to intervene–"

"Don't be stupid," Jessan interrupted. "Gerea is in the House of Apollo. Even the King won't be able to intervene in the House of Aphrodite, *if* he'd listen to you."

"Still, he may have some influence–"

"He won't." Meggie felt Jessan's eyes on her. "It's a pity you don't look more like Aphrodite," he mused. He drew in a sharp breath and let it out.

Meggie froze in Brav's embrace. "I can make myself look like Aphrodite."

"It wouldn't work," Jessan objected. "He's already seen you."

Meggie pulled free of Brav's hands. "He hasn't seen what I can do," she said quietly. "None of you have." She took a few steps back, so she was standing in the light and they could see her clearly.

Her instinct was to raise her hands to hide her face, but she stopped herself. That was what she'd always done before, but that had only been when she was in public. She didn't need a gesture. All she needed was determination.

She stood in the light of the streetlamp and let herself change. Her hair changed from her own chestnut brown to Cera's flaming locks. It grew longer, spilling down to her hips. She grew taller, her figure more athletic, until she looked just like her cousin.

She'd been doing this for years, ever since before she'd gotten her first job. There was no way a fourteen-year-old could pretend to be a thirty-two-year-old woman without some kind of magic. Her mother taught her how to control it when her powers first manifested when she was twelve. It took hours the first time, sitting in front of a mirror with her mother, trying to make a pimple disappear. It had been difficult at first, so she'd just changed small things, but the older she got, the easier she found it. Now, outside the barrier that surrounded Earth, it was ridiculously easy to change everything.

The Guardians stared at her. Jessan whispered, "Cera", on a longing, aching sigh.

"I can look like anyone I want," Meggie said, hearing her own voice take on Cera's throaty tones. "Show me what I need to look like. Tell me how I need to act. I can change you, too. Gorgos won't recognise us, I promise."

*   *   *

Back on the ship, the other Guardians all attended to their duties, while Brav saw Meggie back to her cabin.

"This is a bad idea," he said as the door closed behind them.

Meggie smiled grimly. "It won't even be the most dangerous thing I've done today."

Brav ran his hands through his hair. "Gods, Meggie." He turned away from her.

She came up behind him and lay a hand on the bunched muscles between his shoulder blades. "Teach me how I need to behave."

He let out a huff of laughter and turned back to her. "Well, imagine everything you went through today, but backwards." His expression turned serious. "Meggie, Aphrodite is a very… physical person. She's the goddess of love, but that's not exactly right. Aphrodite is all about lust. Love gives. Lust takes. And believe me, Meggie, Aphrodite *takes*."

"Didn't I prove today that I can… that I can be…?"

Brav's hand came up to stroke her hair and she remembered the way his hands shook in her hair when she took him in her mouth. "I know that what you had to do today embarrassed you. I know you didn't want to do those things with me. I'm sorry. Truly I am. That's why I think impersonating Aphrodite will be too much for you."

"Brav…" She was going to tell him about Colin, but her courage failed her. "You didn't make me do anything I didn't want to do."

She felt the tremor return to his hand for a moment. He pulled his hand away. His face was bitter.

"Just last night, you told me that kissing me was a mistake. You told me I'd gotten the wrong idea when you begged for my tongue in your mouth. And now, less than twenty-four hours later, you're telling me that what you really wanted to do in that bathhouse just now was to suck my cock."

The harsh words hurt Meggie, but she could see the hurt that was making him lash out. "I wanted you," she said honestly. "It was—exciting, to be able to see you. Touch you. Wash you. Kiss you. And if pretending to be Aphrodite means that I have to… to do intimate things with you, then that's what I want to do. For my sisters. And for us."

"Ha!" He wasn't ready for her honesty. Her rejection had hurt him more than she'd known. He was vulnerable to her, Meggie realised. Vulnerable, and needing her so much, but worried that he'd lose everything if he pushed her too far.

In that moment, she hated Colin more than she ever had, and that was saying something. He hadn't just hurt her when he'd assaulted her. He'd taken *this* moment from her, too. This moment that should have been beautiful and special and he was *here* when he had no right to be here, ruining something he had no right to ruin.

Brav lashed out as he stalked towards her. "You think you could pretend to be Aphrodite? Well, look at *this*. This is how Aphrodite behaves."

He reached past her and punched a line of text into the console behind her. It brought up a video of a formal dinner. The woman at the head of the table was Aphrodite, Meggie knew that without being told. They *did* look a little alike, but as Brav had said, Aphrodite was hard around the eyes.

Aphrodite was giving orders, enjoying her food, enjoying the entertainment of dancers that whirled before their view. The music stopped and the dancers left. "Dessert!" Aphrodite cried gaily. "Master of the Wardrobe, to me!"

A man separated himself from the row of guards behind her. He came around in front of the table and bowed. Then, he crawled under the table. Meggie stared as he lifted Aphrodite's skirt and put it over his head. Aphrodite's face tightened in pleasure, her cheeks starting to flush. Meggie could see small movements under her skirt, where the Master of the Wardrobe had his head between her thighs.

"Oh, my God, is he…?"

"Eating her pussy," Brav said bluntly. "Watch another minute and you'll see her orgasm. Aphrodite *loves* everyone to watch her come."

"I don't want to watch." She started to turn away but Brav caught her and turned her back to the view screen.

"Watch!"

Meggie watched as Aphrodite's head tipped back. Watched the woman's thighs tremble. Watched the guard's shoulder muscles work as he pumped his fingers inside her.

"And *that's* what you want me to do to you?"

My God, I hope that question's rhetorical, Meggie thought, because yes, absolutely, that was what she wanted him to do to her.

She looked back at Brav. The question was not rhetorical. He wanted an answer.

She felt herself blushing and she looked down at the floor between their feet.

"Aphrodite doesn't blush." His hand tilted her face up to his. "Can you sit up at a banquet and demand that I lick your pussy?"

Determined to show him she wasn't afraid, determined to show herself that damned Colin Walt no longer had any power over her, she cried, "Yes!"

Brav's face was like a thundercloud. "Well, then, let's get started," he snapped. He picked her up again and threw her over his shoulder. Meggie gasped at the caveman move as she flipped over him. He deposited her on the small table and kicked the chair out of the way.

CHAPTER TWELVE

She was still wearing her slave outfit. He dispensed with the golden bra, tossing it to the floor where it landed with a clatter. He opened her belt, which was the only thing that held her dress closed and covered her front.

She put her hands over her sex.

Brav regarded her scornfully. "You're not ready for this, Meggie."

Meggie pulled her hands away. "It won't be the first time I've had a man do things to me I'm not ready for," she snapped. Feeling herself tremble, she shifted to the edge of the table and opened her legs. "Master of the Wardrobe," she whispered, "to me."

He stared at her, his hot gaze going from her flushed face, down to the pert curves of her breasts revealed by the slit in her dress that reached the hem, then back up to the space between her thighs.

"Show me," she whispered.

The next moment, Brav was on his knees before her. His big hands landed on her knees. She bit off a cry as he pushed her legs further apart. He curved his hands gently around her calves as he moved forward into the place he'd made for himself.

"So beautiful," he murmured.

Meggie's hands came up to his shoulders. She liked to hold on to him. Liked the feeling of his hard muscles under her hands. He was still wearing the vest he'd worn in the slave market, so there was nothing to stop her slipping her hands beneath it to caress the warm, smooth skin of his shoulders.

Brav's hands were moving, long, slow strokes over her thighs now. Every stroke slid slightly higher until he could trace the crease where her thigh met her body. Meggie whimpered and leaned back a little, still holding on to him as she opened herself further to his inspection.

"Gods, so beautiful." He leaned forward and placed a kiss to the top of her bare thigh, then slowly kissed lower. Meggie fell back further until she was lying back on the table. All she could see was the top of his head as his lips explored the softness of her inner thigh. She could feel herself pulsing between her legs, longing to feel him touching her there.

She whispered his name and stroked his shoulders. No one had ever touched her like this. Not ever. Colin Walt had certainly never wanted to bury his mouth in her most secret places. She felt a shiver go through her whole body as Brav's big, warm hands caressed her legs.

The dress fell open, the sides falling back, so that she was completely naked for him below the waist. The dress still clung to her breasts, but the nearly sheer fabric did nothing to hide the aroused peaks of her nipples.

Brav moved higher and everything inside Meggie clenched as he pressed a gentle kiss to her dark curls. His hands soothed her legs as they clenched around him. "Brav," she cried, burying her hands in his thick, dark hair.

"Will you let me in, sweetheart?" he asked, tracing her labia with one finger. "Will you let me taste you—worship you?"

"Yes," she gasped. "Oh, God, please." She clutched tighter at his hair.

He pulled his head out of her grasp and moved away. One of his hands came to cover her sex, but it wasn't to caress her, it was to shield her. He shook his head and took his hand away, only to close the dress around her body. He pulled her to sit upright and knelt back on his heels.

He regarded her steadily. "What did you mean when you said it wouldn't be the first time a man did something you weren't ready for? Did you mean the way I treated you down on Clarion Quint?"

Meggie closed her legs, suddenly feeling very exposed, but it was important she didn't let him keep thinking that he had done things to her against her will. "No," she said quietly. "It wasn't you."

Brav's eyes narrowed. "Tell me about it, sweetheart."

Meggie felt tears sting her eyes and she wrapped her hands

around her waist. "It was years ago." She didn't dare look at him. She knew that if she did, she wouldn't be able to say a word. "God, these lights are so bright." Why couldn't he have asked her in the darkness of the night, when they'd been down on the planet?

Brav rose to his feet in one lithe motion. "Lights, change setting to candlelight." The room dimmed until it was lit by a warm, rosy glow. "Come here, sweetheart." He lifted her in his arms, high against his chest this time, not over his shoulder, and carried her to the bed. "Lie next to me, baby."

He lay her on the bed, and came down behind her, sliding one muscular bicep beneath her head and wrapping the other around her waist. She felt surrounded by him, protected, safe. "Better?" he asked.

She nodded. Even though he couldn't see her face in this position, he could see the movement. She knew what he was doing. He was making a safe space for her, one where she was protected by his body, one where she could open herself up to him emotionally without having to look him in the eye while she shared all her secrets.

She felt his tender kiss at the nape of her neck. "Tell me what happened, sweetheart."

"I was fourteen."

She heard his groan of "Gods!" behind her. "Fourteen?"

"Our mother had died. Teresa was only five. Dad—didn't take care of us very well. We needed money, so I tried to get a job." She shrugged, a nonchalant gesture of her shoulders moving against his chest.

"So young, sweetheart."

"Too young," she agreed. "I pretended I was older. I could make myself look older. I thought I got away with it for a while, but a fourteen-year-old still acts like a fourteen-year-old. No one wants to employ a woman in her thirties who acts like a fourteen-year-old."

She didn't speak for a moment, thinking back. Then she continued.

"The man who hired me figured out that I wasn't as old as I said I was. He said he would fire me." She swallowed hard. "I said I needed this job. I needed the money." She tried not to shiver. "I said I'd do anything."

She felt the shiver of horror that ran through Brav. "Sweetheart—" he began, but cut himself off.

"He made me…" She had to close her eyes, even in the dim room and knew that she would never have been able to speak these words if they were face to face. "He wanted sex. And I needed that job so badly. So, I let him."

She felt Brav shaking behind her. "That son of a bitch," he growled. "I'll fucking kill him. Gods, sweetheart, you were a *child*."

"I consented. I... I let him."

His arm was like steel beneath her head. "You were a *child*. You weren't capable of consent. I'll fucking kill him. What's his name? Where does he live?"

"It doesn't matter." She shrugged again.

"Of course, it fucking matters!" he shouted. He gathered his composure with some deep breathing. "Give me his name, baby girl."

"He was already punished. He was... he was harassing other women, too. He lost his job."

Brav's voice was deep and rough in her ear. "He should have lost his fucking balls. Did they castrate him?"

"No! They... they don't do things like that on my world."

"Then they damn well should." His arm was tight around her waist. "What was his name?"

Eventually, she gave it to him. He would probably never be back on Earth again, she thought. And even if he did come to Earth, he probably would have forgotten it by then.

"We'll find another way to rescue your sisters, sweetheart," he assured her. He pressed a kiss to her bare shoulder, exposed by the transparent fabric now wrapped around her body. "I love you, Meggie. I don't want to hurt you or frighten you ever again."

Meggie turned in his arms, finally able to look at him. "Brav, no," she said gently, her hand going to his lean cheek, feeling the scratch of evening stubble there. "You haven't hurt me. You haven't frightened me. Not ever. I've felt so safe with you."

Brav closed his eyes for a moment, savouring her touch. "Today in the baths..."

"I wanted you so much," she whispered. Her hand slid down his bare chest, letting her fingers tangle in the springy hair. He'd shucked off the vest when he'd climbed into bed behind her. Her hand slid lower, to his belt, then lower still. She felt him begin to respond.

"Meggie, wait." He caught her wrist and pulled her hand away from him. "No, baby, not tonight. Not after everything you've gone through." He kissed her fingers and sat up. "You must be hungry.

Stay here, sweetheart, and I'll get you something to eat."

He went to the replicator and came back with a tray holding soup and Joradan bread. This time, she didn't feel anything special as she ate the comfort foods. Nothing could be more comforting than the way he was sitting behind her, holding her between his spread legs as he fed her supper.

He turned his back while she got into her nightgown, tucked her in and bent to kiss her forehead. "Goodnight, sweetheart."

She caught his hand. "Brav, wait."

"Yes, sweetheart?"

Her heart turned over at the caring in those words. "Brav, would you sleep next to me tonight?"

He stroked her hair back from her face. "It would be my honour."

He sat on the edge of the bed to remove his boots and then pulled off his pants, leaving just a wide band of stretchy black underwear. "Don't worry, sweetheart. I won't undress all the way."

She lifted the covers for him and he lay down next to her. She went into his arms, resting her head against his chest. She felt happier than she had ever felt in her whole life. It didn't take his whispered words above her saying, "I love you, Meggie," for her to know that she really was loved.

She pressed a light kiss to his chest. "I love you, too, Brav."

His arms tightened around her for a moment, then relaxed in case he hurt her. "Goodnight, baby girl."

"Goodnight... darling." She'd never used a love name like that for anyone but Teresa, but with Brav, everything felt right.

*   *   *

Six hours later, they arrived at Jiliar. "Why does every planet look like Earth?" she asked. "I mean, it's blue and green, mostly, with a few deserts. I thought alien planets would be... well... alien."

"Alien planets still need oxygen for humans to live there," Kairn explained. "The gods settled these planets millennia ago, changing them from their natural state to one that would support human life. They brought plants and animals from Earth, terraformed the lands and oceans. There have been some changes in the last few thousand years, but if a planet isn't mostly blue and green, then you don't ever want to land a shuttle there without life-support gear."

Meggie had spent most of her waking hours learning about Aphrodite. She was still determined to impersonate the goddess, and Brav had come around at least enough to support her decision.

She was wearing a golden gown this time, but it wasn't all that different from the chiton Brav had first made for her, except it was split from neckline to hem, the same way the slave's garment was and tied with a gold sash. She'd changed her figure so that full breasts pushed at the gold silk and a neatly trimmed thatch of curls was visible through the slit in the skirt when she walked. She wore a golden circlet on her hair, but, as he'd told her, jewels could be easily replicated, so they were worn for adornment, but not as a sign of status. Anyone could replicate a jewel.

Instead, status was shown by the quality of her slaves.

All the Guardians had dressed like the guards in Aphrodite's retinue. Meggie had nearly melted on the spot when she saw Brav dressed in the revealing costume.

"Mmm, very nice," she'd murmured, running her fingertip beside the leather straps that crossed his muscular chest.

He'd gone very still and said nothing.

"Brav?"

She noted the quiver in his tense jaw.

"Brav, are you OK?"

He bowed. "Yes, my lady." He looked her up and down. "Forgive me. It's just… you look just like her."

A thought began to tease at Meggie's mind. "Brav, you've taught me a lot about Aphrodite's court. How did you learn all this?"

He bowed again. "Common knowledge, my lady. Excuse me." Then he'd left her alone, confused and a little hurt at the way he'd been so distant.

They were only an hour behind Gorgos's ship. The plan was to arrive as quickly as possible, to keep Gorgos off balance, and to hope to avoid the real Aphrodite in case she arrived early for the visitation.

"This is vessel Aphrodite Prime, informing you that we will be landing outside the palace in five minutes," Jessan stated, speaking into the comm unit.

"Five minutes!" the operator squawked. "But—you don't have permission—"

"My mistress is the goddess Aphrodite," Jessan growled. "She doesn't need your permission. So, I suggest you clear the landing site or I'll flatten anything that's on it."

Another voice came on the line. "Vessel Aphrodite Prime, your ship is… not what we expected."

"Keeps the fucking godhunters off her ass," Jessan retorted, and Meggie remembered that Tarn had said much the same thing the first night they'd had dinner together.

"Moan," Brav ordered softly.

Meggie let out a soft moan, her cheeks flushing wildly. She was sitting in a chair in the cockpit, firmly strapped in, Jessan in the pilot's chair beside hers, while the other Guardians seated themselves on a bench behind them, harnesses attaching to the wall at their backs. She'd changed their appearance, so that they wouldn't be recognised, just as she'd changed her own.

But right now, she had to moan. Aphrodite powered her ships with pleasure, so Meggie had to sound like she was having an orgasm. Strapped into her chair. In a room with men who wanted to be her brothers-in-law.

On an embarrassment scale of one to ten, it was worse than that time the tampons fell out of her bag at a school assembly.

"Tell Gorgos to be ready for his visitation," Jessan barked. "My mistress is going to be very angry with him as soon as she's finished coming."

"We will be ready, Aphrodite Prime."

Jessan glanced over at Meggie and she was surprised to see a flush on his high cheekbones. "Sorry I had to be so blunt, sister."

"Don't mention it," Meggie muttered. "And I mean that. Please, let's never mention any of this to anyone."

Jessan chuckled and turned his attention back to the controls.

Then it was the moment of truth. She stood straight and tall—well, at least a *little* taller, because Aphrodite was no-one's idea of tall—her head back, her chest thrust slightly forward because Brav told her that Aphrodite liked to show off her bust.

She'd thought that the goddess of love would be tall and slender, like a supermodel, but tall and slender Aphrodite was not. She was short and curvaceous, and every luscious curve screamed of seduction and sex. Even though she was shorter, she was bigger than Meggie. *Everywhere.* Her bust was bigger, her hips were bigger—even her hair was bigger. She'd thought Aphrodite was going to have straight hair, maybe a light curl, but Aphrodite's hair curled wildly in a cloud around her head, barely held back from her face by artful ribbons.

The door opened. Meggie went first, not bothering to check to see if the Guardians were following her.

CHAPTER THIRTEEN

Gorgos was waiting for her, dressed in a gold-edged toga that strained over his round belly. Meggie regarded him with scorn. He was wringing his hands. A very little research had turned up the reason why Gorgos was worried Aphrodite was going to leave him a smear on the carpet.

The man was a petty thief.

"Well?" she demanded as soon as her feet touched the ground. Gorgos hurried to her and knelt at her feet.

"Great Aphrodite. Powerful, beautiful Aphrodite. My planet is honoured—"

"Shut up."

Gorgos swallowed his next words.

"Tell me why I shouldn't nuke this little backwater piece of *sludge* from orbit." She kept her voice serene, but stern.

"Most beautiful goddess, I can explain! It was all a—a misunderstanding! I just wanted to *visit* Roylon Tertius. I never intended to take your divine diadem—"

Meggie fixed him with a stare that was *just* shy of what she needed to turn him to stone. "Have you still got it, little man?"

"Yes—yes, I saved it for you."

"Well, where *is* it?"

He snapped his fingers—although he was sweating so badly, he had to snap them several times before they made a sound. A slave came forward, bearing a small box.

"Give it to my guards," Meggie ordered casually, keeping her attention on Gorgos. "Now, tell me, little man." She leaned forward and smiled. "Why do you deserve to live?"

"I bought you a gift!"

Meggie examined her nails. "I'm very quickly getting bored with you, little man."

"Bring them out!" Gorgos shouted, running his hands over his hair. He was sweating, she saw, his hair damp at the temples.

There was the sound of creaking and squeaking. Meggie frowned, then stopped. Aphrodite didn't frown. It might give her wrinkles.

A cage came into view, on wheels. Inside the cage were her sisters.

Don't blow it now, she thought. *Don't seem too eager.* "So what?" she scorned. "What do I want *girls* for?"

"They're virgins, divinity!" Gorgos assured her. "All three of them. And this one has powers!" He pointed through the bars at Cera, his finger an inch from her face.

Cera snapped her teeth at him. Gorgos withdrew his finger hurriedly.

"Such spirit," Meggie mused, secretly glad. Cera still had her fire. She might still be screaming inside, but she still had enough spirit to try to bite Gorgos's finger off. Meggie allowed a slight smile to curve her lips. "I think I might like them after all. Get them onto my ship."

The three women were released from the cage. They didn't recognise the Guardians who came forward to take hold of them because Meggie had changed their appearance. All the better. If any of them showed any signs of recognition now, it would be disastrous.

"I'm leaving," Meggie announced. "I don't want to stay on this backwater a moment longer than necessary."

"But, divinity, I had planned a feast—"

"Eat with *you*?" Meggie asked, scorn in every line of her beautiful face. "I'd rather go hungry. I'm getting out of here."

"But—you always stay for the whole three days of the visitation…"

Meggie froze. Aphrodite always stayed here? And right now, they were surrounded by Jiliaran troops. The moment Gorgos realised she wasn't Aphrodite, they were all dead. She had to do what Aphrodite always did.

Meggie shrugged one curvy shoulder. "Fine. But this banquet had better be good."

Gorgos was watching her with narrowed eyes. She stalked past him, then stopped. She had no idea where she was going, but she could pretend irritation easily enough. "Well? Hurry up, you stupid little man."

Gorgos hurried.

*   *   *

An hour later, she was in her own private quarters that Gorgos insisted she occupy. Only Brav came into the suite with her. Meggie had insisted that the others go with the women who were now her slaves.

Gorgos had protested that his guards would keep the women safe.

Meggie had rounded on him. "Trust your guards not to violate my virgins?" she shrieked, and something inside her broke when she saw Cera's face. She'd seen that look on her own face in the mirror once, many years before, and knew what it meant. She was too late.

She turned to Gorgos, fury building inside her hot enough to kill. "If one of your guards so much as lays a *finger* on my property, I swear to you, I won't punish them, I'll punish you. My guards go with them. My guards stay with them. That's *final.*"

The Guardians had gone with her sisters back to the cells.

The suite was luxurious. There was an enormous, soft bed with silk sheets and curtains that billowed down around it in translucent clouds. There were comfortable chairs scattered around on the finely patterned carpet, elegant tables, and even clothes and jewels. Every moment, another slave came into the room with newly replicated trinkets for the goddess.

And the bathroom—it wasn't even a room. It was a suite all of its own. Like the bathhouse on Clarion Quint, the bathing suite had three rooms, one for undressing and preparation, one that was warm, for washing and massage, and one that was hot, already full of steam with a cold plunge pool at one end.

"Very good for the skin," the slave informed Meggie, as she showed her around the suite.

The slaves serving her all had feminine characteristics, Meggie noted, but they weren't *quite* human. Their skin was a pale aqua colour, and it pulsed with light. When they were pleased, the lights pulsed brighter.

"Pleasure entities," Brav explained when Meggie asked about the lights in a whisper. "Genetically modified to feed on pleasure, much like the goddess's ship. You must let them please you. Aphrodite allows them every intimacy. And I do mean *every* intimacy."

They bathed her. Meggie tried not to be embarrassed, but it wasn't easy. Brav stood inside the door of the bathing chamber and watched her as the pleasure entities bathed her.

All Meggie could do was tell herself that they weren't quite human. They probably didn't have the same standards as her, she told herself. They were designed to feed on pleasure. They did her hair and her makeup and her nails, pampering Meggie until she felt like she'd float away on a cloud of bliss. They pulsed with light every time she sighed happily.

For them, it probably wasn't sexual when they washed every inch of her body, sliding soapy hands over her skin. And then, when they took her out of the bathing pool and spread her out on a mattress, covering every inch of her back and the backs of her legs and calves with sweet oil, that probably wasn't sexual, either. Not even when they rolled her onto her back and performed the same massage on her front.

Meggie sighed and caught Brav's eyes as he watched them massage her. It probably wasn't sexual for the pleasure entities. It was certainly sexual for Brav.

And then they took her from the massage mattress and dressed her in a gown exactly the same as the one she'd worn earlier and guided her from the room.

*　　*　　*

Meggie entered the banquet hall self-consciously. Like the slave dress, this one was open all the way down the front. The only difference was that this one was made of gold silk and tied with a golden sash. The only things that held it together were her belt and wishful thinking.

The banquet hall was crowded. Everyone there was human, but there must have been hundreds of them. Gorgos was up on a small throne at the top of a dais. At the other end of the banquet hall was another dais, higher, and it didn't have a throne. Instead, it had a bed with billowing white translucent curtains tied to the tall bedposts.

Music was playing and a troupe of dancers were entertaining the diners reclining at the two long tables that ran either side of the long banquet hall. Brav walked immediately behind Meggie. The music stopped as they entered the room.

"Goddess!" Gorgos cried, slipping off his throne and hurrying down the steps to meet her. He held out his hand for hers, clearly intending to kiss it.

Meggie let herself sneer at the little man and kept her hands at her side. He reminded her of Colin.

"We are blessed with your presence," Gorgos said hurriedly. "Please, Goddess, make yourself comfortable. Perhaps you would bless us with pleasure before we begin our meal? I'm sure you'd like to relax after your journey."

Meggie held her head up and didn't reply, trying not to show the way she trembled. She crossed the room and ascended the stairs, knowing that everyone was watching her. Pleasure before the meal? Her heart pounded.

"Feel free to choose one of my guards to pleasure you, goddess," Gorgos offered, walking backwards to get back to his own throne. It was awkward watching him trying to go up the stairs backwards. "Or, of course, as many of them as you please."

A troop of guards approached and paraded to the divan to range themselves in front of Meggie. Behind them, at the other end of the room, Gorgos lifted the hem of his tunic and wrapped his stubby fingers around his cock.

Knowing she was being watched by the filthy man as he jerked off, Meggie's panicked gaze darted from one guard to the next. They were all huge. Whatever they ate here on Jiliar, it was clearly loaded with steroids, judging from the way every man's abs rippled beneath the leather straps that couldn't be called a breastplate. She looked from face to handsome face.

Her panicked eyes landed on a face that was vaguely familiar beside her and she remembered that she'd changed Brav's appearance, too. Her heart beat so hard and fast it was a wonder they couldn't see it pounding against her excuse for a dress. "Why would I want your guards when I have my own?" she asked.

Gorgos frowned. "But these are *your* guards, goddess. You sent them in advance of your arrival."

Meggie tossed her head, Aphrodite's curls cascading over her shoulders. "I want this one. I've spent long enough training him."

Brav bowed. "If my lady would like to recline, I will please her, as she has taught me to please her," he said, in a voice that *everyone* could hear.

Meggie strolled the length of the room as everyone watched, and ascended the staircase. When she reached the top, she sat on the edge of the bed.

Brav stepped away from her. She nearly protested before she realised he was just pulling the curtains around the bed. He turned to glare at Gorgos. "My lady doesn't need to see your ugly mug when she's having an orgasm."

The guards closest to the bed all turned on their heels, so that they were facing the assembled guests rather than the bed. Meggie felt a little reassured that what was going to happen at least wasn't quite so public. Now all she could see through the thin curtains was the long red cloaks they wore.

Brav distracted her by swinging her legs up onto the bed. "No," she whispered, but he was just helping her lie down. She felt exposed, despite the barrier of the curtains. They were gauzy and any one of the dozen men not more than a few metres away could have made out every movement of their bodies by just turning their heads. Then they were enclosed—together.

"What's going to happen?" Meggie asked tremulously. "What do I have to do?"

CHAPTER FOURTEEN

Brav came to sit beside her at the head of the bed. "Relax, Meggie. I think you're worried about something that isn't going to happen tonight." He didn't touch her.

"You're not going to… take me? But… I think Gorgos expects it. If he realises…"

A spasm crossed his face. "Against your will? When you're not ready for me? Absolutely not. Never." His voice roughened. "Meggie, Meggie, what were you thinking, agreeing to this?"

His hand cupped her cheek and the tenderness of it made tears sting at her eyes. "I had to save my sisters," she said, and closed her mouth tight against the sobs that threatened to escape.

"We're going to get through this." His hand trembled against her cheek. "I won't take advantage of you, Meggie. I won't hurt you. And I won't let anyone else hurt you, either."

Meggie closed her eyes. "It doesn't *have* to hurt… does it?"

"Sweetheart." His voice deepened with tenderness. "Gorgos expects you to find your pleasure. That doesn't require penetration. All that is required is that you have an orgasm. Aphrodite doesn't always allow her guards inside her. She likes—variety. But tell me now if you can't take this, and I will go out fighting for you. Say the word, and we will stop this here and now."

Brav's hand lowered to clasp hers.

"Or we can proceed," he assured her. "It is your pleasure, in this bed, that is expected. Not an assault—pleasure. If you are willing to continue, I am here to help you. I can pleasure you in any way you choose. I am required to obey. And, quite frankly," he looked her up and down, "I want to."

She gasped and stared at him wordlessly.

"You can look at this as an opportunity," he suggested. "Any sexual act you have ever dreamed of, I am ready and willing to perform. Or you can ask me to tutor you in the ways of pleasure, show you all the ways we can please each other. We will *not* do anything you don't want to do."

"But what if I don't want you to touch me?" She wasn't sure that was true, though. Having a handsome warrior ready to fulfil all her sexual desires really didn't sound all that bad.

"If you don't want me to touch you, then you can touch yourself. All that is required is an orgasm. It doesn't matter what brings you to that peak."

Not one man of her acquaintance had ever spoken to her like this. She wasn't sure she'd even heard the word "orgasm" spoken aloud since she'd done Sex Ed in school. And Sex Ed had not prepared her for this situation.

"What if... um... what if I *do* kind of want you to touch me?"

His eyes flamed. "Then I will be very careful, baby. Very gentle and slow. Kiss your mouth. Your neck. Your shoulders. Touch your beautiful breasts. Bring them to my mouth. As for your orgasm..." He shrugged. "For this first time, I think I would put my hand between those beautiful, soft thighs, and let you rub yourself against me, come that way."

"You wouldn't... penetrate me?"

"Not if you didn't want me to."

She let out her breath in a sigh. "OK," she said.

"That's not enthusiastic consent, baby." He lay back on the pillows and put his hands behind his head. "Let me know when you've finished masturbating."

This time, her sigh was a gasp accompanied by a quick slap to his chest. "Bastard."

"Possibly. But someone sighing 'OK' in a sad little voice is not sexy. So, I'm changing the rules, as of now. I'm going to lie here. If you want me to touch you, you'll have to come to me."

"What?"

"You heard me. You'll have to swing your leg over me and straddle me. And *then* I might consider giving you multiple orgasms."

"Multiple orgasms." She repeated it silently, noting the way he watched her mouth. She flicked her tongue out to wet her lips and his eyes narrowed. She looked down to his crotch. The intimidatingly large bulge there said that he was more than a little affected by the idea. "Fine," she snapped.

She twisted so she could swing her leg over him and settle her weight on his thighs, carefully avoiding any connection between his shaft and her body. "Are you happy now?"

"Will be in a minute," he muttered and sat up.

She'd thought he would dive right in. Slam one hand over her breast, another between her legs, but he didn't. Her body was braced tight for it.

Instead, he reached behind her to loosen her hair. Aphrodite's riotous curls fell around her shoulders in loose waves and he sighed. "Aphrodite is physically perfect, but her heart is not beautiful. Your heart is beautiful, Meggie. I can see your beautiful heart in your eyes." His hands slid through her hair to hold her cheeks. He'd said her heart was beautiful once before, Meggie recalled, and felt her body softening. "You are so beautiful."

He leaned down. His lips were soft against hers, causing pleasant tingles to run through her body. He didn't eat at her lips, just slid his mouth gently across hers until she was chasing the pleasure of his kiss. Then he let go of her face to slide his hands through her hair. Her own hands were on his wide, nearly bare shoulders, bracing herself.

She wasn't sure if she could call this their first kiss. They'd both used the Averones as an excuse for their first kiss and pretended it never happened. This—this could be nothing but a kiss. His tongue probed gently at the seam of her lips, asking for admittance.

Meggie opened herself to him and made a soft sound of pleasure at the feel of his tongue exploring her.

He brought her hair around, so it spilled over either shoulder. His big fingers combed through it. As he stroked down, his fingertips passed over her full breasts, then, slowly, over each nipple. She went very still. She tried not to jerk when sudden pleasure shot through her but wasn't successful.

"You have beautiful hair, sweetheart," he whispered. "So lovely. One day I'll run my hands through it. And such lovely breasts. I can't wait to really feel *you* in my hands. Until then, I can at least please you. So many pleasures that I can show you here." His big fingers strummed her nipples gently and she arched back in pleasure.

"Brav," she whispered.

"Feel good, sweetheart?"

"Feels good. Don't stop."

Eventually, he abandoned her hair and cupped her breasts in his palms. She sighed and pressed herself closer to him. His hands were tender on her soft skin. She nearly came out of her skin when he thumbed her nipple, gasping, her hands clutching at his shoulders.

He took his time, strumming his fingertips over her nipples or rubbing his hands all over them until the pleasure made her shake in his arms. Every time he touched her nipples, it was like a cord pulled tight between them and her pussy. She'd never felt such an electric, dragging feeling between her thighs before, but she knew she liked it.

His lips followed a path from her mouth to her ear, pressing nibbling kisses along her jawline. She sighed sharply when his teeth nipped lightly at her earlobe. His tongue traced a line down her neck to dip into her collarbone. She wrapped her arms closer around his neck and brought his lips back to hers.

One of his hands drifted down over the dress to the slit beneath the belt. She didn't feel shy anymore. She grabbed his hand and pressed it between her legs. It was only when the pressure of her hands on his made his finger push between her swollen folds to touch the softness between that she realised how wet she was.

"This is so embarrassing," she muttered.

"Not embarrassing, baby," he muttered right back. "So sexy. So hot."

"But I'm… wet. I'm dirty."

"Wet is good, sweetheart." He turned his hand so that it slipped further between her folds. "Wet is very, very good." She cried out as he finished opening her outer pussy lips and pressed the side of his fingers into the sensitive slit.

Meggie couldn't help herself. His other hand was still on her breast and she wanted to come. Now!

As he'd suggested earlier, she rubbed against his hand, holding it in position against her in a spot she knew she liked more than anything. She might not have ever found pleasure with a man before, but that didn't mean she didn't know how to chase a quick orgasm with a hand between her legs. Somehow, knowing that the hand belonged to Brav made the sensations even more electric.

The release that barrelled through her was sharper than any she'd ever known. She rose up on her knees a little to keep riding his hand. When the spasms died away, she collapsed onto the broad chest that was heaving beneath her while his hot cock branded her belly through his leather trousers.

Before the last echoes of her orgasm had died away, Gorgos called for the dancers to return. Her head resting against Brav's broad shoulder, her legs wide open around his thighs, Meggie watched the dancers through the curtain. They were dressed in gauzy veils and they gyrated to an erotic rhythm as the meal resumed.

One of them kept looking up at the dais where Meggie was slumped in Brav's arms. The woman was beautiful, her slender limbs toned with muscle, her body moving with a sinuous grace. Meggie watched, her heart still pounding, as the woman slid her veiled body against a male dancer. He slid his hand down her thigh and opened her legs, thrusting his hips into the space between her legs.

The dancer bent back, her back arching until her hands reached behind her and she supported herself upside down. She lifted her other leg to wrap around the man's waist. He was supporting her, now.

Meggie turned her head further. They weren't just rubbing together, she realised. The male dancer was inside the woman, thrusting his cock into her pussy in rhythm to the music. Another dancer joined them, kneeling in front of the woman, pressing a passionate kiss to her exposed folds.

Meggie watched them fuck, watched the woman's face flush, watched her thighs tremble as she came. Watched the man as his face contorted and he came inside her.

The other dancers were fucking, too, she realised. So were some of the people at the tables. Those that weren't, including Gorgos, were looking up at her and Brav expectantly.

She was still spread out over him. He was still hard against her belly. "Do you like to watch?" he asked. "Does it excite you, baby?"

Meggie sat up and let her gaze snag with Brav's. "Yes," she answered bravely. She shifted down a little until she felt his hard shaft press between her legs. She bit back a moan. "Yes," she repeated, and rubbed against him again. Her outer lips were still parted and her clit stung with pleasure, still sensitised from her earlier orgasm.

Brav groaned and thrust up against her. "That's it, baby," he urged. "Ride my cock until you come. Let me give you pleasure."

"Make me come," she ordered breathily. "They're all watching. After a show like that, they'll expect it." Meggie braced her hands against his nearly-naked chest and let the rhythm of the music and the rhythm of her body take her over.

CHAPTER FIFTEEN

When Meggie woke up the next day, it took her a moment to realise where she was. She'd woken up in so many different beds lately that it was hard to keep up. She was warm, she was comfortable.

She was alone.

She turned her head on the pillow and gave in to tears.

She was alone. She'd felt alone ever since her mother died, but she'd had Teresa to take care of. In these last few days—God, had it only been a few days?—she'd gotten used to not being alone. Ever since they'd rejoined the Guardians, Jessan, Tarn, Kairn and Mac had made it clear that they were there for her. Brav had always been there, even when he'd been emotionally distant. He hadn't just been there for her. He'd worked his way into her heart.

And last night, he'd been in her bed. His hand had been between her thighs and he'd brought her to a stunning orgasm. Then she'd ridden him to another orgasm before eating her dinner. After the banquet, he'd been… polite. He'd escorted her back to her suite and taken up his place outside her door. He was so distant. She'd never felt such overwhelming sensations with another person before. How could he be so distant when she'd wanted nothing more than to melt into him?

A chime from the door interrupted her tears.

She hesitated. Meggie wasn't sure she had the right to refuse the pleasure entities to enter. She knew for certain that she didn't have a key.

The person didn't push the door open. Meggie pulled the covers higher. She had nothing to wear. She'd hated the dress they'd put her in and deliberately balled it up and stuck it under the bed. She was naked under the covers.

"Come in?" Her voice changed from tentative to bitter. "You might as well. I haven't got a key."

The door opened.

"Brav," Meggie said, shock and delight taking her voice, leaving her to just form the name silently.

"It's the same as last night, I suppose," he said, surprising her with the bitterness in his voice. "You couldn't stop me, so you submitted enough to get it over with."

"No!" She sat up straighter, then blushed and pulled the sheets higher as she nearly exposed her breasts. "That wasn't what happened at all!"

"Really? Then what happened? You were overcome with lust for a slave? No, wait! Better yet, you fell in love with the man who treated you no better than the piece of shit who abused you as a child?"

Meggie felt his words hit her like sledgehammers. Her chest felt like it had been caved in and she couldn't speak.

"I brought you breakfast." He reached back into the alcove outside her bedroom and retrieved a tray. "Where do you want it, *goddess?*"

It felt like another blow. "Brav–" she uttered brokenly.

"On the table I suppose," he continued relentlessly. He put the tray on the table and pulled out the chair. "Well, goddess, come and get it."

A sudden anger surged inside her. How *dare* he define what they'd shared last night in such terrible terms? "Fine." She threw back the bedcovers, utterly careless of her nudity, and swung her legs out of bed. She stalked across the deep carpet to the table and sat down in the chair.

All of a sudden, her bravado deserted her. She crossed her arms over her body. She heard Brav's muttered, "Fuck."

He whirled away from her and strode to the wall. He spoke to the replicator. The replicator. She hadn't even realised there was one. There were so many wall panels with symbols on them and she hadn't taken the time to learn which ones indicated the replicator.

So, she'd slept naked like an idiot.

Brav returned with a chiton. "My lady–" his voice was hoarse and broken. "Please, take the dress. I didn't realise they hadn't given you any clothes."

Meggie stood up and raised her arms over her head, defiantly allowing him to see her full nudity. It wasn't the first time he'd seen her naked. Once, when he'd rescued her from the shower and again when he'd shown her what Aphrodite would expect from her Master of the Wardrobe. Last night, he'd had his hand between her legs and she'd opened her gown for him. So, why was it that at this moment she felt so very exposed?

Brav moved around behind her and dropped the folds of the chiton around her body and tied the belt between her breasts the way she'd liked it the first time she'd worn a dress like this. She wrapped her hands around her waist, feeling like if she didn't, she was going to fly apart. His hands fell onto her shoulders and he turned her around to face him.

"Meggie," he began, then stopped, staring at her face. "You've been crying."

That was it. She hit him, flailing her hand at his chest—not hard enough to hurt, but enough to show her displeasure. "Of course, I've been crying, you *bastard*."

He dropped to his knees before her, slowly, like they couldn't hold him up anymore. "I am so sorry," he whispered. "So very, very sorry."

Meggie brought her hand up to cover her mouth to try to stop her lip trembling. "You don't even know what you're apologising for."

"I hurt you," he answered. "Last night. I took advantage of you when I swore I wouldn't. I know that nothing will make up for what I forced you to do last night, but I need you to know that I deeply, deeply regret it."

He was only a few inches lower than her, but the desperate expression on his face made it seem like he was miles away and couldn't do anything to get closer.

Meggie reached out her hand to touch his lean cheek. He hadn't shaved and his skin was bristly with stubble. "I was crying because I thought you regretted touching me." He closed his eyes tightly, as if holding back tears at the tenderness of her touch. "I was crying because I thought you didn't want me anymore."

"Not want you?" The disbelief on his face was like cool water easing a burn. "I'll want you until I draw my last breath. The only thing I regret is that you couldn't consent to what we shared last night. I can't forgive myself for that, Meggie."

"What do you mean, I didn't consent?" She was so surprised that her head jerked back. "You refused to touch me until I begged you. I consented—Brav, was that why you were so unhappy this morning? Because you thought you hurt me?"

His lips trembled and she wanted to kiss them. "Meggie, I'm not a free man anymore. I'm a slave." She watched his Adam's apple bob up and down as he swallowed hard. "I don't deserve you."

Meggie gave in and traced his vulnerable lips with her fingertip. He shuddered. "Brav, think back to our last night on Gerea's shittiest ship. I slept in your arms. I told you I loved you. That hasn't changed."

He searched her face. "But I'm a slave. How can you respect a slave? Meggie—you don't know…" He looked down at her feet. "It's not even the first time. Aphrodite caught me six years ago. She held me for five years." His voice lowered to a desperate whisper. "I couldn't tell you before. I was so ashamed."

Meggie took a step forward, all the space that was between them and wrapped her arms around him. His face pressed into her breasts, one of her arms was across his shoulders, the other slipping behind his head. "Brav, I love you. I don't care about any of that. I just love you."

Finally, finally, his arms came around her. He buried his face against her, groaning, "Meggie, Meggie, I love you so much."

He rose to his feet, keeping his arms around her, and took her mouth in a wild, sweet kiss.

Was this another first kiss? Meggie wondered. This was their first kiss in private. Then she stopped thinking and surrendered to the pleasure of his mouth exploring hers.

When Brav finally broke the kiss, they were both breathing hard and Meggie felt dizzy. She clung to him.

He guided her gently back to the table, but this time, he didn't pull out a chair for her. This time, he sat down and pulled her into his lap.

"Now," he said, reaching for the food, "let's see about some breakfast."

He insisted on feeding her. She managed to get him to eat a little. He insisted at first that he'd already broken his fast, but when she made it clear that she wasn't going to eat the abundance of food on the tray, he polished it off, drinking deep swallows of the coffee-like drink he told her was called Krith.

She began to worry. Had he really been hungry? It took some probing, but he eventually admitted that he hadn't allowed himself breakfast, punishing himself for what he thought he'd done last night.

"What's going to happen tonight?" she asked. "Gorgos said that Aphrodite stays for three nights." She laid her head on his chest. "I could never have gone through this with anyone but you."

"Hmmm." Meggie liked the low, possessive growl that rose in his chest. "Speaking of tonight, have you thought about what you want me to do to you?"

Meggie felt herself blushing a bright, hot red. "No," she said honestly.

"I've thought of nothing else," Brav confessed. "I was awake all last night thinking about what we did together as I guarded your door, hating myself for it, but fantasising about everything else I want to do to you."

Meggie's blush got hotter. Greatly daring, she asked, "What did you have in mind?" Sitting on Brav's lap as she was, she couldn't help but be aware that he was aroused and she found that she was very curious what made him shift suddenly beneath her.

Brav's arm was around her shoulder, supporting her where she sat on his lap. Now, she noticed his other hand, resting lightly on her thigh. He started to draw little circles, pulling at the fabric of her chiton. He bent forward and caught her earlobe between his teeth.

She whimpered. He made a small sound of male pleasure at the noise.

When he spoke, his mouth was still close to her ear. She'd never known her ears were an erogenous zone before, but as his hot breath feathered over them she knew she'd been wrong.

"The way you react to me, sweetheart, I'm starting to wonder if you might like it better if it was a surprise."

For one reason or another, Meggie had spent an awful lot of time in the last few days without underwear. If he kept talking to her in that deep, growly voice, she was going to leave a wet spot on the back of her dress. *Wet is good, sweetheart,* he'd said. *Wet is very, very good.* Right now, she felt very, very… good.

"I think I like surprises," she moaned. The hand on her leg

slipped inside, between her knees, and her thighs shook.

"Hmmm." *God!* There was that noise again. If he'd lift his hand just a *little* bit higher, she'd probably come before the Krith even got cold. "One thing I need to know first, sweetheart."

"Anything." She moved on his lap so that her head could fall back on his shoulder and her thighs opened a little more.

"Hmmm." He growled. She whimpered. His breath was still hot on her ear. "Tell me, baby, have you ever used any toys before?"

"I had–" she had to stop for the shiver that wracked her body. "I had a Barbie doll when I was a little girl."

He shook with laughter behind her. "Unless a Barbie doll serves a very different function from what it sounds like, that isn't what I meant." His hand clenched in the fabric of her dress. His other arm dropped to her thighs too, now that he didn't have to hold her up. Both his hands were fisting in the fabric now and she realised he was pulling it up.

Her breath was coming faster, and so was his. She could feel his heart pounding in his chest behind her, feel the heat of his rigid cock beneath her bottom. "Brav," she whispered. She shifted again so that her back was to his front and he was fully behind her, opening her legs so that they were hooked over his and she was completely open to him. Her hands fell to his forearms and she clutched at the muscle there.

That earned her another male growl. "Toys," he repeated in her ear. The hem of her chiton had reached her thighs now. "I'm talking about toys that big girls play with, Meggie."

He slid his hands below the fabric now bunched at her hips, probing the soft flesh of her inner thighs. She arched into his touch, begging him mutely to go higher.

"Toys that big girls use to make themselves feel good," he growled. He pulled her legs even further apart. The motion made her labia part and she cried out in helpless need. He stroked a finger either side of her petals, tangling in the downy curls.

She sobbed.

"Toys," he went on, "that big girls use… here."

She arched like a bow in his lap as one finger slid into her secret folds.

"Well, Meggie? Answer the question." He held his hand away from her body while he waited.

"I've forgotten the question." She'd forgotten her own name.

"Have you ever used any toys… here?" Again, that light, teasing touch that made a short scream rip from her throat.

"No! Never! God, Brav, please, please–"

"Uh, uh." Both his hands were on her thighs now. "One more question for a good girl to answer." He pressed a kiss to her neck and she shook from head to foot in his arms. "How would you feel about me putting a toy inside you?"

"God, Brav, I want you inside me so much. Please, please–"

"Uh, uh." He pulled her back sharply, so that the heavy shaft of his cock branded between her buttocks. Then he was closing her legs and pushing her off his lap. He raised his right hand to his mouth and sucked at his fingertip. "You're delicious, baby. Can't wait to get my tongue in you. And anything else that comes to hand."

She fell back against the table, hardly able to stand up. "Brav, I want you," she panted.

"I know, baby." He took two quick strides and hauled her up against him, pressing a hard, passionate kiss to her mouth. "Tonight. Tonight, I promise, I'll fill you up."

And then he *left*. He *left*.

He looked a bit like walking was painful. *Good*, Meggie thought. *Oh, my God, I'm dying.*

CHAPTER SIXTEEN

After breakfast, the pleasure entities returned to prepare Meggie for the day. "Senator Gorgos will be pleased if you would join him, goddess—"

"No," Meggie said sharply. She wasn't going to spend any more time with the disgusting man than she had to. "Take me to the dungeons. I want to see the gifts he bought for me."

The pleasure entities didn't have a lot of choice. They tried to convince her to spend a pleasant day with Gorgos, but Meggie was sure it would make her sick. She flatly refused and insisted on going to the dungeons.

Inside… inside were the people she loved.

They were all held in a single room, lit now by a single light in a sconce on the wall. Teresa had been lying on the floor, her head in Kairn's lap as he spoke softly to her, but she jumped to her feet when she saw Meggie. Mac had been crouched by her feet and rose to his full height, a growl developing in his chest, when the door opened. Meggie realised that with the light of the hallway behind her, they couldn't see her. Teresa stopped to lay a hand on his arm as she waited beside him.

Cera rose to her feet, too. "What the fuck do you want?" she demanded.

"It's all right," Jessan said, rising to stand beside Cera. "This is the goddess—the one who sent us to guard you. Remember?"

Cera went so still Meggie wasn't even sure she was breathing. She waited until the door closed behind Meggie.

"Is that you, Meggie?" Cera breathed.

"It's me." Meggie let the glamour drop from her features. Suddenly, her dress didn't fit quite like it had a moment ago. "I'm here. I'm going to get you out of here, I swear it."

Teresa swept past Mac and cannoned into Meggie's arms. The small, soft weight of her sister was enough to bring tears to Meggie's eyes.

"It's OK," Meggie assured her, wrapping her arms around the sister she had given everything to keep safe, again and again. "I've got a plan to get us out of here."

"What can we do?" Jessan asked.

Meggie shook her head. "I can handle this. Just—just be patient, OK? I just have to get through three days. Then we can leave here and we'll be safe."

"Where is Brav?" Tarn asked. "We can't leave without him."

"Don't worry. He'll be with us," Meggie answered. "I've changed his appearance, too, but he's still my guard. He's sleeping now. He guarded my door last night."

"Meggie, how wonderful!" Teresa breathed, but Meggie noted that the others all looked sceptical. Jessan's brows drew into a frown.

"Sister, can I speak with you privately?"

Meggie looked around the small room. There didn't seem to be a lot of privacy available. "Where?" she asked. "I can't—I can't get you out just yet."

"I can provide privacy." He raised his hands over his head and as he lowered them, a shower of silver sparks fountained over them, enclosing them in a shimmering veil. "They can't hear us or see us now, and I'd like an honest answer. What are you doing to win our safety?"

Meggie bit her lip. When she spoke, her voice was breathy. "Please don't make me tell you."

Jessan closed his eyes and his face twisted. "Sister, you don't have to do this," he urged. "We'll find another way."

Meggie looked away from his intense blue eyes. "Look, it's nothing bad. It's fine. And in two days, you'll be free and it won't matter."

"It will matter, sister. And if the others knew what you had to do to impersonate Aphrodite as I do, it would matter to them, too." He put his hands on her shoulders. "Sister, if this is a hurt that you will carry with you later, that will matter to all of us."

She met his gaze now. "I'm not being hurt, Jessan. It's… embarrassing, but I'm not being hurt. Brav is with me. He's… helping me. I'm not being forced into anything I don't want to do."

Jessan searched her eyes and she wondered if he was seeing into her mind. She tried not to think of leaning back in Brav's arms in their white-curtained haven while he stroked her until she came. He mustn't have seen it, she decided, because he didn't look shocked or appalled at her wanton thoughts. Eventually, though, he seemed to come to a decision.

"All right." He glanced over his shoulder, as though he could see Cera through the shower of silver sparks. "Cera wanted to warn you. She couldn't say it in front of the others—she told me mind to mind. There is a man named Baelor. He is a great threat to all of us. He frightened her badly. She believes he and Gorgos are working together. Be careful, sister."

"I'll be careful."

The shower of silver sparks stopped flowing and the last of them fell to the floor where they shimmered like opals in the dim light before fading away. Meggie heard footsteps approaching and hastily changed her appearance back to that of Aphrodite.

Reluctantly, she left the room. She wished with all her heart that she'd had time to say goodbye to Teresa. That she'd had time to talk to Bess and Cera. That she'd had a chance to tell Cera that she considered them sisters, too.

But there wasn't time. She'd only just started a casual saunter when an enormous man carrying a sack on his shoulder came around the corner. "What are you doing here?" he asked in surprise.

Meggie drew herself up to her inconsiderable height, given that he was nearly twice as tall as she was. As he drew closer, it became apparent that he was a giant. The little pleasure entities barely came past his knees, and Meggie herself wouldn't have reached much past his waist.

"I'm a goddess, I can do what I want." She looked him up and down scornfully. "What are *you* doing here? Why carry such a heavy weight when you can replicate whatever you want?"

He shifted the sack on his shoulder and spoke evenly. "I'm bringing wheat to the kitchen. It's cheaper to bake than it is to replicate. And slave labour is completely free." He regarded her blandly. "I suppose a goddess doesn't have to concern herself with things like that."

Meggie tried not to show she was ashamed. "I really didn't know," she mumbled, then gestured to her pleasure entities and hurried back to her own suite.

In the afternoon, or what passed for it on the ship, the pleasure entities came to prepare her for the banquet that evening.

Meggie dutifully rose from her chair and followed them. Now that she knew where the replicator was, she'd made herself a jigsaw puzzle to pass the time. She'd been tempted to spend the day on her bed with her hand between her thighs, after the way Brav had heated her up this morning, but something told her it would be all the sweeter tonight if she waited.

She wanted her next orgasm to come from him. All day long, she'd been thinking about it. What kind of toy would he have? How would it feel to have something inside her? Would she freeze up and think of Colin or would she melt in Brav's arms again?

And there was another point of anxiety. She'd seen Brav naked. She'd had her hand wrapped around his cock, and very nearly her mouth. She knew how big he was. Colin hadn't been big and he'd hurt her badly. What if Brav's idea of a toy for big girls was a phallus as thick as his arm?

She followed the pleasure entities to the bathing chamber and let them bathe her. Brav arrived silently and stood guard at the door. Uncaring of her nakedness, Meggie emerged from the bath and went to the mattress where they massaged her last night, lay down and let them prepare her for the banquet.

*   *   *

This time when she arrived in the banquet hall, Meggie didn't hesitate. She sashayed straight to the divan.

"Time for you to choose your lover again," Gorgos announced, already spreading his legs so a slave could get between them.

"That one," Meggie said quickly, pointing to Brav, who was still disguised.

Gorgos frowned. "I didn't think you'd be so predictable. You usually like a change of lovers."

"My lady will find a new pleasure tonight, I promise you that," Brav snapped, and pulled the curtains closed around them. Then Meggie was secluded—in name only—with the warrior beside her.

He lay back, as he had last time, hands under his head while a grin stretched his sensual lips. "Same rules as last night, baby."

"Rules?" He wasn't wearing a shirt. He wasn't wearing a shirt. And his chest was *mouth watering!* Meggie couldn't drag her gaze away from the muscular expanse, the dark hair in the centre of his chest, the flat copper nipples, the washboard abs… and then his belt, and the black leather trousers that hid the rest of him from view. As she watched, a bulge started to form there and her eyes flicked guiltily back to his. "Um, what rules?"

"One orgasm minimum." She was never going to get used to him saying the word orgasm like it was an everyday thing. Although for him, it probably was. "And you can choose any means you like to get you there. You can do anything you want to yourself." His eyes became heavy lidded as he looked over her lush curves. "I will do anything you want to you."

"What about you?"

He blinked. "What about me?"

"Well, don't you want one, too?" No way was she going to say the word "orgasm" out loud.

His lips curved in a sinful smile. "Want to touch me, do you, sweetheart?"

She blushed. "Maybe."

"Anything you want, sweetheart. Just say the word and I'll do it for you. Or if you want anyone else in here. Or if you want me to use anything on you or for you."

"Like what?"

His voice roughened. "Like tying up your hands to the bedposts with silk scarves. Like a phallus to thrust inside you."

Her voice dropped to a whisper. "You mentioned that this morning." She looked him up and down. "Why use a toy, though? I thought — um…" she gestured to his crotch. "I thought, well, you have one of your own."

He laughed out loud.

"Shush!" she cried, leaping forward to clap her hand over his mouth. "They'll hear you."

"Yes, Meggie, I am fully equipped to serve you." He reached up to touch her face and she realised that she still had her hand over his mouth. She pulled it away in a hurry and he took his hand from her cheek.

He reached under the pillows and brought out a long, thin box. "I thought you might find this helpful. You've never been opened with pleasure before. You'll be tight inside and this will open you up a whole lot easier than my cock. Open the box."

She did as he bade and gasped. Inside… it looked like a vibrator. It was long and slim, and it looked like silver. "I had no idea you had… that kind of thing… here!"

"Take it out of its box, baby."

She lifted the little silver wand. It was nowhere near as large as his own cock and she wrapped her fingers around it with a rushing sense of relief. "It's warm," she murmured.

"Of course, it's warm. Did you think I'd fuck you with a cold toy?"

She felt the blush rising in her cheeks again and refused to answer.

"To turn it on, you have to tell it what to do."

"How do I do that?"

"It works like the replicators work. You just have to think of… vibration." He chuckled softly. "I think you'll like how it responds to what you're thinking."

That moment, the little wand came alive in her hand buzzing lightly in a way that sent a shock of pleasure through her, even though it was only in her hand. She dropped it, and it fell into the bedsheets, half hidden by a fold of silk.

"I can't do this," she stated. She looked up at him pleadingly. "Brav, help me. I don't know what to do."

His expression gentled and he held out his arms. "Come here, sweetheart."

She stretched herself out next to him, feeling her breasts pillow against his hard muscles. He put his arms around her and stroked her back, long soothing strokes that gentled her and made her feel safe.

"You don't have to do anything you don't want to do, sweetheart. This is *your* pleasure. You tell me what you want to do. What you want me to do with you."

She looked down at him. He meant it. She took her courage in both hands, because it was hard to admit out loud what she really wanted. Reaching down between them, she took hold of the silver wand, still warm, but no longer buzzing. "I want you to use this on me," she said. "Show me how I can use it to make myself feel good."

He took the wand from her, his much larger hand enveloping hers for a moment. "Are you sure, sweetheart?"

She met his eyes fiercely. "I'm sure, Brav."

He sat up and scooted back to sit up against the headboard. "Then come here to me." He gestured to his lap. "Sit with your back to my chest."

Heart pounding, Meggie crawled up the bed and sat between his spread legs. His hard shaft branded her lower back, but he didn't pull her closer, didn't thrust against her.

"Why not have me facing you?" she asked.

"Facing me would be nice," he admitted, his voice a low rumble. "But I want you to focus on what you're feeling tonight. I don't want you getting distracted by what you think I'm thinking or feeling, or getting self-conscious because you're gasping and moaning as I bring you pleasure."

"Am I going to gasp and moan?" She'd meant to be teasing, but it sounded serious.

He leaned forward and took her earlobe gently between her teeth. All at once, she was flooded with as much heat as she'd experienced that morning and she was pretty sure her eyes crossed.

"Gasping," he murmured in her ear, his hot breath fanning over her cheek. "Moaning. Sighing. Everyone else in this room is going to be *so* jealous." He sucked her earlobe into his mouth and a choked cry escaped her. "And if I don't get you to say the word 'fuck' out loud at least once, I'm going to think I'm not doing my job right. Now, just relax back against me, baby." His chest was so hard behind her, his shaft even harder. "I'm going to make you feel so good."

He pressed a light kiss to the side of her neck, just below her ear as his arms came around her. Her own hands fell naturally onto his forearms as his hot, wet mouth trailed down her neck to where it met her shoulder. He opened his mouth and sucked.

Her hands gripped his arms in a convulsive movement, and for a moment, his arms tightened around her. "Does that feel good, baby?"

"Yes," she gasped.

He continued to trail his lips around her neck and shoulder, sliding the neckline of the golden gown to the side so he could caress her bare skin. One hand rose to stroke gently over her breast while the other was tucked tight around her waist.

Meggie gasped as his palm stroked over her nipple. She'd never felt anything like this when she'd touched herself. When he touched her, it was like an electric shock ran through her body. He played with her breasts so gently that it was only moments before she was gasping, moaning and sighing beneath his touch, just as he'd promised. Her hips began to arch restlessly, jerking suddenly as pleasure spiked at a particularly gentle touch.

His hand slipped into the open front of the gown and he drew a soft circle around her areola. She jumped, arching her back to push more of her breast into his palm. "Brav, please!"

"Yes, baby, anything you want. Anything."

"Please, more!"

He cupped her breast and massaged while she moaned, louder than before. His voice was deep in her ear. "Let's try the toy now, baby."

She didn't have time to worry that he would press it between her legs before he'd brought it up to her breast. He touched the warm, vibrating silver want to the tip of her breast through the silk of her gown and she jerked and sobbed with pleasure.

His other hand was opening her golden sash. The gown fell open either side of her as his hands smoothed the silk from her flesh. She was ready, so ready, to feel his hands on her skin. Ready to feel the warm, silver wand against the sensitive skin of her bare nipples.

"Please," she whispered, and he obliged, touching the wand lightly to her naked breast.

Something inside Meggie clenched tight suddenly and her hips thrust forcefully forward. His other arm slipped down to press against her hip as he caressed her nipple with the wand again. Meggie's head fell back against his chest and she looked up at him.

He was intent on her body, so she looked down. Her gown was open all the way, since there was nothing to fasten it below the waist, and she was fully exposed. Her breasts were bare, thrusting towards the buzzing toy, spilling slightly to the sides as she arched backwards. She could also see the curve of her belly, and below that, the soft dark curls between her thighs.

She grabbed the hand that wasn't holding the wand and slid it over her belly and between her thighs. She looked back up at him, meeting his eyes. "Touch me, Brav," she whispered. "I need to feel you here."

He bent his head and kissed her, taking her mouth in a passionate exploration as his big hand slipped further between her spread thighs. One finger teased gently between her curls, finding her slit.

"So wet, baby," he gritted.

"You make me so wet," she whispered, and then his finger was between her folds and she was lost.

He explored her as no-one had ever explored her. He stroked a wet path between her outer and inner pussy lips, all the way down to her well, then back up to the head of her slit. She bucked, gripping his wrist, trying to get him to press her clit as he had last night, but he kept his touch gentle. He circled her tiny bud of pleasure, almost, but not quite touching where she needed him.

The wand was stroking down over her belly now and Meggie was moaning openly. He slid it over her mound, and over her outer lips.

"Please, Brav! Oh, God, please!"

"Spread a little wider for me, baby," he urged, and she opened her legs without any hesitation. Opening her eyes, she could see the outline of the guards, standing in ranks at the foot of the bed. Each one of them was just a large shadow. Beyond them, the whole court was watching.

Knowing that they were watching just made Meggie hotter. Then Brav touched the little wand to her throbbing clit.

Her orgasm was immediate. She arched off the bed, chasing her pleasure while Brav growled in her ear. While the guards stood with their backs to the curtains. While the rest of the court joined in the orgy at the table.

Brav didn't stop touching her, though, and in moments, had her rocketing with another orgasm. By the time he slid the wand lower, to the entrance of her body, she'd lost count of how many times she'd come.

She was nervous, but the wand was warm, and she was wet. The feeling of the heated silver moving through her slick folds was intense and she reached up to grip Brav's shoulder behind her as he slowly pressed the toy against her entrance. She gasped, but tried to keep herself open for him.

The wand moved slowly inside her slick folds. Meggie felt a moment of resistance at the head of her channel. It had been fourteen years since she'd had anything inside her, but the wand moved past her resistance smoothly, to press inside her and buzz inside her warm, wet sex.

"Are you OK, baby?" Brav asked in her ear.

"Feels so good," she gasped. She moved experimentally, feeling the wand shift inside her. "Oh, Brav! Please—please!" Her other hand moved to grip the thick muscles in his thigh.

She wanted to tell him to thrust the wand inside her. Wanted to tell him to fuck her with it, but she couldn't.

His mouth lowered to clamp around her shoulder and she felt a brief sting as his teeth scraped her. It made her jerk on the wand. The muscles in his forearm shifted as he slowly withdrew the wand.

Meggie gasped and thrust herself towards it. Brav followed her movement, thrusting the wand inside her. It was even deeper, this time, and the buzzing had changed to a deep, pleasurable throb that echoed Meggie's own racing heart and throbbing clit. Her body clenched around the invader and she felt a new delight as her inner muscles clamped down on the warmth thrusting deeply into her body.

The pleasure pushed her past every inhibition. "Oh, God!" she moaned. "Fuck me deeper, Brav. Fuck me harder."

Brav just growled, withdrew the wand nearly to the tip, and thrust it into her again. And again. And again. Meggie lay sprawled in his arms, between his spread legs, his cock pressed tight behind her, while he fucked her tight pussy with the throbbing silver wand and the whole court watched.

Meggie moved faster, chasing another orgasm as it rose within her. It was different this time. Deeper. Sweeter. *Wilder.* She kept her eyes open, looking at the row of warriors through the curtains as her lover fucked her deep and hard with the silver wand.

Then his other hand slid down to search between her folds. He found her clit and massaged it gently. The twin sensations of the wand thrusting and throbbing inside her, as well as the firm pressure of his big, callused finger hard against her clit was too much—enough to send her flying again.

She arched and writhed in his arms, gasping out his name as she found her pleasure. He slowed the rhythm of the phallus inside her as she subsided into his embrace, her hands relaxing on his thigh and bicep. He withdrew the wand gently, but she still moaned. The sensation of the wand leaving her body was nearly as intense as when he'd first entered her with it.

She turned to him, reaching up for a warm, searching kiss. His hands moved gently over her body, soothing her.

CHAPTER SEVENTEEN

After the banquet, Brav closed Meggie's gown, then lifted her into his arms. She looped her arms around his neck and buried her face in his shoulder. He smelled musky, his skin still hot and slightly damp from their passionate encounter. He carried her from the banquet hall.

They didn't talk on the way. When they reached her rooms, he laid her on the bed. "I'll be back in a minute," he said.

It really was only a minute, and although Meggie could happily have fallen asleep in under a minute, she made the effort to stay awake. He returned and scooped her into his arms again.

Meggie didn't realise he was taking her into the bathroom until he lowered her into the warm water. "Oh, Brav!" she exclaimed. He was still with her—the tub was large enough for six, so there was plenty of space for them to share. The water came up to Meggie's chest.

Brav's expression was serious, but it wasn't grim or distant like it had been last night. "I thought you may need something to soothe your muscles," he explained, scooping water over her with his cupped hands.

Meggie leaned back in his embrace. "You mean because you fucked me hard tonight?"

Brav's head lowered to kiss her bare shoulder. "You don't know what hard is yet, baby."

She quivered with remembered pleasure.

He washed her all over, his hands slow and gentle on her skin.

She turned in the water so she could loop her arms around his neck again. "Brav."

"Yeah, sweetheart."

It wasn't a question and it wasn't an answer. Meggie sighed and lowered her head to his shoulder. Her body floated close to his.

All of a sudden, she wanted to cry. He felt it, of course, just the barest tremor of a sob rising from deep within her.

"Sweetheart, are you OK? I didn't hurt you, did I?"

"Oh, no, Brav, it was wonderful. Perfect, in fact." She pushed her face against him. "Brav."

He heard the pain in her voice and drew back so he could sit on the underwater bench seat at the edge of the deep bathtub with her in his lap. "Tell me, sweetheart," he urged.

Meggie's arms were still around his neck, but she pulled back enough to see his face. "I love you, Brav," she said seriously. "Everything we do together is beautiful. But I wish—I wish so much that it was the first time for me. I wish I'd never known any pain. Because this is how it should be. I was never so angry with Colin as I am in your arms. Now I know what he took from me, and I hate him so much."

Brav's arms tightened around her. "He'll never hurt you again, sweetheart," he vowed. "I swear by my very blood and bones."

He washed her tenderly. When the gentle movement of his hands between her thighs made her hips start to twist again, he pulled away and soothed her. He dried her off and took her back into the bedroom.

This time, he made a nightgown for her in the replicator. She sat on the edge of the bed and raised her arms like a child for him to dress her. He put the nightgown on her, then tucked her into bed.

"Aren't you sleeping next to me?" she asked drowsily.

He stroked her cheek and the soft area below her ear. "Not tonight, sweetheart. I've got to guard your door. But sleep well, my beautiful, beautiful mate. Know that I love you with all my heart."

Meggie was asleep even before the door closed behind him.

*　　*　　*

Meggie woke the next day, thinking, *After tonight, it will be over. After tonight, we can all go home.*

What would happen when they all went home?

For the first time, she found herself seriously considering the future. She'd never given it much thought, even when she was young. All she'd ever had time for was thinking about today. All that the future had ever promised her was more days like the ones that had passed. Get up, go to work, go home, call Teresa. Get paid. Sleep in on Saturday. Clean the house. Get slightly older.

And now?

Her chest felt tight as she dared to hope. Now, Brav might be with her. Now, she might be able to leave behind the job she'd hated for the last fourteen years. She might be able to become a teacher as she'd always dreamed. She might have children. She might travel, not just the world, but the galaxy.

Teresa was grown up now. She hadn't spoken to her father in years. He neither needed nor deserved her concern. There was nothing stopping her from living a life she'd never dared dream of.

She replicated herself a fresh chiton for the day, tying the golden sash around Aphrodite's waist. She looked down at her body. Aphrodite's body. Brav certainly seemed happy exploring it, but was that because it was Aphrodite's body? How would he feel if her breasts weren't so big, her curves not so full? Years of hunger had left her lean and she was never going to develop the curves Aphrodite flaunted.

She replicated herself a big breakfast, determined to plump out her slender figure, not even sure if calories taken in Aphrodite's body would help Meggie's butt. She put her fork aside before she was even halfway through it. It was impossible to take pleasure in food when she was feeling insecure. She wished that Brav was with her. She was sure that he'd reassure her.

He'd probably kiss her until her eyes rolled back in her head. That would be reassuring. She pushed her chair back from the table and went to the door.

Brav wasn't there. Instead, the giant she'd met outside the dungeons was guarding her door.

"Where is Brav?" she demanded, shock making her tone sharpen until she sounded every bit as imperious as the real Aphrodite.

The giant bowed. "Your favoured guard is resting, goddess. He has entrusted you to my care."

"And *can* I trust you?" Despite herself, her confidence wavered. This guard was big enough to break her in half with one hand.

The giant bowed again, but Meggie caught the flicker in his eyes as he caught her uncertainty. "Brav saved my life, goddess. I owe him everything. I would serve you to the last drop of my blood."

Unsure what to do, Meggie went back into her room and closed the door. Brav had been afraid that she wouldn't be able to respect him because he'd been a slave. The more she heard about him, the more she respected him. He was an honourable man, a faithful friend… and she fell more in love with him every day.

Just a few moments later, there was a chime from the door.

Meggie had just sat down at the table again. She was about to call, "Come in," when one of the pleasure entities drifted out of their cubby and opened the door. They hadn't done that when Brav was the one who was knocking, so Meggie had a pretty good idea of who it was. She braced herself.

It was Gorgos.

His round, red face was creased with worry. He hurried over the expensive carpet and stood hesitantly across the table from her. He was trembling all over. A dozen guards followed him into the room and arranged themselves in ranks in the corner.

"Well, what is it?" Meggie snapped, picking up her fork again and prodding at the now-cold food.

"Goddess… please. I beg you to consider performing the Donation of the Goddess. The moons are all in alignment. The people are ready. You've spent the whole visitation in your chambers. I… I hoped that you would perform the Donation of the Goddess today, even though I am no longer in your favour."

Meggie looked up. "I don't want to," she retorted. "I am *extremely* displeased with you, Senator Primus. I just want to leave. I'm tempted to leave right *now*."

Gorgos flung himself at her feet

"Goddess, please!" he wailed. "Please perform the Donation! My whole planet needs this! If you do not perform the Donation, the whole sector will know that I have displeased you! Our trade partners will sever agreements with us and the whole planet will suffer. Forgive me, Goddess. I am a poor servant, but I beg you, do not punish our entire planet for my own modest mistakes."

He knew the right words to say, Meggie thought sourly. The piece of shit kneeling at her feet was a liar, a thief and worse. She remembered what he'd said back at the baths: that he'd like nothing so much as to beat Aphrodite to death and molest her corpse.

But it hadn't occurred to Meggie that staying in her room would hurt anyone. She couldn't even ask if this was true, the real Aphrodite would know this. Her heart pounded. If she stayed in her room, people would suffer. Economics isn't an exciting subject until you're wondering how to put food on the table.

If she stayed in her room, somewhere on this planet, another fourteen-year-old girl would go to work for her family and her life would never be the same.

She was going to answer, but she'd taken too long. Gorgos clutched at her feet. "Please, please, please! You liked the three virgins I gave you, didn't you? I can have them tied up in the temple and you can watch your favourite guard deflower them all."

She drew her foot back and showed considerable restraint by not kicking him in the teeth.

Lips pursed in displeasure, Meggie took the napkin from her lap and draped it over the table. "Jiliar is a fair planet," she said slowly. "I would not wish her to suffer." She allowed herself a stern glare. "But know this, Senator Primus, if anyone touches my virgins, I shall have your hands removed."

There was no chime at the door this time when it opened. Brav's face was like a thundercloud when he saw Gorgos at Meggie's feet.

"Get away from her," he growled, striding forward. He didn't even glance at the guards as he stepped between Meggie and the Senator. "Did he touch you, Goddess?"

"Not a finger, not a finger!" Gorgos intruded before Meggie could answer. The guards had changed position: now each man stood with a blaster in his hand. They didn't dare point them at a goddess, but Meggie knew they wouldn't hesitate to shoot Brav.

"He didn't touch me," Meggie replied, quieter. Brav's eyes met hers, searching, trying to be sure she was telling the truth. What he saw must have satisfied him. He gave her a little smile.

Gorgos was still talking. "The goddess is so gracious to our planet. She has agreed to perform the Donation of the Goddess."

The smile was wiped off Brav's face. His eyes widened. "You didn't…" he whispered.

Meggie's heart skipped a beat. He looked genuinely horrified. Cera and Jessan could speak mind to mind. Right now, she'd give anything to be able to speak to Brav privately so she could know what she'd just gotten herself in for.

"What time is the Donation?" Brav asked, still not taking his eyes off Meggie.

"Everything is prepared," Gorgos offered. "You must come now. The whole planet awaits."

"I must prepare my mistress," Brav growled.

"There is no time," Gorgos cried. "The Donation must begin now, as the rising of the sun and setting of the moon coincide."

Brav's face was pale now. Meggie had never seen him so pale. His eyes darted around the room like he was looking for a weapon. His eyes skidded over the guards, still with their blasters in their hands. What in God's name had she agreed to?

In the end, Meggie *had* to follow Gorgos from the room. She let him lead the way and she and Brav walked a short distance behind him. The guards followed them.

"Do you have a plan?" Brav whispered, not even turning his head to look at her.

"No," she whispered back.

There was a short, tense silence, then Brav whispered, "Faint."

Meggie took a few stumbling steps and gave a small cry as she crumpled. Brav's hands caught her before she could hit the floor.

"Senator! Wait!" he called.

Gorgos turned to see Meggie limp in Brav's arms. "What's happened?"

"My lady has fainted. She cannot participate in the ceremony. She is unwell. I must take her back to her chambers." He lifted Meggie's limp form high against his chest and cradled her there.

"No," Gorgos snapped. "She promised. I've been waiting for this for years. She doesn't need to be conscious to spread her legs. Get moving."

A quiver of fear ran through Meggie. Brav refused to budge. "I will not jeopardise my lady's health," he said stubbornly.

Meggie could practically *hear* Gorgos scowling. "Take her!" he cried.

Meggie's eyes flew open as she felt new hands taking hold of her. "No!" she cried, and remembered swiftly that she was supposed to be unwell and changed it to a moan. "No, I'm not well…"

Things seemed to happen so fast. Brav slipped her down to her feet, but kept her body pinned to his with his left arm. He lashed out at the guard who tried to take her from him, landing a powerful blow on the man's jaw that knocked him out cleanly. And then there was another, and another. Brav was handicapped by holding Meggie, but his arm was like iron around her.

Gorgos's voice, even more terrifying for its very calmness, cut through the sudden tumult.

"Kill him if you have to," he said. "She's going to perform the Donation of the Goddess, whether she wants to or not. Take her."

Brav was a powerful man, a skilled fighter, but there were too many of them. Even though it took four of them to control him, it was mere minutes before the guards had him securely and his helpless eyes met Meggie's.

"Please, no! Stop!" she cried and all at once, she was back in that moment when Colin first laid his hands on her. She was fourteen years old again and he was so much bigger than she was. She felt like her limbs were filled with water, hardly able to hold her up. The guard had to support her to keep her on her feet as she moaned, "No, please, no. Please."

"You agreed to this," Gorgos reminded her. He looked her up and down, leering. "I waited years for this." He turned to the guards. "Collar her."

Meggie only had a moment to remember the silver collar that had sat around Cera's throat when they were sold in the slave market before she felt the cool circle fall around her shoulders. The guard activated something at the back of it and it clicked into place. It wasn't tight around her neck, but it did something worse.

It tore her powers away from her in an instant. One moment she was standing there in Aphrodite's lush form, the next she was wearing her own skin. As her ability to maintain the illusion was stripped from her, Brav's appearance changed, too. Gorgos's mouth fell open. He looked from Meggie to Brav and back again.

"I know you," he whispered. "I remember you. I remember you both. You were at the auction." His eyes bulged as his face turned puce. "You were *stealing* from me! You were going to steal my virgins and I *need* them for when the *real* Aphrodite arrives as planned this afternoon." His eyes narrowed again. "Arrives this afternoon. And I will be able to give her a great gift. In the meantime, there is no reason that you could not still participate in the Donation of the Goddess. You can change your shape, you must have at least a little Alterran blood in you. You won't give as much value as the real Aphrodite would, but you can still give me your powers."

Meggie's flesh crawled as he looked her up and down.

"Take me," Brav begged. "Sacrifice me. Take my blood. Take my life. Just let her go, please, and I'll give you everything."

Gorgos ignored him, still looking Meggie up and down. "And you still look a little like her. You don't have the figure, of course, but there is a definite resemblance. I could do anything I wanted with you."

"You lay one hand on her, you piece of filth, and I swear to every god that I will kill you!" Brav shouted. One of the guards holding him just pressed a blaster to his chest and pulled the trigger. The muzzle pressed so close to Brav's chest that Meggie could barely even see the flash of green light.

Meggie screamed as Brav went limp. "Brav, no!" Gorgos was still looking at her with anticipation. "Oh, God, help!" Meggie cried. "Please, no, please. We weren't doing any harm—"

A big hand clapped over her mouth, muffling her cries.

"Well done, man," Gorgos approved. "I can do without listening to the whining of a woman and a thief."

Meggie pleaded, but her pleas went unanswered. The guards held her arms tightly and dragged her along.

"You can't do this!" she cried. "I'm the goddess Aphrodite! You can't treat me like this!"

"A thief and a liar," Gorgos gritted. "Even if you *were* the real Aphrodite, I wouldn't let you back out now. I've been waiting years to treat you like this," Gorgos snarled. "Years to tie you up and force you to open your legs for me. Waited years to sit on your throne and take everything you've got."

Meggie's legs crumpled beneath her. The guard had to catch her and carry her along with him.

CHAPTER EIGHTEEN

They carried her through long hallways, Brav dragged behind her. By the time they came out into the open, Meggie was nearly hoarse from crying and begging them to let her go. Brav was still unconscious.

The temple was situated at the end of a vast plaza, perched atop an impressive set of stairs, white columns leading to a carved, gleaming pediment. The plaza was packed with people, watching avidly as the goddess Aphrodite was carried, half-insensible through the crowd. Gorgos waved to them as he passed. There was a low hum of conversation and a smattering of applause, but clearly no-one was pleased to see either the goddess or their Senator Primus.

Meggie wasn't sure what she'd expected to see in the temple. Perhaps just an empty space. Gorgos had mentioned a throne, so perhaps something like the Lincoln memorial with a giant stone figure seated on a chair. The people were just as packed in here as they were outside, but they were more enthusiastic as they cheered for their Senator Primus. Meggie reached out to them, past the guard's encircling arms, begging for them to save her, but they ignored her gesture.

They looked... hungry. They were unmoved by her hoarse pleas and just looked at her like they wanted to devour her.

At the far end of the temple there was another set of stairs and a throne, but the throne wasn't at the head of the stairs. The throne was at the bottom. At the top of the stairs was an open space between two pillars. A heavy golden chain as thick as Meggie's arm ran from the top of one pillar to the throne below the stairs.

'Sacrifice *me*,' Brav had said. Meggie closed her eyes. Gorgos was going to kill her. Kill her and do terrible things to her corpse. She stared at the pillars. So, this was where she died. They were going to tie her up to the pillars and sacrifice her.

Of all the ways she'd thought she was going to die, this was not one she'd anticipated. In her darkest moments she'd wondered sometimes if she'd die by her own hand, if it wasn't for the fact that Teresa needed her. All those years of suffering, all those years of wishing that things were different, dreading the days ahead—now that she might finally have something to look forward to, here was the end of everything.

What was going to happen to Teresa when she died? Her mind felt heavy and dull. She'd expended all her energy. There was no way she could fight, no hope of getting free. It was no different than when Colin had hurt her. There was no way to get free. So, she just trembled as the guard clamped a manacle around each wrist and attached them to another gold chain hanging from the tops of the pillars.

When he knelt to place manacles around her feet, Meggie found reserves of strength she didn't know she had. She kicked out, fought, but the guard just grabbed her ankle and clasped the cool gold around it, holding her legs apart.

Gorgos stood at the foot of the stairs, watching as she was prepared. Brav's still form was draped at the top of the stairs at Meggie's feet. He was still breathing, but what did that matter? It wasn't going to be long until they were both dead.

When Meggie was secured, Gorgos began to ascend the staircase. He didn't take his eyes off her for a moment. Her mouth formed protests that made no sound, her throat raw from screaming.

"You look so much like her," he murmured as he drew near. He reached out a hand to stroke a stubby finger down her cheek. "I've been dreaming of this for years."

A feminine voice rang out. "What kind of travesty is this?"

Gorgos turned so quickly he nearly fell down the stairs. A woman stood at the entrance of the temple, her face and figure the same as the one that had stared back at Meggie in the mirror for the last few days. Meggie recognised that lush figure, the cloud of dark hair—Aphrodite had arrived.

"Goddess!" Gorgos cried, stumbling down the steps. "We didn't expect you until this afternoon!"

Dark eyes narrow, Aphrodite retorted, "That much is evident. How dare you conduct this travesty of a Donation when I have made it clear to you again and again that I will share neither my power nor my pleasure with a pig like yourself?"

"She is a liar and a thief, goddess!" Gorgos cried, hurrying down the stairs towards the real Aphrodite. "She has powers—she changed her appearance to look like you! I thought it was you! It wasn't my fault that I was deceived by her. I bought you a beautiful gift. Three virgins, goddess, each of them young and lovely."

Aphrodite waved a dismissive hand. "What use do I have for virgins?" she asked. Her gaze drifted past Gorgos to where Meggie was chained at the top of the stairs. "And who is the little slut you thought you'd use for your fake ceremony?"

Gorgos opened his mouth to answer, but Aphrodite held up a hand for silence. Suddenly, there was pressure in Meggie's mind. She gasped. She'd never felt someone else in her mind before. There was a sudden silence in there, as though someone was waiting to talk.

Meggie thought, *"Hello?"* and felt stupid just thinking it, but the presence in her mind made her feel like the other person was waiting for something. All of a sudden, the image of her mother's face came into her mind, so clear it was as though she'd just stepped out of the room rather than having died fourteen years ago.

Finally, the presence in Meggie's mind spoke one word. *"Nemesis."*

The voice was satisfied, but the word wasn't reassuring. Nemesis. That was something to do with vengeance, wasn't it? Did Aphrodite want revenge for Meggie's crime of impersonating her? Meggie twisted her hands, so that she gripped the chains that bound her to the pillars. She sent a thought back, one slightly more fitting than saying hello.

"Don't let him kill us," she thought. *"Please, I have a younger sister to look after. I have a man that I love. I have two cousins who are like sisters. If I die, they will be lost. Please, goddess. I beg you."*

Aphrodite's expression didn't change. She looked back at Gorgos. He quailed and Meggie knew that he was feeling that intense pressure in his mind now.

"I'll deal with these imposters myself. And you, little man. You know the punishment for stealing."

"But I bought you a gift! Three virgin girls!"

Aphrodite scoffed. "Virgins are bad enough. What do I want girls for? Hold out your hands."

"Goddess—divinity, no!"

One moment, Gorgos was holding his trembling hands out in front of him, the next moment, they were gone. All that was left were stumps, pumping blood. Gorgos screamed in agony. The next moment, the skin was blackened and seared. The blood no longer flowed, but the smell of burning flesh filled the air.

The crowd was absolutely silent, but one man spoke. He was just sauntering into the temple as though he was late to a party, but not particularly upset at being late.

"Mercy," he drawled.

Gorgos cut off his cries immediately and stared at the newcomer. It was a man in his mid thirties, of average height, not quite middle-aged. He was lean and dressed all in black, with just a hint of gold braid at his collar and cuffs. In a word, he was nondescript: dark hair, dark eyes and a face that could easily be forgotten, were it not for the scars on his cheeks and the hint of cruelty in his eyes.

He said it again, and it was clear that it was an order. "Mercy."

It was the same man who'd come to take Leona away. The same one who swore that he'd do terrible things to Cera and kill the rest of them. Meggie hung her head, hoping to avoid being recognised.

"Baelor." Aphrodite's hands had tightened into tiny fists. "What interest does Everius have in this affair? This little man was caught stealing from me. He has forfeited his life."

"And yet, you will show him mercy." Baelor bowed, a short, simple gesture that somehow conveyed a world of sarcasm.

"I am not in a merciful mood. The servants of Everius are not welcome in my House. Get in your shuttle and leave, and I shall mete out justice as I see fit."

Baelor bowed again. "I shall depart, most gracious of goddesses, but I shall take Gorgos with me." He approached the two at the foot of the stairs slowly and steadily.

"No. He's mine."

Baelor reached them "Fairest of goddesses." His voice was steely. "My Master has claimed him. He is no longer yours."

Aphrodite's knuckles showed white. "What use does Everius have for a petty thief?" she demanded. "He tried to steal money from me to pay for a gift he gave me." Aphrodite gave a mirthless laugh. "I thought your Master had grander ambitions."

"My Master is astute and sees beyond your immediate need for retribution. Guards—kindly bring the Senator Primus of Jiliar to my shuttle. Oh, by the way." Baelor had already started to leave the room before turning back to Aphrodite. The guards were obeying his orders as the goddess gritted her teeth. "Before we go, he's going to need hands."

"I can't heal him." Aphrodite glared at Baelor, a thin smile on her face. "I can perform minor healings, but I can't replace body parts."

"Oh, I know that he will never have his real hands back. But you are also of the line of Hephaestos. You know how to forge a pair of hands. See that he gets them."

Meggie's mouth fell open as Gorgos's hands changed, swelled and grew. In another moment, he had hands again.

Not flesh, as Baelor had said. Not his real hands, but hands nonetheless. They looked like they were made out of dull, grey metal.

Gorgos gave a whoop of delight and scratched his nose. He drew his hand away with a cry of pain. There was a new, bloody area on his nose.

"It bit me!" he cried.

"It didn't bite you, you idiot," Aphrodite drawled. "I'm afraid metal-working is not my specialty. I made you functioning hands, but I couldn't smooth them for you. The texture may be something of a surprise, especially on sensitive areas. If you'll take my advice, you'll never jerk off again."

Gorgos's lip curled in sheer hatred. He started to fling himself towards Aphrodite.

Baelor flung out a golden line of light that wrapped itself around Gorgos's neck. Gorgos screamed and caught it with his new metal hands, just in time to stop it from pulling tight around his neck.

"Come now, Gorgos Ironhand," Baelor instructed smoothly. "The rest can wait for another day."

Gorgos followed him, with one last, burning look of utter loathing at Aphrodite.

Aphrodite's voice sounded in Meggie's mind. *"So, you have powers to change your appearance, do you?"*

"Yes, goddess."

"Is this your own form?" Aphrodite asked.

"Yes, divinity."

"If you can change your shape, why wouldn't you fix that ass?"

Meggie ignored the mean sally. *"You said that you had minor healing powers,"* Meggie thought as Aphrodite proceeded down the space in the middle of the temple. She glanced down at Brav. *"Can you heal him?"*

"Heal him?" Aphrodite asked. Her face was bland, but quizzical. Vaguely intrigued. *"That's the first thing you thought of?"*

"I love him," Meggie replied, simply, honestly.

Aphrodite nodded. She was at the foot of the stairs now and seated herself in the marble throne. Her voice spoke in Meggie's mind again. *"You look just like my sister, Nemesis. Are you an Alterran?"*

She wanted to agree, but she had to say, *"My mother's name was Megara."*

"Tosh." Aphrodite waved a dismissive hand and arranged the skirts of her chiton. *"I didn't mean her married name. Before she married, Megara was Nemesis, daughter of Zeus."* She regarded Meggie, still curious. *"I thought she died three thousand years ago. I thought I was the only one left."*

"Artemis survived, too," Meggie assured her. Conversation was good. Conversation was better than dying a horrible death. *"Did you know Artemis? She's my aunt."* Establish a connection. She'd read that somewhere, or seen it on a TV show. Humanise yourself.

"Of course, I did. She was my sister. I remember the day she came back to our father's House with her new husband. I never saw a couple whose bond was so bright."

Meggie wasn't sure what bond she was talking about, but this was good. This sounded positive. She might actually get out of here alive. She glanced down at Brav at her feet. Maybe even all of them get out alive. *"Please heal him,"* she begged.

Aphrodite shook her head and Meggie's dismayed cry sounded loud in the quiet room.

"I cannot, sister."

"But you said you had healing powers!"

"He was shot in the heart, sister. It's a miracle he's alive at all. I can only heal him temporarily. I can grant him an hour of health, and then he will die. Unless…" her expression grew crafty. *"Do you know the purpose of this throne, sister? The purpose of those pillars?"*

Meggie shook her head.

"They are to transfer power. And if you truly are the daughter of Nemesis, you will be able to share your power with me. Will you do that, sister?"

Meggie's answer was swift. *"Anything. I'll do anything. My sisters are here, too, and their guardians. If I give you my power, will you release them all?"*

Aphrodite nodded her head. *"I will return anything that is not my own. I am no thief, sister."*

"Then, yes," Meggie said quickly. *"Tell me what I have to do."*

"This device is very ancient. It works from blood or lust."

"Lust?" Meggie was startled.

"Lust," Aphrodite repeated. *"You won't have to give your life, sister. All you have to do is give yourself to the man you love. That doesn't sound too onerous now, does it?"*

"No..." Meggie looked around. *"But there are so many people... I don't know."*

Aphrodite shrugged. *"Your choice. I will release your sisters, of course, and their guardians, no matter what you choose, but if you aren't willing to perform the Donation, your lover is dead."*

"I'll do it. Heal him. Heal him now."

Aphrodite bowed her head and placed her hands on the arms of the throne, clasping the golden dolphins carved there. A golden glow shivered up the chain from the throne to the pillars. It seemed to run along the floor like water to encircle Brav's still form, rippling around him like water on a shoreline. He opened his eyes.

Meggie was the first thing he saw, manacled to the pillars. He jumped to his feet, looking around.

"Let her go!" he shouted.

Aphrodite just smiled. "Not yet."

Brav hurried to Meggie and took hold of the manacles on her slender wrists. "Wait, Brav," she whispered. "Brav, listen."

His hands wrapped around the manacles as if he would tear them to pieces with his bare bands.

"Brav, listen, she's going to let us go. She's going to let all of us go. But you were badly injured, and she needs more power to heal you."

"I won't see you sacrificed," Brav growled. "I'd sooner die. You know that, Meggie, don't you? You know I'd give my life for you and be glad to do it."

Meggie wished her hands were free, if only so she could reach up and caress his dear face. She let her voice soften, let him hear the love in her heart. "I know that, Brav. But you wouldn't want me to be alone, would you? I need you with me. I sometimes think I've spent my whole life alone. I can't keep on this way. Don't you want to save me from my loneliness, too?"

His voice lowered, for her alone. "Sweetheart, you know I would do anything for you." His hand touched her face, just as she'd longed to touch his face earlier.

"She said it doesn't have to be a sacrifice of blood," Meggie went on. "She said it could be a sacrifice of pleasure. Don't you want to share that with me?"

"Of course I do, darling. So much. But this ceremony, Meggie, once it's begun, it can't be stopped. It isn't like being at the banquets in the evening when you can call a halt when you're feeling overwhelmed. If the Donation isn't carried to completion, those golden chains are going to electrocute you."

Meggie shivered. "What will it take to complete the Donation?" she asked in a small voice.

Brav's face was serious. "Once the Donation has started, you can only be released after we make love. And I won't be able to use a wand on you this time. It will take my body filling yours to get you free. I know you're afraid of that, Meggie. I won't do it to you if you're frightened."

She wanted so *much* to be able to touch his face. Wanted to reach out and feel his skin under her fingertips.

"What I want more than anything is a future with you. I understand that we're going to make love and I'm not afraid. I want you, Brav. I love you." She stared up at his dear, handsome, concerned face. "What does it take for the Donation to start? How do I know if it's already started?"

"If it is a sacrifice of pain, the Donation starts with the first bloodletting. If the sacrifice is one of pleasure, it starts with the first kiss."

She rose up on her toes and planted a small, soft kiss on his lips. His eyes closed as he savoured the sensation. "Meggie, Meggie," he breathed. "This wasn't how I planned for this to be."

She pressed another kiss to his lips. "I love you, Brav."

CHAPTER NINETEEEN

He shivered this time, then glanced around. "There's no curtains this time," he commented. "Are you sure you can do this, Meggie? Really sure?"

She glanced down, suddenly nervous at the thought of the spectacle they were providing and her eyes fell on her golden sash. "It might–" she cleared her throat. "It might be easier if I didn't have to see them. You could use my sash to cover my eyes."

She saw the sudden flare of lust in his eyes. He liked this idea. Another downward glance showed he was definitely reacting to the situation. His hands came up so that he could cup her face. "I'll look after you, baby," he promised.

As his hands drifted down her body, Meggie felt herself reacting to him, too. His touch was so gentle, so soft, as he skimmed his fingers over her breasts and landed on the sash at her waist. "Are you really sure, Meggie?"

"I'm sure, honey." She gave him a tiny, encouraging smile. "Cover my eyes, Brav. Make our own private world where there is nothing but love."

That earned her a kiss, his body moving closer to hers, as his sensual lips shaped hers. She wrapped her hands around the golden chains that restrained her as she strained towards him.

She was so distracted by the kiss that she didn't realise he had undone the sash until she felt her dress release. She glanced down at where his hands were slowly drawing the gold silk sash from around her waist, then back up to his eyes. She wanted his face to be the last thing she saw before she gave herself to him completely.

He was so handsome, she thought, drinking him in. His dark eyes, dark hair and square jaw were the most beautiful thing she'd ever seen. His attention was wholly on her, gauging her reactions, making sure she was comfortable and ready for what he was going to do.

"I love you so much," she whispered.

Then the world faded away as he raised the golden silk to cover her eyes. He tied it gently, but securely, at the back of her head.

It helped. After that, nothing existed for Meggie but Brav and the next touch of his hands.

"I'm here with you now, baby," he reassured her, hands falling to her shoulders and smoothing across the narrow bones. "Just me, baby. Just me and you. Together. Loving each other."

His hands skimmed along her arms where they were raised above her head. When he reached her hands, he paused and let his fingers tangle with hers, letting her feel the tenderness in his touch. He wove his fingers through hers for a moment, then slipped them free, moving down the sensitive inside of her arms now.

Behind the golden silk blindfold, Meggie's eyes closed suddenly tighter at the sensation. Deprived of her sense of sight, Brav's touch seemed even more devastating than before.

He skirted around her breasts, barely touching the outer sides before moving down to her waist. She sensed him moving closer, felt the heat of his body, and then finally felt him press against her as his arms banded around her waist and his head lowered for a kiss.

'Give yourself,' Aphrodite had said. That's what this felt like. It felt like she was becoming his. She didn't feel shy or nervous anymore. All she knew was Brav, his warm body, his gentle hands and his tender lips moving over her own. She found herself chasing his kiss, wanting to feel more of him. She moaned and opened her mouth, inviting the invasion of his tongue.

He heard her unspoken plea and deepened the kiss with a groan.

She was giving herself, but he was giving himself, too. There wasn't any going back after this. Meggie met his tender exploration with a tentative passion and when he opened for her, inviting the invasion of her tongue into his mouth, she followed willingly.

Exploring him was like nothing she'd ever known. He made a soft sound of desire and pressed closer until she could feel his swollen arousal pressing at her belly. His hands slipped lower to cup the small mounds of her buttocks. She'd worried that he wouldn't like her figure, but he didn't even seem to have noticed. He didn't care about the size or softness of the flesh that filled his hands. All he cared about was that it was hers.

Meggie let herself soften further against him, let him grind himself against her as their mouths devoured each other.

They kissed until they were breathless, their hearts beating a frantic tattoo of passionate need. Brav's hands moved restlessly up and down her back and his body pressed close to hers. Meggie pressed herself right back against him, as much as the manacles and golden chains would allow. She loved to hiss him, but it wasn't enough.

"Oh, Brav, more, please, more," Meggie moaned the next time their lips parted to mingle their hot breath against her face. "Oh, Brav, please."

He fell to his knees at once and Meggie felt a shiver run the entire length of her body from her toes to the top of her head. "Oh, yes," she whispered and thrust her chest towards him.

The dress was open all the way down the front. There was nothing stopping him from sliding his hands inside and smoothing over her waist, her sides, her chest. Meggie felt like she was on fire with need of him. When his hands finally cupped her breasts, her thighs quivered with reaction. When she felt his hot mouth open over her nipple, her knees nearly gave way.

She sobbed as he drew deeply on her sensitive nipple, sucking it as far into his mouth as he could, filling his mouth with her flesh. Familiar tingles of pleasure ran from her nipples to the junction of her thighs. Meggie thought back to the last two nights when she'd laid in his arms and he'd brought her to peaks of pleasure she'd never known before.

"So full," he murmured, his lips still so close to her skin that she felt each word form against the puckered, pink flesh.

This time, if anything, the sensations were even more electric and with every pull of his passionate mouth moving from one breast to the other, Meggie felt warmth and wetness growing between her thighs. She moved restlessly against him, wanting more of his hot mouth on her breasts, so desperate for more that she couldn't stay still.

There was nothing to stop his hands from sliding between her thighs, held open for him by the chains that bound her to the pillars.

Not that Meggie would have done anything to stop him. She canted her hips forward to give him easier access.

If she had stopped to think about the people watching, she might have been embarrassed by the noises she was making, but the blindfold created a private space where only she and her lover existed. She couldn't hear them. She couldn't hear anything beyond the sound of her own pounding heart and her own rasping breaths where they mingled with Brav's own elevated breathing.

His fingers drifted through the small nest of dark curs that guarded her sex and Meggie's hands gripped the golden chains tightly.

"Love the feel of you here," he muttered gruffly. "Do you like it when I touch you here, baby?"

"Oh, God, yes, Brav," Meggie moaned. "Touch me, honey, please touch me."

He pressed a kiss to her thigh and the muscle quivered beneath the loving benison. "Tell me what you want, baby. Tell me what you want me to do to you."

He traced her slit gently, lightly and Meggie whimpered. "Open me," she commanded, too deep in need to be shy. "Brav, please, put your fingers inside me. I want you to fill me up."

His fingers traced the outer lips of her pussy softly and she sobbed, ready to beg some more if that was what it took.

"Inside me, please," she begged.

He pressed another kiss to her skin, this one to her opposite thigh as his hand lowered to slide between her shaking thighs. She felt his finger circling her entrance, and a drenching rain of desire washed over her.

She'd had his fingers inside her before, and the little silver wand, but each time she'd known that the experience wasn't going to end with his cock inside her. Now, knowing that soon he was going to join his body to hers, Meggie flowered open for him and his finger slipped inside her easily.

"Fuck," Brav muttered and stroked inside her, adding a second finger and stretching her wide. Meggie threw her head back, her blindfolded gaze on the ceiling she couldn't even see as the man she loved filled her with his thick fingers. He plunged them deep into her warm well, spreading her slickness against her inner walls as he fucked her with deep, powerful strokes.

And then she felt something else. His breath? Warm against her flesh where her pussy lips spread to allow his fingers to fuck into her. She didn't have to question the moment his lips touched her there. His lips, his tongue.

"You taste so fucking amazing, baby," he whispered, his voice a hoarse rasp of desperate need.

Muscles danced inside her, gripping at his fingers as he opened his mouth and circled her clit with his tongue.

Fresh wetness flowed from her body to bathe his hand. She heard her own voice, high and sharp as she moaned and sobbed his name, beyond anything but the feeling of his big fingers fucking her, thrusting deep and slow into her willing body.

The orgasm washed over her with the power of a freight train, powerful and unstoppable. Her channel convulsed around his fingers as her whole universe narrowed to this moment, this man, and the feeling of his fingers inside her and his mouth on her clit.

He slowed his rhythm as she came down from the peak, gentling her as she trembled from head to foot. When she would have collapsed if not for the golden chains holding her up, Brav rose to his feet.

Meggie opened her mouth, searching for him. When his lips met hers this time, she tasted herself on him and shocked herself when she realised that she liked the taste. She slid her tongue into his mouth to chase more of her flavour and Brav fed it to her with passionate intensity.

"Take me," Meggie whispered when his lips burst from hers. "Take me, Brav. I want to feel your cock in me now."

Brav shuddered and his tongue stabbed into her mouth, owning her.

"Next time, I'll undress you," she promised. "Next time, I'll take your cock in my hand and guide it into me, but this time, Brav, you'll have to do it. I want you so much. I want to be yours, Brav. Just yours. Yours forever."

For the first time, she wished that she could see as she heard his shaking hands trying to deal with his clothes. She heard the slight sounds of the fastenings of his trousers opening and the slide of fabric against skin as he pushed his underwear aside.

The manacles and chains around her ankles stopped her closing her legs, but they didn't stop her spreading them wider. Brav groaned at her eager submission.

"So beautiful, baby," he rasped. "So beautiful opening yourself for my cock. Promise you I'll be gentle, baby. Tell me if you want me to slow down or stop."

He moved closer, fitting his body into the space between her thighs.

Meggie was so desperate to feel him inside her she wasn't ready for the sudden shock of fear that shot through her. The only time she'd ever had a man between her thighs, she'd been hurt and humiliated. She stiffened.

Brav drew back. He raised his arms to behind her head and untied the blindfold. Meggie blinked and tried not to cry as his face came into view.

"It's me, baby," he told her solemnly. "It's only me, sweetheart."

Meggie wanted to cry. "I'm so sorry," she whispered. "I'm so afraid."

Brav's face twisted with pain that Meggie knew was for her. He wrapped his arms around her waist beneath her gown and she felt his bare chest pressed to her breasts. *Her* breasts, she realised. The body that had been assaulted when she was so young had been a different body. It had never known pleasure like she'd known with Brav. She pushed herself closer to him, feeling safe and loved in his arms. She inhaled his familiar spicy scent, feeling the faint roughness of his chest hair against her cheek.

"Nothing for you to be sorry about, baby," Brav murmured, holding her close to him, one hand across her hips, the other pressed between her shoulder blades. "We can take as long as you need, sweetheart. "

Meggie drew in a deep breath. "I'm all right now I can see you," she told him, and it was true. She had felt unsafe her whole life until she met him. And then every single moment she'd spent in his company, he'd protected her, cared for her, provided for her. She trusted him with her life—she could trust him with her body.

"Are you sure, baby?" He looked down into her face, searching her expression.

"I'm ready, Brav," she replied, clear and determined. "Make love to me, Brav. Show me what it is to love."

He groaned and buried his face in her shoulder. He kept one hand around her waist as the other reached down to grip his cock. Meggie looked down at his big hand encircling his shaft as he brushed the tip over her pussy, over her slick folds, over her aching, swollen clit. She gasped in renewed need and empty muscles inside her spasmed with wanting him.

The head of his cock felt huge and smooth against the entrance to her pussy. Meggie shifted her legs even further apart to make space for him there. Brav gave a soft groan and pushed forward.

Meggie sobbed and Brav froze. "Sweetheart?"

"Feels so good," she replied. He was inside her. Just the broad, slick head, but still inside her. "More, Brav, more."

His big hands steadied her and he pushed forward further. Even the first thick inch of his shaft made Meggie feel like she'd come home. This was where he belonged. This was what had been messing her whole life: Brav, inside her. This was home. This was home forever, here, with her body becoming one with the man she loved.

"Baby?" Brav asked. "Are you taking it OK?"

All she said was, "More."

And he gave her more. He pushed inside her in slow, gliding thrusts that stretched her body slowly but inexorably to receive him. When he finally reached the heart of her, when she felt his hips come flush with hers, she lifted her face to his to receive a kiss every bit as deep and searching as the press of his shaft inside her. She took his tongue into her mouth, completely open to him.

He stayed there a moment, as deep inside her as he could reach, their mouths joined in a slow, sensual kiss. When their lips parted, Brav leaned his forehead against Meggie's. "Am I hurting you?" he asked in a shaken voice.

"Not hurting," Meggie assured him. "Brav, I love you."

"Oh, baby, I love you, too. So much. Are you ready for me to move inside you now?"

"Oh, yes," she whispered and moaned when she felt the pull of his body withdrawing from hers, his thick shaft creating a delicious friction as he rubbed her inner walls. She wanted to clutch at him, wanted to feel her nails dig into the thick, heavy muscles of his shoulders and neck. She had to content herself with clutching at the chains and straining her body towards his as she chased the return of that intimate connection.

He paused for a moment at the entrance of her body, the head of his cock barely lodged inside her, then surged forward. Meggie moaned loudly, her passionate cry lost in the sound of Brav's fierce grunt. She panted, trying to control her breathing, trying to comprehend the intense pleasure she felt at the fierce pull and push inside her body.

Brav withdrew again, and again surged into her body. Meggie sobbed. No amount of controlled breathing was going to help her with this. Her hands formed into fists around the golden chains. Brav's hands steadied her hips, pulling her so hard against his cock that his pubic bone rubbed against her.

His ragged breathing bathed her face and his desperate gasps for air sounded loud in her ear. Meggie lost all sense of time, lost all sense of anything except the drive of his body into hers. She kept her eyes on his face, taking in the fierce set of his mouth, the sweat that beaded on his brow, dampening the lock of hair that fell over his forehead. His eyes were glittering with erotic intensity as he drowned in her gaze and lost himself in her body.

And yet, despite his need, despite the fierce friction inside her tight folds, he was still controlled, still careful with her.

Meggie wished it could last forever, but the tension in her body was already building to a point. Brav's muscles were tense, and his rhythm was speeding up. "Meggie, Meggie," he chanted. "So tight, Meggie, so sweet around me. I can't last much longer, baby."

"God, yes, Brav," Meggie gasped. "Yes, yes. Come inside me."

The next thrust was stronger, deeper, as if her words nearly drove him to the brink.

"Gods, baby," he muttered. "Fuck. Meggie, I want you to come with me. Can you do that, baby? Can you come all over my cock while I fill you up?" His hand slid from her hip to slide a finger over her clit.

Meggie couldn't answer. The breath locked in her throat as the tension suddenly pulled tight inside her and she shattered. She felt her inner muscles clasping him, milking him. Brav threw back his head and gave a loud shout as the feeling of her coming all around him pushed him over the edge with her.

He drove himself deep into her, pushing hard to the very heart of her and let go. Her eyes flew wide at the feeling of warmth pulsing inside her. His face was contorted into a rictus of pleasure as he shuddered and lost himself completely.

When he was finished, he wrapped his arms around her and buried his face in her hair. The manacles around Meggie's wrists and ankles suddenly glowed bright. Out of the corner of her eye, Meggie saw the light flowing down the chain to the throne where Aphrodite waited. The goddess closed her eyes and shuddered as the light flowed into her.

It was only then that Meggie realised that there was a man kneeling between Aphrodite's knees, his head under her skirt. Meggie wasn't sure if Aphrodite shuddered from power or pleasure.

She took her eyes off the goddess. It didn't matter which. All that mattered was that Brav was going to be OK.

The manacles released. Meggie's arms fell and landed on Brav's shoulders. She wrapped him in a tight embrace and enjoyed the feeling of his heart pounding against hers. His broad chest was heaving and he clutched her close as his body subsided within her.

"Love you," he whispered. "Mine now."

"Oh, Brav," Meggie replied. "Yours forever."

Meggie regretted the moment that their bodies parted. Brav smiled gently at her to ease the feeling of disconnection. He pulled up the stretchy black band of his underwear and closed his trousers.

"Meggie," he whispered. "What happened to your clothes?"

She looked down. Her dress was still open, still gold, but this dress was subtly different from the one she'd worn as Aphrodite. This one was fitted to her own natural body and flowed over her slender shape. Her hair, still strewn across her shoulders, had also changed. The chestnut locks were now frosted with gold at the tips.

Meggie remembered what Leona had said to Cera. "I think it's my goddess-form," she replied. "Oh, Brav. I've been playing a part my whole life. Finally, I can be myself. And this is who I am."

Brav had to bend to the floor to retrieve the golden sash that held her gown closed. Her hands fell on his arm as he tied the belt around her waist. The collar inhibiting her powers came easily away from her neck and was discarded on the floor.

"Are you OK?" he asked, eyes searching her face again.

Meggie smiled and kissed him. There were no words for how OK she was right now. She looked over at Aphrodite and tried not to feel embarrassed about the slave even now getting to his feet and wiping his mouth with the back of his hand. "I did what you asked," Meggie reminded her. "Is Brav going to be OK now?"

Aphrodite pushed the tumbled hair back from her face. "Yes, he'll be fine. I keep my word."

"And we can leave? You promised I could take my sisters and my friends with me if I completed the ceremony." She blushed despite herself when she described what she and Brav had just shared as a 'ceremony.'

Aphrodite waved a dismissive hand. "I promised, sister, and I keep my word. You and your sisters and their guardians can go."

Meggie took Brav's hand. "Honey, we can go home!" she cried.

But Aphrodite spoke again. "I said nothing about *him* leaving, sister."

Meggie froze. "But you promised…"

"I did no such thing. I said that you could take what was yours."

"If he's not mine after what we just shared, then he never will be mine."

"He can't be yours," Aphrodite retorted. "He's *mine*. He's my slave, albeit a runaway, but still mine. I said you could fuck him. I didn't say you could keep him."

"No," Meggie whispered. She turned to Brav. The sudden pallor of his face was only highlighted by the sharp spots of colour still vivid on his cheeks after their loving. "No, Brav, I'm not leaving you."

A thousand thoughts, a thousand emotions flickered across Brav's face, one after another. Suddenly, he stooped to wrap Meggie in a tight embrace again. "Go," he whispered into her ear. "Go, Meggie, and be happy for my sake."

"I can't leave you here," she protested, but he pulled back to stare into her face. Making memories, she realised. Imprinting her face into his memory forever.

"She'll never let me go. Let me know that I can at least purchase your freedom, Meggie. I may only be a slave, but grant me this one last dignity."

Aphrodite's guards were already coming up the stairs. They took hold of Brav's arms and he let Meggie go. He let them take him away.

"No!" Meggie cried, following after them. "No, please, you can't take him."

"He belongs to me, sister," Aphrodite said, her eyes hard. "He belonged to me before you even met him."

There wasn't a damn thing Meggie could do. She watched the guards take Brav. They headed for Aphrodite's ship. She watched as they marched him up the ramp and he turned for one last look at her, and then he was gone.

CHAPTER TWENTY

Dashing the tears from her face, Meggie watched until the door slid closed behind him, then headed for the palace dungeons.

She knew her way by now, and even on rubbery legs with a mind half-broken with grief, it only took her a few minutes to reach them. Thinking that the guards probably wouldn't know everything that had transpired in the temple, she assumed Aphrodite's appearance again.

The giant was standing guard outside the door. "Open the door," Meggie demanded. "They're coming with me."

He didn't comment on her red eyes or flushed face, he just bowed and opened the door for her.

Meggie didn't have the heart to make it an emotional meeting. She kept up her persona as the imperious goddess. "You're coming with me," she said. "All of you. Now."

They scrambled to their feet and followed her. Meggie was sure that each and every one of them noted her red eyes and flushed face. At least they couldn't see the way she was still sticky between her thighs. She led them past the giant, heading for the ship port. She hurried them on board.

Jessan's face was set as he strode past her into the ship. "I knew this would happen," he gritted. "Sister, you shouldn't have."

That was all it took for Meggie to lose it. She strapped herself into a seat, but tears were streaming down her face and she buried her face in her hands as she sobbed.

Jessan sat in the pilot's chair, his hand gripping the control stick so tightly his knuckles were white. Bess tried to go to Meggie to comfort her, but Jessan spoke up. "Tarn, get the ladies in their seats *now*. We're leaving."

"Yes, sir." Tarn guided Bess back into a seat, gently but firmly.

Meggie tried to control herself, but even when the sobs stopped, the tears still flowed.

"Where's Brav?" Jessan asked, keeping his eyes on the controls and off Meggie where she sat beside him.

Meggie drew in several ragged breaths before she could say, "He's not coming."

Jessan exploded. "The fuck he isn't!" He surged out of his seat. "I'm going to find that son of a bitch and I'm going to fucking kill him. And take his godsdamned *body* home. Where is he, sister–?" he stopped suddenly and sat back down as though his knees had given way. "By the gods, girl… is he alive?"

Meggie wiped the tears away and tried to pretend that fresh tears didn't take their place. "He's alive. Aph—Aphrodite has him. She's going to keep him as a slave. He told me to go on without him."

There was no way she could keep the sobs inside after saying those words. She buried her face in her hands again.

"That's where he was five years ago," Tarn mused. "I'd bet my life on it. And now Aphrodite is taking back her own, is that right, Meggie?"

Meggie nodded, glad Tarn had asked her the question in such a way that she only had to nod her head. She couldn't speak anymore. She felt like the bottom had dropped out of the world.

"I'm not leaving him here," Jessan gritted. "I won't do it. I won't."

In the row of seats that lined the back wall, Cera unbuckled her harness. She stepped forward and laid her hand on Jessan's shoulder. His hand came up to cover hers almost absently, as if she'd been putting her hand on his shoulder all their lives instead of this being the very first time. "Take off, Jessan. I know what we can do. And the first step is getting away from here."

Jessan didn't even glance back at her, he just nodded and adjusted the controls. Cera returned to her seat and buckled her harness again.

A moment later, the ship began to rise. It shook violently during lift off and Meggie was glad of the harness that kept her in her seat. Jessan jerked at the controls until they were in orbit, then he turned back to Cera.

"What's your plan?"

And as Meggie listened, her tears dried and hope bloomed in her heart again.

*   *   *

An hour later, Meggie and Cera were ready, and Jessan was shaking with frustration.

"I should go with you," he gritted.

"Well, you can't, so stop griping about it," Cera suggested airily, in a way that had Jessan grinding his teeth together. "Meggie's even bigger than you, now. She can punch her way through whatever needs punching." Cera looked down at her own body, now that of one of Gorgos's guards. "I'm no slouch myself."

Meggie shifted uncomfortably. She had changed her shape to that of the giant she had encountered several times while on Jiliar. She was confident that she had his appearance right, but holding the disguise wasn't as easy as it had been before she'd given up part of her powers to Aphrodite.

It had taken her last bit of energy to transform Cera. When she'd come to changing Jessan's appearance, she'd watched his familiar face flicker, then settle back into his own features.

He'd looked down at his hands. "Do I look any different?" he'd asked, frowning.

Cera scowled. "You look just as ugly to me now as you ever have. What gives, Meggie?"

Meggie insisted that she was trying, but to no avail. She couldn't do any more. Her powers would need time to recover from what she had donated to Aphrodite during the ceremony. So now it was just Cera accompanying her to the planet and Jessan had to stay behind or risk recognition.

"I don't like it," Jessan growled. "I should be there with you. There's more to defending yourself than sheer size."

"I don't care if you don't like it," Cera retorted. Despite her sharp tone, the hand she placed on his arm was gentle. She moderated her voice and murmured, "We'll be OK."

He wasn't happy about it, but he didn't say any more.

Cera looked back at Meggie. "Ready?"

Meggie nodded. She caught Teresa's eye, noting that her sister was seated beside Kairn, holding his hand. Mac was on her other side looking rough and wild, kneeling adoringly at Teresa's feet.

"I'll see you soon," Teresa assured her, but Meggie saw her grip Kairn's hand a little tighter.

She'd never teleported anywhere before. She'd never expected to. It felt… odd. Like taking in a too-deep breath and feeling parts of herself expand that had never stretched before.

She wanted desperately to ask if Cera had always known she could do this, but she was already in her giant form and she didn't want to call attention to their deception. The conversation could wait until later.

Everything looked different from the giant's perspective. Even Cera, in a form nearly as big as Jessan's, looked small beside her. They'd had to appear somewhere Cera had seen, so they were in the corridors outside the dungeon where Cera and the others had been held.

Another guard approached. He glanced at them and nodded, but Meggie caught his arm. "Hey," she said, "we're supposed to take Aphrodite's new slave back to her ship. Where is he held again?"

The guard lifted his wrist and checked the *custodia* strapped there. "47A."

"Thanks," Meggie rumbled. They went on their way.

She breathed a sigh of relief. They had gotten away with it!

Then the guard called back at them. "By the way, Geraint?"

Meggie froze. She didn't even know the giant's name. Should she respond? Pretend she didn't hear? Was it a test? Had she given herself away?

"We're late," Cera snapped. "Be quick about it!"

The man kept speaking anyway. "I just wanted to thank you for helping with the loading yesterday. Much appreciated."

"No worries," Meggie replied, without turning, then walked on. No worries? Did a giant from another planet express himself that way? She had no idea. She walked a little faster.

The numbers of the cells were on the doors. Brav's cell should be just around the corner. Meggie swaggered around it—

And came face to face with herself.

More or less, anyway.

It was the giant. The real one.

Cera threw a punch, but he caught it easily. "Easy, my lady," he said.

Cera's eyes flared bright gold, but the giant just held her hand and waited. Cera strained.

"What's going on?" Meggie demanded, looking from one to the other. Cera was working hard, but nothing seemed to be happening. Eventually Cera slumped, her fist still held in his hand as she breathed hard, trying to recover.

"My powers don't work on him," she admitted, her voice low.

"None of your powers do, unless we consent," the giant confirmed. "I am a Nephilim. The gods cannot trick us or control us—never again."

Meggie's eyes, matching the giant's own eyes, went wide. "Do you mean to say that you saw who I was from the beginning? And didn't tell anyone?"

His head went back with sudden pride. "Are you surprised that a slave has honour?"

In her haste to assure him, Meggie started to babble, "No, of course not," but she was cut off.

Another man had come around the corner in front of her. "Hey!" he shouted. "No fighting! I'll have all three of you on report!"

The giant let go of Cera's hand quickly. He bowed. Meggie and Cera followed suit. "Forgive us, Hamertan. It won't happen again."

"Like hell it won't," Hamertan muttered. "I know what you lot are like, always brawling..." his voice trailed off. His eyes trailed from the giant to Meggie, noting just now that they were identical. "How are there two of you?" he asked slowly.

The giant frowned and for a moment Meggie's heart thudded faster with fear in case he revealed them. But then he laughed incredulously and said, "Are you seriously telling me that you didn't know Geraint and I were twins this whole time?"

"Twins?" Hamertan repeated, still looking from one to the other.

Cera failed to conceal a smirk. "Did you think Geraint just worked *extra* hard?" The snigger she let out was not even partially concealed.

"You're on report!" Hamertan shouted. "All three of you! I want you in my office by the evening bells and I'll give all three of you the lash."

Cera was clearly ready to argue but Geraint held up a hand. "We will abide by your decision, Hamertan. We will be in your office by the evening bells."

"Humph!" Hamertan regarded the three of them suspiciously. "If you're not, I'll have the lot of you executed. So, you'd damn well better show up. Cowards."

"Yes, sir," Geraint said evenly.

Hamertan strutted away down the corridor.

"You can't," Meggie whispered, even once Hamertan was out of sight. "You can't take the lash for us."

"He won't," Cera put in. "He'll come with us—once we've rescued Brav, he can come back with us. Is that what you want? Will you help us rescue our brother?"

Brother, Meggie noticed. Jessan called Brav his brother. Had Cera gotten the term from him?

Geraint nodded. "I would have helped you even if you hadn't offered me my freedom."

He turned and raised the *custodia* on his wrist to the panel beside the door. Inside the dark cell, Brav leaped to his feet. Meggie hurried past Geraint, crying, "Brav! We've come to—oof!"

Brav's fist landed in her belly and she bent double with the sudden shocking pain, just in time for another blow to catch her on the jaw and rock her head back. Her knees crumpled. Geraint caught her before she could hit the floor and shoved her back towards Cera.

He subdued Brav, wrapping his massive arms around the Guardian warrior as Brav fought and snarled.

"Now, goddess!" Geraint shouted. "I can't hold him much longer!"

There was another unsettling moment, and then they were back on the ship. Meggie fell to her knees, overcome by the pain from Brav's powerful blows. Cera dropped beside her, still in her male form, her large hand falling between Meggie's powerful shoulders and stroking in a soothing gesture. Teresa and Bess came to kneel at Meggie's other side.

"What happened?" Teresa cried.

"Brav hit her," Cera told her shortly.

Teresa sucked in a harsh breath and let it out in a filthy curse. Meggie, still winded and aching from Brav's heavy blows put her hand on Teresa's to calm her. Her giant hand dwarfed her sister's.

Brav was still shouting and struggling against Geraint's restraining hands.

Jessan strode up to Brav and shouted, "You're home, man! You're home! You can stop fighting!" He caught Brav's face between his hands and forced Brav to look at him and recognise him.

Brav went still. In his rage, he hadn't even recognised his friends or the familiar ship. "Jessan?" he asked quietly, his voice rough from shouting. "Is this real? Or have I lost my mind?"

"It's real," Jessan assured him. "You're home now, Brav. You're home."

Brav looked around as Geraint let him go. Meggie felt the ship accelerate and didn't even know who was in the pilot's seat. Her head felt like it had already exploded. She heard Brav ask for her. "Where is Meggie?"

From her position on the floor, Meggie raised her hand. "Here," she said, and whimpered because speaking *hurt*.

"You're not Meggie–" Brav began, then stopped. "Oh, no. Oh, no."

Her eyes were closed and she hadn't even realised. She let the glamour drop and she and Cera were returned to their own forms. She felt Brav's hands gentle on her arms as he turned her to him.

He swore when he saw the mark he'd put on her face. His hands shook as he touched her and Meggie felt the healing warmth pass between them.

"Gods, Meggie, I'm so sorry," Brav whispered. "I swear by all the gods, by my own mother, I didn't know it was you."

The pain drained away as the healing power from his hands suffused her with warmth. Meggie opened her eyes. Brav's face looked tortured above her own. "Where else did I hurt you, baby?"

She took his hand and placed it on her belly and the golden glow returned as he started to heal her there. "Gods, Meggie, I'll never forgive myself for this. Not for this… not for any of it. Meggie, Meggie, I'm so sorry."

"It's OK," she assured him. "I know you didn't know it was me. But, Brav, we're safe. We're going home. We're all going home."

It was only as she said it that she realised it was true. She stared at Brav, then at Teresa, Cera and Bess so close beside her. All of them together, as they'd only been for a few short hours in the fourteen years since Meggie's mother died.

She'd made it. She'd done it. It all flashed through her mind. Being beaten by the Malia warrior back in Leona's house. How terrifying it had been at the slave auction. Facing Gorgos. Impersonating Aphrodite night after night. When Gorgos had tied her to the pillars and threatened to do the most awful things to her.

When Brav had lain so still at her feet and she was sure she'd lost him forever.

She wanted to say something, but it was all too much. She opened her mouth, but only to gasp in a ragged jerking breath of air before she started to cry. She reached for Brav.

He drew away.

Teresa put herself into Meggie's arms and crooned soothing words. Her sister was small and plump and she gave beautiful cuddles. Meggie felt enfolded by the person she'd loved the most in her life, even as she felt the sharp ache of Brav's withdrawal.

She wanted to talk to him, to ask why he would pull away from her now, just when everything she'd ever dreamed of was in her reach, but she couldn't stop crying.

She felt another presence in her mind, as she had when she'd spoken telepathically with Aphrodite. This time, she recognised Cera as she delicately probed Meggie's mind. She saw what happened on Jiliar, and somehow, with a light, deft touch, she took the pain away. Meggie felt the moment that Cera saw Baelor in her memories.

Cera stood up sharply. "Take me back," she ordered.

Jessan had been leaning over Tarn's shoulder where the other man sat in the pilot's seat. He turned to stare incredulously at Cera. "No," he said.

Cera stalked towards him. "I said, take me back!" She pointed to the ship's controls. Meggie felt the change in the engines as they responded and Cera wasn't even touching the controls.

"What are you doing?" Jessan demanded. "We're not going back there!" He grabbed her hand and pulled it away from the controls. A moment later, the ship turned back towards its previous course.

"Baelor is there," Cera retorted. Her face was white with anger, two vivid patches of pink on her cheeks. "I swore I would kill that man, and I will." She reefed her hand out of Jessan's grasp and pointed to the controls again.

Jessan pulled her bodily away from the controls. "You can't do that!" he cried. "You'll get us all killed, Cera! Stop and think about what you're doing!"

She fought him. He flipped her around so her back was to him and wrapped his arms around her body, pinning hers to her sides. "Leave it," he ordered. "Baelor is the Steward of Rhodes. Going after him isn't worth it. How do you even know him?"

"He was the leader of the Malias who took us from home," Cera retorted hotly, bursting free from Jessan's arms. "You don't know what he did to me."

Her heated words fell into a silence and all of a sudden, everyone had a good idea of what Baelor had done to her.

Jessan reached out a trembling hand towards her. "Cera, baby—"

"Don't you fucking touch me!" Cera pulled away and ran down the hall.

Meggie and her sisters followed her.

Cera found the guest cabin as if she already knew where to go, although she'd never been on Tarn's ship before. When Meggie, Teresa and Bess reached her, she had her arms wrapped around her waist and she was breathing hard.

Bess put her hand on Cera's arm. "Cera, why didn't you say anything?" she asked. "We didn't know—"

"You knew. But I didn't want you to know. So, I altered your memories." Her fingers were white where they gripped her waist. "It's one of the few things I can still do while I'm wearing the collar. I don't think they realised I could get through it at all."

Bess tried to put her arm around Cera's shaking shoulders, but Cera pulled away, backing up until she hit the wall and slid down it. Her arms wrapped around her knees.

"Was that why the slavers tried to sell you as virgins?" Meggie asked. "Because you altered their memories?"

Cera swiped away a tear that had escaped her iron control and nodded. "I put the thought in their heads. I thought it might keep their hands off us.."

Meggie sat down beside Cera. She didn't try to put her arm around her. "I'm sorry I didn't get to you sooner."

Teresa sat beside Meggie and Bess sat on Cera's other side. "You saved us," Teresa said softly, putting her head on Meggie's shoulder.

"You both saved us," Bess said, not daring to try to touch Cera again.

Cera buried her face in her knees.

The door slid open to reveal Jessan. His face was etched with agony. He went to Cera and pulled her arms away from her knees, reaching them around his neck.

"No!" Cera cried, but he put his arms around her anyway, leaning over her knees so he was embracing her whole body. Cera fought for a moment, then her hands clung and she began to sob.

CHAPTER TWENTY-ONE

It took two days to return to Earth. They had to use the large replicator in the cargo bay to make some more beds. Cera, Bess and Teresa slept in the single cabin with Meggie, while the giant Geraint joined the Guardians in the dormitory.

When they arrived back in Earth's orbit, the familiar blue and green planet spinning below them, Brav didn't head to the Earth to land. Instead, he flew Gerea's shittiest ship around to the dark side of the moon.

There was a spaceship there, glimmering with lights. None of the Guardians seemed surprised or discomfited, so Meggie wasn't concerned. "What's that?" she asked. "Has it always been there?"

"That's Solace Station," Tarn answered. Brav hardly spoke to her these days and he made it quite clear that all his attention was occupied with piloting the ship. "That's our headquarters." He threw a quick glance at Brav. "We'll take you in there before we take you back to Earth, just so you can get checked out."

"No one's checking *me* out," Cera said flatly.

"Yes, they are, baby," Jessan retorted, not taking his eyes off the screen. Meggie had a good view of his profile and noticed that his face was white.

"They are not. I won't allow it."

"Yes, they are, Cera." His face was taut. "You need to know if you're pregnant. I don't want you finding out when you're alone."

Cera swayed, as if his words had hit her like a blow. Bess guided her into one of the seats at the back of the room. Jessan clenched his teeth so hard a nerve ticked in his jaw.

Pregnant. It was all Meggie could do to keep from laying a hand on her own belly. The possibility of pregnancy hadn't occurred to her until now. Glancing over at Brav's shuttered face, she was glad that she'd shared everything with him, despite his withdrawal afterwards. She almost wished that there was a small part of him she could carry away from her time with him.

One thing was for certain. Their time together was over.

He hadn't touched her again. Hadn't said any sweet words, not even when they were alone on the several occasions that Meggie had orchestrated it. He hadn't tried to get her alone. She recalled, bitterly, that every time he'd ever touched her, it had been to do with the mission.

And his words of love?

What did words matter, when he was on the other side of the room?

He'd had a long talk with his brothers when they'd reached a safe distance from Jiliar. Meggie knew that they'd all gone down to the dormitory, and they'd come back looking emotionally wrought. Brav's eyes had been red. He hadn't even tried to talk to her once.

In Solace Station, the staff at the hospital were kind, if impersonal. Meggie had no wounds to tend to. The others were similarly not wounded, but the trauma of what they'd suffered would stay with them. The medical staff offered counselling. Teresa and Bess took it. Meggie knew it would be a long time before she could talk about what she'd done.

After her examination, Cera went straight to the room she'd been allocated and locked the door. Meggie saw her striding past and turned to Bess who was just coming into her cubicle.

"Is she–?"

Bess nodded.

Meggie slipped off the bed.

"Where are you going?" Bess asked, following Meggie as she left the room.

"I'm going to sit with her."

Bess followed and Teresa soon joined them.

Meggie activated the chime at Cera's door.

The words, faint, but distinguishable, came from behind the door. "Fuck off!"

Meggie slid the door open anyway. "We're your sisters," she said firmly. "We're not going to leave you alone right now." She let her voice gentle. "We're here for you, Cera."

Cera stared at her, then started to cry. She even let them hold her.

Late in the afternoon, the door chimed. Meggie, hoping it was Brav, tried not to show her disappointment when Jessan and Tarn were revealed. Tarn bowed. Jessan's face was pale, his eyes shuttered. "The Station Council would like to speak with you ladies, if you are well enough."

Meggie glanced back into the room. Cera was already rising to her feet, the others following her.

"We're fine," Cera announced, her eyes still red.

Jessan made an incoherent sound. He'd guessed. One glance at her face, and he knew. "Cera," he whispered. He reached out for her, like he couldn't help himself.

Cera swept past him. "I guess you don't get your dream after all," she said cryptically.

"You're my dream," he murmured.

Meggie saw Cera's jaw clench. "Not anymore. Now, let's get *moving*. I am really ready for today to be *over.*"

Meggie had been a little anxious about appearing before the Council. She'd thought they'd be seated on a high ledge above them, looking down on the human women, but they were brought to a comfortable room instead.

It's like the Oval Office, she thought. All the Council members were seated on lounges and armchairs, and a boy was going around the room, handing them cups of Krith.

When the Council members saw the women arrive, they rose to their feet. Every one of them was immensely tall and muscular and if it wasn't for the time Meggie had spent on Tarn's ship with the Guardians, she would have felt even more intimidated.

They bowed. Teresa caught Meggie's eye and Meggie had to struggle not to laugh at the appreciation in her younger sister's expression.

"Please, ladies, be seated. May we offer you a cup of Krith?"

"Thank you," Meggie said, taking the cup that the boy was already offering her. She sat on the sofa. Teresa sat beside her. Cera and Bess sat on a sofa nearby. Cera refused the Krith. Meggie wondered if pregnant women were supposed to drink it, so she just held it in her hand, just in case. Tarn and Jessan took up positions by the door, as if they were guarding the room.

"My name is Draex. I am the Station Marshal. I'm pleased to be able to tell you that your mother, Artemis, has reached her destination safely. She is at Desiderus Nonus, a station far from here, and will soon be reunited with her mate Reganus. Thanks to her, we finally have a chance against Everius."

Draex was the tallest of the lot. His hair was pure silver, flowing over his shoulders, although he didn't look all that old. He sat in a chair facing them, so that they didn't have to crane their necks to look up at him. He even leaned forward, lowering himself further. Meggie was impressed by the small consideration. She'd had plenty of bosses who didn't bother to show any consideration and loved to stand over their employees. This was a nice change.

"Can you tell me about the barrier that Artemis placed around the Earth?" Draex asked.

Cera replied, her voice low. "She maintained it with her mind. With her power. She asked me to maintain it while she was gone. And I failed." Her voice dropped to the faintest whisper.

"No." Jessan took a step away from the door, moving towards Cera, but a glance from Draex stopped him.

"No," Draex repeated. "I don't mean to contradict you, but that isn't right. The Malias were already in Earth's atmosphere when Artemis left. What happened is the fault of Everius. Not you."

Cera's face twisted as she struggled to hold back tears. She gripped her hands together so tightly her knuckles were white.

"Council members, would you excuse us, please?" Draex asked, but it was clearly an order. The council members each bowed to the women, then left the room until only Tarn, Jessan and himself remained. "None of this is your fault," he said softly.

Cera trembled from head to foot. Jessan left his place by the door and knelt beside her. She wrapped her arms tight around his neck and shook with sobs she could no longer contain.

Draex allowed time for the storm to pass. It had never occurred to Meggie that Cera would hold herself responsible for their abduction. He was very perceptive, this man. Kind, too.

"The reason the Malias made their way to Earth was because Everius's power has grown. There is no defence that can be maintained by one person against the power Everius wields today. That is why we have brought Solace Station to remain in synchronous orbit behind the moon. The Guardians of the House of Valor will protect the Earth now."

"Do they know you're here?" Teresa asked.

Draex shook his head. "No. Not yet, but it must be soon. We must be careful when we liaise with the government of your planet. The arrival of foreign warriors in your orbit could easily be perceived as a threat. It is imperative that your planet knows that we are here to protect you."

"I may be able to help," Bess said. "I work in foreign affairs and I've liaised with members of several governments. I'll reach out to some of my contacts and set up a meeting."

Draex nodded. "Thank you." He put his cup on the small table beside him, the gesture clearly indicating that the meeting was over. "Tarn and Jessan will see you back to your rooms. You are welcome to stay on Solace Station as long as you like. After everything your people have done for us, we are forever in your debt."

"What did he mean, forever in our debt?" Teresa asked when they'd left the room and were heading back to their own quarters.

Tarn answered. "The Guardians have a long history with the Alterrans, from your mother's first youth. Aside from anything else, the Alterrans have always been matched to the Guardians as brides." Tarn's eyes caught Bess's momentarily. "A Guardian would do anything for the woman he loves."

"Does Draex have a wife?" Teresa asked.

Tarn shook his head. "No, Draex is committed to his duties as a leader." Another glance at Bess, as though he couldn't help himself. "A leader cannot always choose to follow his heart."

That night, unwilling to leave Cera alone, they all spent the night in her suite, despite the fact that they each had one of their own. Bess shared the bed with Cera, while Teresa and Meggie slept on the couch and a quickly replicated cot in the living room.

The suite was bigger than any hotel suite Meggie had ever seen. It was as big as a comfortable apartment, and even had windows and a balcony overlooking a huge park with a lake sparkling blue under an artificial sky.

The next day, Meggie went for a late breakfast in the Refectory. While each room had its own replicator, many of the Guardians still chose to eat communally, and the long tables in the huge room were packed during mealtimes. There were several Refectories across the ship, each as large and as busy as the main Refectory.

Meggie slept in. She'd expected to toss and turn all night, given that she was sleeping in *yet another* different bed, but she'd put her head on her freshly replicated pillow and gone straight to sleep.

When she'd woken, the others had already gotten up, leaving her a note to say that they would be exploring the gardens if she wanted to join them after breakfast.

After lunch was more like it. The Refectory was nearly empty at this time of day, just an hour or so before noon. There were a few small groups of Guardians, talking quietly as they ate, or reviewing documents. She was just collecting her tray from the servery when she turned around and saw Brav, catching him in the act of spinning on his heel and taking that first step away from her.

"Brav," she called, and from the guilty way he froze instantly, she realised that he was trying to avoid her. Fury bubbled up in her. She slammed her tray back on the pile.

"How dare you!" she cried. She hurried forward, so that she was standing in front of him and could see his miserable expression. "After—after *everything*, how *could* you just walk away from me like that?"

He closed his eyes. Like her, he had dark circles under them and his jaw was rough with dark stubble. "Meggie–"

She crossed her arms over her chest, but he didn't continue. "Well?" she prompted.

Brav shook his head. "I'm sorry, Meggie. That's all I can say."

"Sorry for what?" she asked. "Sorry that you said you loved me? Sorry that you made me love you? Sorry that you fu–"

She couldn't go on. Couldn't make herself turn everything they'd shared into something ugly. She wished she still had the tray in her hands because she wanted to hit him with it.

Brav's face was shuttered. For a long moment, he said nothing, then he took her arm. "You're coming with me," he stated.

"I damn well am not!"

He didn't even argue with her, just hustled her from the Refectory.

CHAPTER TWENTY-ONE

His room wasn't far away. Most of the ship was quickly accessible because instead of elevators, they had transporters. You stepped into them and named your destination, then found yourself there, in a flash of blue light. They even had little maps on the walls of the transport docks, like you'd find in a subway station.

A few minutes later, Brav was sliding open his door and pushing her inside. She'd expected that the room would be furnished in minimalist stainless steel, but she'd forgotten that most ancient cultures weren't really into minimalism.

There was a fireplace as the centrepiece of a living area, burning clean and bright and warm, but without smoke or soot. In front of it was a long sofa and a fur rug was stretched before it on the floor. The dining table was heavy and polished to a high shine, the chairs were strong—they probably had to be, to bear the weight of a heavily muscled Guardian—and the supports were beautifully carved. She couldn't see a bed, so she assumed that sleeping quarters and a bathroom were behind the other closed door.

Her heart thumped hard when he set the entry door to privacy mode behind him. His face was like a thundercloud.

"I won't let you cheapen what happened between us by shouting it out in the Refectory," he snarled.

"Cheapen?" she asked. "What is there to cheapen when it apparently meant nothing to you? It might have just been sex rather than making love, but I gave myself to you, Brav, and you don't seem to realise that." She bit her lip. "That hurts, you know?"

A nerve ticked in his jaw. "We made love," he replied shortly.

Meggie flushed. "Sex," she corrected.

He took a cautious step towards her. "We made love, Meggie. It wasn't just sex between us. We made love."

Tears threatened. "You shouldn't say things like that."

"Why not?" She felt, more than heard, the next cautious step he took towards her.

"Because it hurts me."

He stopped. "That's what I'm sorry for," he said abruptly, the harsh tone back in his voice. "I'm so sorry I hurt you, Meggie. I'm sorry that you were forced to… to do all those things with me. First in the bathhouse, then later, on Jiliar. And that last day—if I hadn't been sleeping, if I'd been there with you, you never would have agreed to perform the Donation of the Goddess. And when I hit you—gods, you'll never know how sorry I am.

"I've done everything I can to make things right. It's not enough. Gods know, it will never be enough." He stopped, closing his eyes tightly, his jaw flexing as he clenched his teeth. "Meggie, there's something I need to tell you."

"I'm listening." She sat down on the couch. Anything to indicate to him she was open to what he had to say.

"If you go back to Earth—*when* you go back to Earth, I mean— I know you won't want to stay on Solace Station because I'll be here… you don't need to worry."

"Worry about what?"

"About Colin Walt."

Meggie was glad she was sitting down. She blinked. "What about him?"

Brav swallowed hard and crouched down before her. "That's why I'm coming to breakfast so late, not because I was trying to avoid you. I was up all night last night searching your planetary databases. This morning, I spoke with the peacekeepers and took them down to Earth. They took Colin Walt into custody. He will stand trial for what he did to you. And he will be punished appropriately." Brav crouched at her feet and looked up at her. "I seriously considered killing him for what he did to you, baby, but I wasn't sure how you'd react to that. What happens to him now is up to you. You are the only one who has the right to decide his fate."

Meggie was reeling. Colin was in custody? And Brav had made that happen for her. He'd remembered Colin's name, and the moment they'd come back to Earth, he'd hunted Colin down. He'd made sure that she would be safe.

Brav looked down at his clasped hands held between his knees. "Meggie, I'll understand if you want to press charges against me, too. You have every right."

"What?" Surprise made her voice sharp. "What are you talking about?"

Brav looked up at her, meeting her gaze fearlessly. "You couldn't consent to what I did to you during the Donation, Meggie. There's a filthy name they use for men who do what I did. I should be locked up, and worse, for what I did to you." He rose to his feet and took a few steps away from her, like the restless energy within him couldn't be contained.

"I consented, Brav," Meggie told him softly, seriously, rising to her feet. "I wanted you. I love you."

A shudder rocked through him and he turned away from her to lean one muscular arm against the mantelpiece. "Gods, Meggie, I don't deserve that. I know that I don't deserve to even be in the same room as you. And even after hurting you so badly, after such unforgiveable acts, I still wanted you. You don't know how much I—" He ran his hand through his hair, gripping it like he needed something to hold on to.

Meggie took the next tiny step to breach the gaping chasm that had somehow developed between them. "Tell me, Brav."

He turned to look at her, and she had the sudden sense that he was completely open to her, as though his soul was laid bare for her. "You don't know how much I wished that you were doing all those things because you wanted me. Not because we had to, but because you wanted to. That's why I tried to… to give you space. I want you so much, Meggie, but I want you to be happy more than anything. And if that means giving you space, I can do that." His voice dropped to a heartfelt whisper. "I can do anything for you."

Meggie's shoulders dropped as all her tension dissipated at once. She stared at him, this hard, prickly, *vulnerable* man that she'd fallen in love with.

He'd been hurt before. He'd been taken from his parents, and while the Guardians had clearly done everything they could to fill that gap, it was still a hole inside him. Then, when he'd been captured by Aphrodite, he'd lost that support system, and she'd made him feel ashamed. It had shaken him off balance and he was still learning to find his feet again. Being captured again had been a ferocious blow to his pride. He didn't believe he was worthy of her love. He didn't believe he was worthy of anyone's love.

He wasn't reserved. He'd been open with his words of love, open to showing her how much he desired her, but there had always been doubts in his mind. He needed her so badly, but he was terrified that he would lose her.

So, instead, he was pushing her away.

She didn't just take one step this time. She took half a dozen until she was right in front of him. Then one more step, until her body was pressed against his and her arms were around his neck.

"I love you," she whispered. "I've said it before, and I meant it, Brav. I will always love you." She rose up onto her toes and pressed her face into his shoulder.

His arms came around her, still cautious, stroking her waist with fingers that trembled.

"Oh, Meggie, really?" His eyes searched hers. "Are you sure, sweetheart? I will never deserve you—"

"Marry me, Brav," she whispered, knowing that it would take him *forever* before he dared say the words to her. "Marry me, mate with me, or whatever your people call it."

A rumble of laughter went through him that she felt all the way to her toes. There were other interesting things going on his body, triggering reactions in her, too. "We call it marriage, sweetheart, when we drink the wedding wine. Mating… mating is part of it, but it's not the part that you do in front of your friends."

Meggie bit her lip, shy, but really not shy as she watched the happiness spread across his face. "I don't see why not," she said. "We've done it in front of everyone else."

He threw back his head and laughed and it shocked her to realise that he sounded carefree. She'd never heard him so joyous. He lowered his head and took her lips in a breathless kiss.

"Oh, Meggie, Meggie, Meggie," he whispered when he broke the kiss, his breath feathering past her cheek. "I want to be yours forever. I want you to be mine. I want to spend my life with you. I want to have children with you." He pulled away so he could see her face. "Do you want children?"

She'd spent her life raising Teresa. It had been hard, but she'd loved her sister so much that it had been worth any sacrifice. There was a lot of love in her heart that she wanted to share with the family they would grow between them.

She caressed his lean cheek, rough and unshaven that morning.

He hadn't even stopped to shave. "I want children," she replied. She moved against the pressure growing against belly. "How soon do you want children? Because I want a whole bunch of them."

He kissed her again, a hard, possessive kiss. "I think it might take us nine months to get started, how does that sound?"

She melted against him. "Brav, take me to bed."

He bent to pick her up, but as he did, her stomach rumbled. "Meggie, haven't you had breakfast yet?"

She gripped his shoulders. "Breakfast later," she insisted, but he shook his head, trembling a little when her nails dug in tight.

"I'm going to look after you, sweetheart. Look after you, and our family. That starts now. Breakfast."

He placed her in a chair at the small dining table. "I'll have to petition for a double suite," he commented, shocked joy still lighting his face.

"Right now, all I need is you," Meggie assured him. Her stomach rumbled again. "And maybe some breakfast."

Brav went to the replicator. "Eggs and toast all right?" he asked and Meggie nodded. "Two serves of Heian toast, with Elsan eggs. Krith for two, one extra strong, one weak. And, uh, some Orath fruit balls."

He returned with a tray laden with eggs and toast, a drink that smelled a little like rich, spicy coffee and a plate of small, pale yellow balls that looked like melon balls. "Looks delicious," she said. She reached for the fruit but Brav drew the plate away.

"They're for after the meal," he said, and the look in his eyes made her wonder why. In the meantime, her stomach rumbled again, so she tucked into the food. She paused as she looked at the Krith.

"Can pregnant women drink Krith, Brav?" she asked and watched incredulous joy bloom in his eyes. He pressed his lips together tightly and she caught the sheen of tears barely contained.

"I didn't even think of that," Brav confessed. "All I thought about was loving you." He cleared his throat. "Yes, pregnant women can drink Krith."

Even though the Krith was weak, it was stronger than she'd expected, and it warmed her all the way to her toes. She was careful to sip it after her first try, though.

"Now can I try the fruit?" Meggie asked after she'd cleaned her plate and finished her Krith. "I've finished my meal like a good girl."

The way Brav's eyes swept down her body made every nerve

ending sing back into awareness. "You are a good girl," he drawled, watching her breathing start to come faster. He shifted his chair so that he was sitting beside her.

"What are you doing?"

"You'll see." He brought the plate of fruit close to their side of the table. His voice dropped. "Open for me, Meggie."

Obediently, she opened her mouth and he fed her the first melon ball. It was cool and fresh, the fruit crisp between her teeth, flooding her mouth with sweetness. Flooding *everything* with sweetness. She felt a light shock of sensation travelling through her entire body. She couldn't speak for a moment.

Hands still curved on the table where she'd briefly clenched them into fists, Meggie turned to Brav. "What was that?" she asked. "Is… Orath fruit a sensation food?"

Brav nodded. "Sure is. In fact, it's probably the one my brothers thought I would have fed you the first time."

Remembering the naughty looks the Guardians had passed across the table, Meggie's toes curled. "I see."

"Feed me one." He opened his mouth and took the fruit inside. He closed his eyes and shuddered as the sensation passed through him. "Your turn again."

This time, the sweet sensation that raced through her was stronger. She felt it in every part of her body, but as the sweetness faded from her tastebuds, it concentrated lower down. Deep in her belly. Below her belly. Her heart started to beat faster as she wondered how far this was going to go.

She fed him another fruit and revelled in his groan.

The next fruit he gave her only intensified the sensation. Her whole body felt alive. Her eyes closed for a moment as she relished the sensation, then they flew open.

"Fuck, Brav!"

That sensation was definitely new. She'd felt like she'd had a tiny orgasm, miniscule muscles inside her contracting sharply and leaving her body feeling tingly all over.

Brav chuckled and his finger teased her lower lip into a sensual pout as she panted.

"I didn't know sensation foods could do *that!*"

"There are many sensation foods for lovers. I can't wait to show you all of them. Now, another."

"Wait." Meggie swung out of her chair and into his lap, sitting facing him with her legs wide open around him. She gasped as her newly sensitised pussy came in contact with his hard shaft and lowered her head so that her forehead rested against his shoulder. "Give me a moment. It's… intense."

He let her adjust, his hands smoothing over her waist and hips. "Intense for me, too, baby," he murmured. Her arms slid around his neck. "Ready for another one?"

Keeping her gaze locked with his, Meggie nodded. This time, she took the little round ball of fruit between her teeth and presented it to Brav. Groaning, he leaned forward and bit the fruit from her mouth. This time, the quiver shocked through both of them at the same time. Meggie tightened her legs around his hips as he thrust up towards her, grinding his hard shaft against her tender flesh.

It was even stronger, the contractions pulsing through her intimate flesh more electric than ever. She couldn't stop moving on him, even after she'd swallowed the fruit. "I want to touch your skin," she informed him breathlessly. She unbuttoned his uniform jacket and pulled his shirt from the waistband of his pants. She slipped her hands beneath it.

They both groaned as her hands touched his flesh, sliding up his chest to stroke through the mat of hair on his chest, then down over his tautly muscled abdomen. Her fingers trailed between them, to drift over his hardness and he bucked up again, seeking more of her touch.

"Yes, baby, touch me, touch me. Gods, that feels so good."

Meggie slipped off his lap. His hands reached for her but she danced out of his grasp. Keeping his gaze locked on her, she stepped backwards until she the fur of the rug bristled under her feet.

"Here," she invited. "Here, Brav, it's perfect."

CHAPTER TWENTY-THREE

He rose to his feet. She lifted her hands to the belt that circled
her ribs and bust and let it fall to the floor. She slipped the chiton
from her shoulders and it puddled by her feet. Unlike every other
time they'd been intimate, she was wearing underwear, but she'd
replicated these garments herself.

She hadn't known that he would see her in her underwear when
she dressed this morning, but she'd made lingerie that made herself
feel good. Her bra was supportive, but fashioned out of such a thin
wisp of lace that it concealed nothing. Her panties were similarly
brief and beautiful. She stood proudly, knowing that her figure was
displayed to the very best of her advantage, knowing that he thought
she was the most beautiful thing he'd ever seen.

He devoured her with his eyes. "Meggie," he whispered, as
though words had deserted him.

She reached out to him. He was before her in a moment, his big,
hard hands touching her skin reverently. He cupped her shoulders
and brought her close to him for a kiss and she wanted to weep at
the tenderness of it. Was this another first kiss? It felt so special.

His hands stroking down her arms and back up her sides was
driving her crazy. He never quite seemed to get close enough to her
aching nipples, or that sensitive spot on the undersides of her breasts
that sparked her engines. She shivered. "Oh, Brav, please."

He knew what she meant. On the next pass, his caressing hands
stroked up over her breasts. She felt the drag of her lacy bra against
her nipples. It was unbearably erotic. She pushed herself closer to

him so that her breasts pushed into his hands, wanting, needing the pressure of him against all of her.

"This garment is lovely," Brav murmured, "but if I can't figure out how to get it off you in the next five seconds, I'm going to tear it to shreds."

Meggie giggled, and she loved that she felt free to giggle with him, even when he was loving her. "You've probably never seen a bra before."

"Is that what this is? I like it. But I want it off you."

Meggie turned around and showed him how to work the clasp behind her. She gave a soft cry as the fabric lost its tension around her body. Brav's hands stroked the straps down her arms and encouraged it to release the soft curves of her breasts into his hands.

She leaned back against him as he stroked her, gasping and moaning, as he'd once promised he'd make her do. When his stroking hands went lower, to push her panties from her hips, her own hands hurried to help. She kicked them away and let him take more of her weight as she parted her thighs for him.

He took his time, tangling his fingers in her curls. One finger traced her slit and her thighs trembled so much she was afraid she would fall if it wasn't for his hands on her.

Brav lowered her to the fur rug. It was soft and sensual on her exposed skin. She leaned back, fully, gloriously naked while he was still fully dressed. Brav climbed over her, taking her lips in a kiss before she could lay all the way down. He lowered himself over her as she lay back, one muscular thigh pressing between hers. "Are you sure about this, sweetheart?" he asked.

Meggie slid her arms up his muscled arms and over his shoulders, so that she could stroke his neck and bury her fingers in his hair. "I want you so much," she whispered. "I'm ready, Brav. I want to feel you inside me."

He settled his weight into the cradle of her hips, supporting himself on his elbows above her as he studied her face. "This wasn't how I planned for it to be," he protested, but the hard shaft branding her belly proclaimed that it wasn't much of a protest.

"I didn't plan it one way or another," she admitted. "I don't care about where or how. I only care that I love you and I want to join my body to yours."

Brav brushed her lips with his. "You are the love of my heart," he admitted. "So lovely. So beautiful. And impossible to resist." He settled in for a deeper kiss and Meggie caressed his tongue with her own in the way he had taught her.

"I love you," she said, when their lips parted softly. "I want you inside me, Brav." Her legs opened wider and she coiled them around his lean hips. They both gasped as the motion opened her vulnerable body completely to his. The thick shaft branding her belly slipped lower, between her thighs, to press against her open pussy. She raised her hips to press herself tighter to him.

He surprised her by pulling away. "No," he gasped.

"Are you fucking kidding me?" she demanded, sitting up.

He laughed, a short, desperate laugh. "I don't mean that. I mean, not so fast. Not rushed. I'm not going to make love to you in private for the first time in a hurry." He reached out and tangled his big fingers in the gold-frosted chestnut hair that spilled over her shoulders. He'd done that during the first night on Jiliar, she remembered. He'd stroked her hair over her breasts, over her nipples, until she'd been out of her mind with desire. "Come here."

He pulled her closer to him, pulling her legs over his until she was sitting on his lap again and the hard shaft of his cock was pressed between them. The fabric of his trousers rubbed against her naked pussy.

Meggie moaned and pressed herself closer. "I want you against my skin," she whispered.

Brav's big hands caressed her back. "And you will, baby. But first, I need to taste you. Taste every part of you."

He kissed her mouth first, slow and hot. And all the while his big hands roved over her back, all the way down to her hips, where he rocked against her. Meggie's fingernails dug into his shoulders as she tried to rub her breasts against the hard muscles of his chest.

And then his mouth left hers, sliding down her throat until it latched on the sensitive spot where it joined her shoulder, and sucked. She was going to have a mark there tomorrow, but she didn't care. She threw her head back to give him better access.

Down, his mouth went, drawing a straight path to her nipple. His tongue came out to tease around her taut bud, but Meggie was too excited to put up with any teasing. She slid her fingers into his hair and pulled his head to where she wanted it, pushing her breast closer to his lips.

Brav obliged, opening his hot mouth and closing it on the point of her breast, sucking hard, pulling tight on whatever magical thing inside her drew a straight line from her nipple to her pussy. He opened his mouth wide, like he was trying to get as much of her breast into his mouth as he could, while his hands shaped her body for his pleasure.

Meggie gasped and writhed against him. "Oh, Brav," she gasped. "So good. So good." She trailed her own hand down her belly until her fingertips encountered her soft curls. "I want you here, Brav."

He bent her over, so that she was against the furs again. This time the touch of the soft fur was maddening on her sensitive skin. "Gonna taste you, baby," he whispered. "Taste you and make you come all over my face."

He was between her thighs now, spreading them wide with his massive shoulders, looking up at her with eyes as vivid as the firelight.

But he touched her gently. Meggie jumped as a gentle fingertip traced the outline of her pussy. "Inside me, Brav, *please!*" But he still didn't hurry. He traced all around her outer lips, snagging his finger in her curls, gliding across the soft skin of her inner thighs. She opened her legs wider, inviting him in.

That teasing, torturous finger finally slid through her folds. The feeling was familiar. He'd had his hand between her legs many times by now. She was accustomed to him touching her. She was even accustomed to him thrusting the warm, silver wand inside her body and drawing a ragged climax from her. And yet, this was different.

There was no audience. There was no family to save. There was just Meggie and the man she loved, the man she wanted inside her so badly.

After several years—or so it seemed—of sliding his fingertip between the soft, wet folds, he finally, finally, finally, circled her clit.

Meggie felt her body spasming just from the light touch, felt the moisture well inside her and a drop of it spill down between her legs. "Oh, I'm going to ruin these furs," she moaned.

Brav sat up and pulled his shirt off, quickly followed by his boots and trousers. Meggie's hungry gaze took in the hard muscles of his smooth chest, the washboard abs, the vee of muscles that ran down to his groin, and the thick shaft that stood up, hard and rigid between his thighs.

He was... he was folding his shirt, Meggie realised. "What are you doing?" she asked.

"Making you comfortable, baby," he muttered. He slipped the

folded shirt beneath her hips, then got back into position between her thighs. "Now you can come as much as you like and not worry about the furs. I want to see you flowing under my tongue."

He split her thighs wide again, wrapping his muscular arms around them so he could get in close to where her sex was wet and dripping for him. He lapped a slow glide from the entrance of her channel to the very top of her slit, gathering her juices on his tongue. "Gods, you taste so good, sweetheart." He did it again, savouring her taste.

"Love you," she moaned. Then his talented tongue slid through her folds to find her clit and that was the last sensible thought she had.

She bucked and arched and moaned beneath his oral caress. She felt her own moisture slipping between her thighs to soak his shirt beneath her. Pleasure built on pleasure. She came hard as he pressed his tongue inside her, one rough finger pressing her clit as he thrust his tongue deep into her warm, welling pussy.

She was still gasping as he rose above her, hardly able to return the passionate kiss he pressed to her lips. She felt like every limb was as heavy as lead. She couldn't even raise her arms to circle them around his neck.

"That was *intense*," she whispered as soon as her mouth was free again. "How can it be even better than it was on Jiliar?"

"It'll be better still in a moment," he promised. "How do you want this, baby? Do you want to ride me, like you were earlier?"

"Like this," she whispered, pulling him closer over her. Her legs wrapped around his tight hips again, her heels resting on the backs of his thighs. "I love you, Brav."

His head dropped to her shoulder. "I wanted to take this slow," he muttered. "But I can't resist you, Meggie. You're too beautiful, too sexy, too hot for me to resist."

He pushed her thighs open wider as her arms found the strength to rise and encircle his shoulders. She felt the blunt head of his cock pressing against her secret entrance and gasped. She'd had the little silver wand inside her, and she'd had him inside her once, but she was still nervous.

She widened her thighs further and tilted her hips up towards him. She could feel her own wetness against his heat as he slid against her, breaching her entrance and pressing inside her body. She kept herself open to him, her nails digging into his shoulders again and he groaned at the small hurt and the overwhelming pleasure. "So tight," he muttered.

"So good," she replied, relaxing her inner muscles as she felt him slide deeper into her. He thrust smoothly against her, going deeper and deeper into her slick folds until Meggie felt him bottom out inside her. She gasped in pleasure as the head of his cock kissed her cervix.

"Are you OK, baby?" he asked, raising himself slightly so he could see her face better. The movement pressed him even tighter inside her and for a moment Meggie couldn't speak. He frowned and started to withdraw.

Meggie pulled him back to her, the muscles inside her clamping down on him to prevent him from leaving her. "Don't stop," she gasped. She couldn't manage another word. All she could do was open herself to him again as he repeated the slow, slick slide into her body.

And then there was nothing but sensation. Nothing but pleasure as he fucked her gently, but so deeply that she was sure he was opening her womb. She loved the feeling of him filling her all the way up. Loved the feeling of her own muscles clasping the hot, invading cock that branded her inner folds and kissed the end of her channel with every stroke.

He thrust faster, and Meggie was with him for every stroke, gasping and straining ever closer to him. "Oh, Brav," she gasped. "Oh, please… I need to… oh, God, I just *need!*"

He didn't reply, just slid one hand between them, slid a finger between her folds, and stroked gently over her clit. The sensation was different now that he was inside her, her tender flesh stretched around him. Meggie cried out sharply as he circled the tender button while he thrust deeply into her.

She sobbed his name as pleasure crested within her again. This time, her inner muscles contracted around his thick cock, spasming around his flesh, deep, deep inside. "Come inside me," she whispered, wanting him with her, needing him with her at the peak.

He responded with a deep thrust that seemed to consume her. He pressed hard within her channel and she felt his cock grow even thicker inside her. Felt him throb. Felt the warm wetness spurt inside her as he filled her with his seed. He groaned her name. Whispered words she knew he'd never said to anyone else.

Brav brought his weight down slowly, even now careful not to crush her. He rolled her so that they were lying on their sides, pulling her uppermost leg up higher over his hip to keep them joined.

Lying together afterwards, Meggie stroked little circles on Brav's chest while his hand moved up and down her back lazily.

"Will you live here on Solace Station with me, Meggie? With my experiences as a slave, they've offered me a teaching position—both to prepare the young if they fall into such an experience, and to prepare the warriors in the Espionage Corps. But if you'd rather live elsewhere," he kissed the golden tip of her hair, "I'd go anywhere with you."

She smiled into his skin. "I want to be here with you."

CHAPTER TWENTY-FOUR

They returned to Earth the next day so that Meggie could pack her things, descending in a cloaked shuttle to Leona's house. Teresa went down to Earth with them. Bess said she would go another day, and Cera swore she would never set foot on her home planet again until she'd made mincemeat of Baelor.

Teresa had no firm plans to return to Earth, either. She wanted to stay on Solace Station for a while, both so she could be near Meggie, and, Meggie guessed, be near Kairn and Mac.

Looking around the tiny apartment, Meggie realised that there wasn't really a lot she wanted to keep, especially since she could replicate anything she wanted up on the Station. She packed a bag.

Teresa packed *everything*. They had to make several trips to carry it all from the apartment up to the shuttle parked unobtrusively on the roof. "What have you got in these bags?" Meggie demanded, trying to lift one and failing.

"Stuff," Teresa retorted, sticking her tongue out at her older sister.

Brav reached past Meggie and lifted the heavy bag effortlessly.

"Show off," Meggie murmured, but stroked his bicep where she knew exactly how the muscle bulged under his uniform and only Teresa's presence made her control herself. He took the bag up to the roof while the two women kept packing.

They stopped by Meggie's workplace as she went to pick up a few things she wanted from her desk and tender her resignation. It was Monday morning, Meggie realised. Barely more than a week since the night of Leona's party.

Elise was there with a cake when she came in. There were a dozen people behind her, all of whom burst into song when she opened the door. They'd bought her a bracelet, which surprised her even more. To be honest, she hadn't expected anyone would bother to put in money for her birthday.

Meggie was touched. She gave Elise a hug that the other woman clearly didn't expect.

"Margaret, you look… different," Elise commented. "Your hair looks amazing. It really suits you. Did you have a good time on your week off?"

Meggie laughed and ran her hand through her hair, knowing that she was blushing. "Well, actually," she said, hedging for time as she strove to describe everything that had happened during the last week without saying it was 'nice.' "Actually, I met someone. A friend of the family I'd never met came to my birthday party. We kind of…" her blush intensified. "Well, we spent the week together."

Elise's eyes went wide. "You're *kidding* me?" Her face was suddenly wreathed in smiles. "Margaret, you sly dog! I would never have guessed you would be so adventurous!"

"You have no idea," Meggie said, meaning every word. "I'm quitting, Elise. I'm going to move in with him. I'm going to marry him."

Elise hugged her again. "Oh, Margaret, I'm so glad. Stay in touch, will you?"

Elise meant it, but then, Elise meant everything she said. And when Meggie promised she would, she meant it to. She didn't have to hide any more. She could have friends now and not be afraid.

Meggie promised to keep in touch and took some birthday cake back to the shuttle on the roof where Brav and Teresa were waiting.

"I have something I need to get from Dad's house, too," Teresa informed her.

Meggie went still. "Why would you want to go back there? We haven't lived there for nearly ten years."

Teresa just shook her head, but Meggie knew she was digging in her heels. Nothing could persuade Teresa when she got that look on her face. An hour later, they were landing outside the small suburban house where they'd spent the first four years after losing their mother. As soon as Meggie was eighteen, she'd moved out and taken Teresa with her. Meggie had finished high school while worrying how she was going to pay the rent.

The house was smaller than she remembered. Shabbier, when it had been shabby to begin with. It was an ex-Housing Commission house, made of fibro boards slapped quickly onto a frame, with poky little rooms and a narrow hallway shooting from the front of the house to the back.

Teresa was the one who knocked on the door. Meggie stood a little way back, pressing close to Brav's side. He put his arm around her shoulders. "I'm here," he whispered, pressing a kiss to her hair as she huddled into him greedily.

Their father opened the door. Lewis Croft. Now in his early sixties and showing every hard year on his weathered, haggard face. He scowled at Teresa.

"Whadda ya want?"

Meggie saw the flinch that went through her younger sister's small body. "I'm here to pick something up," she said, her voice quavering.

"What makes ya think I kept any of yer stuff? You've been gone for years."

The curvy line of Teresa's back trembled. "But some of that was important!"

Lewis leaned on the doorframe. "Then you shouldn't of left it behind. I threw out all yer stuff when you left. Same as I did for yer bitch of a mother."

"Mum *died*," Meggie snapped, leaving Brav's embrace to put her arm around Teresa. "It wasn't her fault."

Lewis sneered. "She didn't die. She just walked out one day."

Meggie went cold all over. "She died. There was a funeral."

"No, there wasn't. For some reason, I gave a shit about her kids at that stage, so I pretended there was a funeral. I left you two at home and went to the pub that day."

She tried to keep her composure when everything inside her was trembling. "She's alive? Where is she?"

Her father shrugged. "How the fuck would I know? I only know that I didn't put her in the ground. Should of. But didn't. Now get the fuck off my property before I get my shotgun."

The next moment, Meggie felt Brav's hand settle on her shoulder. He lay his other hand on Teresa's shoulder, so that he held them both in his arms. "Tell me you didn't just threaten my fiancée," he growled.

Lewis drew back in fear and a nasty part of Meggie she didn't want to acknowledge knew that she'd remember that look on his face with satisfaction all her life. "Figure of speech," he gasped. "Sir."

"Glad to hear it." Brav pressed another kiss to her hair. "You poor bastard, you don't even know what you're giving up, do you? You could have had two beautiful girls adore you, and you threw it away with both hands."

Fury twisted on Lewis's face. He opened his mouth to speak, then closed it again several times. Each time, he glanced at Brav's face and knew that he had to keep the hateful words inside. Finally, he just slammed the door.

Teresa made a small sound as her knees buckled. Brav caught her and carried her back to the shuttle, parked around the corner in a park. "I'm OK," Teresa insisted as Meggie opened the shuttle door and Brav lay her in a seat, but her voice was thready.

Meggie climbed in next to her and Brav got into the pilot's seat. "He was a terrible father," Meggie stated firmly. "His behaviour reflects on him, Teresa, not on you."

"'Her kids', he said," Teresa mused, settling back into her seat. "Meggie, do you think he really was our father?"

Meggie stilled, in the process of buckling her harness. "I hope not," she said eventually. "In fact. No. He isn't. Whether or not he was our biological parent, that man wasn't our father from the day our mother disappeared. A real father would never treat his kids the way he treated us. The things I went through… he should have known. He should have stopped it. He should have cared."

"Was it true what he said about Mum, do you think?"

Meggie didn't answer. The shuttle lifted. "I remember the day he told me she died. He said it was a car accident."

"I remember that day, too," Teresa said. "I remember you telling me. There was a ladybug on your uniform."

"I remember the day of the funeral. I remember hurting because I wanted to be there, and he wouldn't let me. Wouldn't tell me where it was. Wouldn't even tell me where she was buried."

They flew in silence for a few minutes, trying to absorb this new information. "I don't remember her very well, Meggie," Teresa admitted. "Do you?"

"I remember her. We were happy. Dad was different when she was alive. He changed after she died—after she was gone."

"Did she love us, Meggie?"

"She loved us." Meggie wished she could put her arm around her sister, but they were still strapped into their seats and it wasn't safe, so she contented herself with taking Teresa's hand. "She loved us *so* much. She wouldn't have walked out on us. I will never believe that."

What *was* she supposed to believe? Meggie wondered, as they flew back to Solace Station. She'd been sure that their mother had loved them, but she'd left them. Without a word. Without a trace.

A suspicion grew, and along with it, equal parts hope and horror. If Megara had been abducted, she wouldn't have been able to return to them. If she'd been killed…

Meggie's mind shied away from the thought. As they cleared Earth's atmosphere and the sky around them grew dark and lit by stars, Meggie wondered if they would ever find out what happened to their mother. She glanced at Teresa beside her. From the stubborn set of her pointed chin, she knew Teresa would not give up until she learned the truth.

EPILOGUE

Leona's hands were shaking as she entered the Infirmary at Desiderus Nonus Station. It had been decades since she'd seen Regan. She ran her hand over her short hair. She'd had long hair when she'd known him. She glanced down at herself. He'd certainly never seen her in a pantsuit before.

A thousand memories flashed though her mind, scenes passing in quick succession. The first moment their hands had touched. Their first kiss at the gateway to the realm of the Fates. When he'd saved her from the House of Women and bathed her so gently. The night when she'd rescued him from flame and terror and she was pretty sure they'd conceived Bess. The morning she'd told him they were going to have a baby. And so many other memories. She'd treasured each one.

She'd thought he was dead. She'd raised her children as a widow. She'd been alone for so long.

Her heart was pounding. The Guardian who was escorting her took her to the room where Regan was held.

"Be careful," the Guardian warned. Leona couldn't even remember his name. She could barely remember her own. "He's crafty. He can be dangerous."

"It will be all right," Leona said confidently. "He loves me." There was not a doubt in her mind that this was true. The man locked in the room before her loved her more than his own life. She was everything to him.

"I won't leave you alone," the Guardian assured her. "Don't be afraid."

"I'm not afraid."

The door slid open and Leona made a small sound she couldn't keep inside, because he was there. Regan. Her breath came fast and ragged and her eyes burned with tears. He looked the same as he had the day they were parted, still young and handsome and hers. All hers.

"Regan," she whispered, the name torn from her throat. "Oh, Regan, darling."

He turned, stopping pacing the floor. His eyes went wide.

Leona threw herself into his arms. "Oh, Regan, Regan," she whispered. "Oh, darling, I love you so much."

His arms closed around her. She could hear the steady beat of his heart accelerating beneath her ear. She raised her face to him, ready to receive his kiss, to know the thrill of his mouth on hers, to hear him whisper her name and the words of love she craved.

His hands slid up her arms where they wreathed around his neck, his touch gentle and warm and sure. He clasped her wrists.

The next thing she knew, he spun her around so he was behind her. One arm came across her body, pinning her hands in place in front of her, holding both her wrists in one large hand. The other was heavy across her chest as he held something sharp to her throat.

When he spoke, it was to the Guardian reaching for his blaster, not to Leona. "Drop it and step away from the door," Regan growled. "Or the bitch dies."

"Regan?" Leona asked uncertainly. His muscular arms were like steel bands around her. He gripped her tighter until she cried out.

"Shut up," he muttered roughly. "You'll never deceive me again. You're coming with me. Now."

THE END? ABSOLUTELY NOT!

The House of the Gods series continues in Book 2: **Defying Zeus**.

If you liked this story, I would love it if you would write a review. It would mean so much to me and it helps other people know if this book is right for them, too. Good reviews also let me know what you want me to write more of!

If you enjoyed Meggie and Brav's story, there is an exclusive short story waiting in my newsletter about their first days together on Solace Station. Colin Walt gets his just deserts and Meggie finds her true calling. Join the Lovers of Gods and Heroes Newsletter by scanning the QR code below.

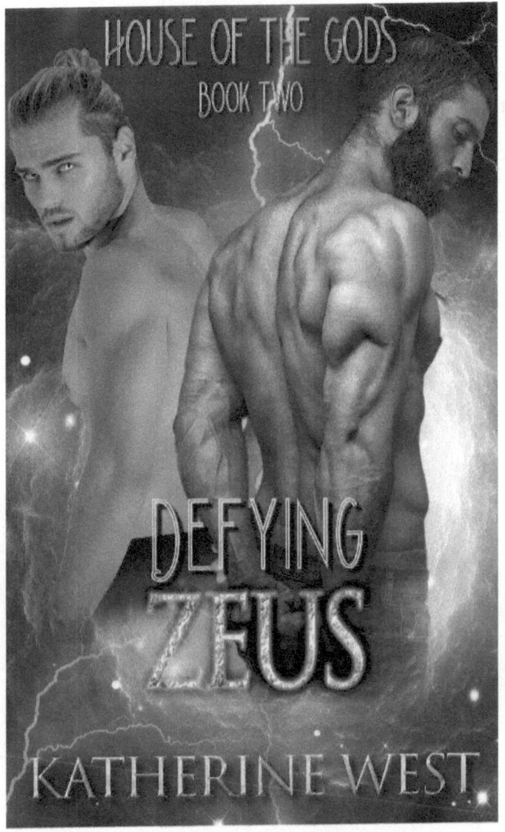

One man is a beast. One is shrouded in secrets. Both men are bound to her soul. To save them, Teresa will defy even the father of the gods.

As a curvy girl with ADHD, Teresa knows how to fight for what she wants, and what she wants is Kairn and Mac, the two Guardian warriors bound to her by the Fates themselves. But Kairn has a secret, and lightning flickers behind his mental shields. Mac opens his heart wide to Teresa, but if the fragile threads bonding his soul to Kairn's are shattered, he will revert to an animalistic, beast-like state that terrifies her.

When a deadly plague is unleashed on Solace Station, Teresa's sister is one of the first victims. The only hope for a cure is to find their mother who disappeared fourteen years ago.

Racing against time and guided only by a cryptic message, Teresa embarks on a perilous journey across a galaxy ruled by ancient gods. Her mother's trail leads to Tenebrae, the prison-asteroid ruled by Zeus. Teresa discovers powers inside her that she never knew as her relationship with the two men develops, but Zeus's guards are right behind them and Kairn's secret could damn them all.

Teresa must defy the father of the gods himself to tame Kairn's lightning and she must gather all her courage to face Mac in his feral state. There is only one way to tame the beast.

And in the end, will all her struggles be in vain if she returns to Solace Station too late to save her sister?

Read this scorching hot romance to find out.

ABOUT THE AUTHOR

Katherine West is shy. Like, really shy. Unless she gets started talking about one of her obsessions, like romance, history, music, art or lacemaking. Then it takes an act of God to shut her up.

She lives in Sydney, in a house where she can see the sunset and is a crazy cat lady with a starter pack of one.

She's been writing books since she was a little girl. Her Year 6 teacher teased her publicly because she wrote long stories. Now who's laughing, Mrs Reynolds?

Katherine is very new at all of this, so let her know if you like her books! She writes steamy science fiction romance (well, "science" fiction that is awfully close to fantasy, but with better healthcare and hygiene) about gods and heroes, and women who are more powerful than they know.

You can join her Lovers of Gods and Heroes newsletter at KatherineWestAuthor.com to receive snippets from upcoming books, extended epilogues and deleted scenes. You can also follow her on Facebook to see her cat and her half-assed attempts at humour.

ALSO BY KATHERINE WEST

<u>House of the Gods series</u>

- Abducting Artemis
- Impersonating Aphrodite
- Defying Zeus

<u>Coming Soon</u>

- Deceiving Apollo
  ...and many more!

IMPERSONATING APHRODITE

Impersonating Aphrodite

Copyright (c) 2024 by Katherine West

KatherineWestAuthor.com

This is a work of fiction. Names, characters, events and dialogue are products of the author's imagination or used fictitiously. Any resemblance to actual events or persons, living or dead, is entirely coincidental.